## WHEN WHITE MAGIC MEETS BLACK MAGIC

With my two babies by my side, I lit the sage stick, set the crystals in the grid, and concentrated, closing my eyes and focusing all the attention in my heart space toward Nicole to send love and peace to the places that were so overcome with fear. I held the vision of her safe, happy, and free in my mind until I could almost see it, like joyful colors in a rainbow swirling together after a storm.

I settled into the vision, completely letting go and allowing the peaceful feeling to wash over me, losing myself in the colors. I was in a trancelike state, only vaguely aware of my surroundings.

But then something shifted. Black edges started to appear around the frame of my joyful space. I tried to focus more deeply on the colors, the peace I'd been feeling, but the black was invasive, creeping in and strangling the light. I could almost feel fingers snaking around my throat, closing around it and slowly cutting off my air. I wanted desperately to open my eyes and shake it off, but I couldn't. It was like one of those awful nightmares that you couldn't claw your way out of, stuck between the fog of sleep and the mobility of being awake, aware but completely helpless. . . .

Books by Cate Conte

WITCH HUNT

WITCH TRIAL

Published by Kensington Publishing Corp.

A Full Moon Mystery

# Witch Trial
## CATE CONTE

Kensington Publishing Corp.
www.kensingtonbooks.com

KENSINGTON BOOKS are published by

Kensington Publishing Corp.
119 West 40th Street
New York, NY 10018

All Kensington titles, imprints, and distributed lines are available at special quantity discounts for bulk purchases for sales promotion, premiums, fund-raising, educational, or institutional use.

Special book excerpts or customized printings can also be created to fit specific needs. For details, write or phone the office of the Kensington Sales Manager: Attn.: Sales Department. Kensington Publishing Corp., 119 West 40th Street, New York, NY 10018. Phone: 1-800-221-2647.

The K and Teapot logo is a trademark of Kensington Publishing Corp.

First Printing: January 2022
ISBN: 978-1-4967-3269-9

ISBN: 978-1-4967-3270-5 (ebook)

10 9 8 7 6 5 4 3 2 1

Printed in the United States of America

For all my rescue babies—my furry family

# ACKNOWLEDGMENTS

A huge thank you to the team at Kensington Books—my editor, John Scognamiglio, Larissa Ackerman, Michelle Addo, the amazing graphics team for the consistently great covers, and the editing and production team—as well as my agent, John Talbot, for bringing this book and this series to life. It has been such fun to write these books!

I would be hugely remiss if I didn't thank Jennifer McKee, my assistant and life organizer. Jen, not much would get done without you around, so thank you for keeping me together.

I am grateful for my crystal guru, Nicole Simonelli, for keeping me well-stocked in crystals and knowledge. It helps make Violet and her shop even better. Jessie Crockett/Jessica Ellicott—this book's plot came together because of your help. I am so grateful for our plotting sessions! Thank you!

My Wicked Author sisters—Sherry Harris, Barbara Ross, Maddie Day, Julia Henry, Jessica Ellicott—thank you for being on this journey with me. Every day I am thankful I am able to celebrate successes and navigate this path with all of you.

I wrote this book during those first months of COVID, when we were in the initial stages of quarantine and life was scary, uncertain, and honestly seemed pretty bleak. While it helped me tap into Violet's mindset as she faced a similar uncertainty—the risk of losing her life as she knew it—it was a hard time in which to live. I am grateful for the people who helped me get through it, and who continue to be my lifeline—the Wickeds, Riham, Teah—love you all.

# CHAPTER ONE

*Saturday*
*Mercury goes retrograde*

"What do you think of this one, Xander?" I pointed to a page in the giant book in front of me and glanced expectantly at my black cat. He sat on the desk watching me intently, his sleek black tail swishing in anticipation of my next move. I was kind of hoping he might give me a hint or a prompt or something. I wasn't sure if my spell casting attempt was going to live up to his expectations, but I had to try. Our relationship was still pretty new, so I felt the need to impress him. I closed my eyes and recited:

> *From my mind, my thinking soars*
> *From my lips, I speak these words*

*From my heart, my intention is right*
*Into the world I spread magickal light.*

I waved my hand—a bit awkwardly, truth be told, as I was still getting used to this whole concept—and waited for something to happen. I was looking for a flash of light, or even for my lights to flicker, but . . . nothing.

Great. So much for Violet Mooney, super witch. And for my new sign that I'd just had made for the shop that read: "Be the reason the lights flicker when you enter a room."

"Shoot," I muttered. "I must be doing it wrong." I opened my eyes and peered at Xander. He still sat there, waiting for something to happen. I could almost read the disappointment in those brilliant yellow eyes.

I felt his pain.

Fiona, my long-lost mother who had appeared back in my life recently with the news that I was a witch, swore I didn't need a wand or anything to help me spell cast— "This isn't a Harry Potter novel, my dear," she'd chided me when I asked—but I still wondered. I'd gotten pretty good at some things relating to my new identity, but some of these grander witchy gestures were still eluding me. "Don't look at me like that," I said to Xander. "I can conjure up a great cup of coffee, at least." I had to take the small victories where I could.

"Vi?" Sydney Santangelo, my best friend and new employee, poked her head into the office. "Who are you talking to?"

I jumped a foot, sending my grandmother's book of spells crashing to the ground, trying to look innocent. Unlike Josie Cook, my mentor and other shop employee (and fellow witch), Sydney had no idea about my . . . heritage. Which wasn't all that shocking, since I hadn't known either until just a few weeks ago. And it still wasn't something I was ready to share with the general public, even if this particular member of the general public was an important person in my life. "What? Nothing. No one," I stammered, adjusting my long lacy skirt. "Just Xander."

"Xander? I don't see him."

I whirled back around to my desk. Nothing. No cat.

He had a knack for that sort of thing.

Syd had stepped fully into the office and was looking at me curiously. "Are you okay? What the heck are you reading that's so big?" She indicated the book on the floor.

I stepped in front of it, letting my long skirt fall over the cover. "Fine, yes, I'm good. It was just . . . one of my grandmother's books."

Syd frowned. "Wow. Kindles are so much easier. And lighter." She turned to go, then glanced back at me. "The lights flickered out there. Did they flicker in here? I hope we aren't getting a storm. I hate winter storms. I wish spring would just come."

"Wait. The lights flickered?" I rushed over to her. "Really? Which ones?"

"I don't know, all of them? Are you sure you're okay, Violet? You're acting a little weird."

"The lights flickered." I clapped my hands together and turned to see if Xander had reappeared to share in my excitement. He was still nowhere in sight. I hadn't figured out if my new familiar was actually a magickal cat, or simply superior at being a cat. "Yes, I'm fine. I'm just . . . really looking forward to the first spring storms too," I lied. "I think winter is going to end early."

I could tell Syd thought I was losing it by the way she cocked her head and squinted at me, but she did a good job of shrugging it off. Today she'd hid her unruly blond curls under a rhinestone cowboy hat, which looked awesome with the lacy dress she wore with knee-high boots. Syd also sold vintage clothing and accessories and loved to dress the part. "Okay then. Anyway, Ginny is here. She brought someone with her."

"She did? Who is it?"

"No idea. She didn't tell me her name. Actually Ginny did all the talking. And she hugged me." She wrinkled her nose and leaned in a bit. "She's kind of weird. You think?"

"Ginny? She's harmless." Ginny Reinhardt was a hugger. She hugged everyone with the same enthusiasm, whether she'd last seen you two days or two years ago. She was also a witch, but I didn't tell Syd that. Syd mostly knew her from her waitressing gigs at the deli down the street and at my boyfriend Todd's bar, Luck o' the Irish. "Can you let them know I'll be right out?"

"Sure. Okay if I go grab lunch?" she asked, taking her coat off the rack.

"Of course. Take your time," I said.

She blew me a kiss and hurried out. "She's coming," I heard her say, then the little bell on the shop door jingled.

I picked up my grandma's book and placed it carefully on my desk, then piled a few other things on top of it. I wasn't sure if Syd would be able to read it even if she did pay attention to it—I hadn't been able to open the cover until I'd accepted the fact that I was a witch—but I didn't want to chance it.

I stepped through the curtain of beads and feathers that separated the main room of my crystal shop, The Full

Moon, from the back room and office area, feeling my energy shift as I stepped back into the presence of all those beautiful crystals. I'd worked with crystals since I was a kid, and their healing powers never ceased to amaze me.

Ginny and her friend were the only ones there. They browsed the display by the window, which had some of my bigger pieces of zeolites under some funky recessed lighting I'd recently had installed. The result was a purple glint on the shimmery clear stones. I loved it and it never failed to catch people's eyes as they walked by. I'd even gotten some first timers who'd come in after seeing that display.

Ginny glanced up, saw me, and waved, her face lighting up. The woman standing next to her paid no attention. She looked vaguely familiar. I searched my brain for why but couldn't grasp it. She was holding one of my bigger free-form pieces of green opal. As I watched, she turned it over in her hand, studying it intently, then placed it down again.

"Hi there," I said, stepping over to them.

Ginny poked her friend, who turned to look at me. "This is Violet. Hey, Violet!" She rushed over and gave me a hug that almost knocked me over. "I'm so glad you're here."

"Wow. Hey, Ginny. Good to see you," I said, hugging her back, although I'd seen her yesterday when I ran into the diner to pick up a grilled cheese for lunch.

She let go and turned to her friend. "Nicole, this is Violet Mooney, who I've been telling you about. Vi, Nicole St. James. One of my best friends." She looked at me earnestly. "Nicole needs your help."

# CHAPTER TWO

I smiled at Nicole. "Hi. It's nice to meet you." I had an impulse to hug her because she looked like she needed it—or maybe Ginny was rubbing off on me—but at the same time I got a vibe that screamed *Don't touch me*.

Nicole St. James looked like she'd rather be anywhere but here. Or maybe it had nothing to do with here and everything to do with her overall state of mind, which I immediately picked up on. Her aura was almost completely gray, and so strong I didn't even need to tune in to see it. Gray auras meant blocked energy centers and a lack of trust. When I turned up my focus, I also saw some dark blue around the edges, which showed me a lot of fear. Her physical appearance backed that up. Her face looked drawn and weary, and her eyes were dark enough they made me think of twin bruises. She was pretty though, with short blond hair pulled back in a barrette and a spattering of freckles across her nose that made her look younger than she probably was.

When I spoke to her she barely met my eyes, just let them skitter over me, then back to the floor. "Hi," she said. Unlike the rest of her demeanor, her tone was curt. Impatient. Like she was very late for something and I was standing in her way.

Ginny sent me a pleading look as if to say, *Sorry in advance but please have patience.*

I smiled back reassuringly. Patience was my strong suit. Most of the time. "So what can I help you with?" I asked Nicole. "Do you want to have a seat?"

Nicole looked from Ginny to me then back again. "I guess," she said uncertainly.

I led her to the back of the store where I did my crystal consults. They were a huge selling point for my shop, and had become popular in the county. They were private sessions where I read people's auras and determined which stones would help them heal. I'd been reading auras since I was a child and I'd always thought I just had a gift for it. Until I found out I had powers that, although they had been mostly dormant all these years, were guiding me to the right healing properties. Which ultimately helped me do even better for my clients who came in looking for physical or emotional relief.

Magick. It still gave me a thrill when I thought about it.

Nicole glanced at Ginny, then back at me. "Not really. I don't think there's much you can do for me. I mean, your stuff is really pretty but I'm not sure how you can help. Plus I have an appointment, so if this is going to take long . . ."

"Just give her a chance, Nic," Ginny said. "I told you,

her crystals are super healing. You won't regret it." To me, she said, "Nicole's been under a lot of pressure lately. She was involved in that whole political battle about the railroad bridge, for one thing."

I looked at her, curious now as everything clicked in my brain. That's why she looked familiar. Our little town of North Harbor had been talking about nothing else for the past few months other than the recently defeated proposal to reroute our existing railroad bridge straight through the middle of our downtown. Proponents swore it would help the economy by providing jobs and that the safety issues relating to the old bridge outweighed any arguments against it. Opponents included environmentalists who said the delicate balance of the river would be destroyed when the current bridge was torn down. And there were also a fair number of opposers in the business community, who didn't want to see buildings taken by eminent domain. "Really? How were you involved?"

"I'm an attorney," Nicole said. "I just changed jobs, but I was with Odin, Steele and Rabner for . . . a long time."

I recognized the name of the firm. It was a high-end corporate law firm that had offices in Manhattan and here in North Harbor. The owner of the largest office building in town that would have been taken by eminent domain had retained them as part of the fight. "So you won," I said. "Congratulations."

She glanced away, but not before I saw a shadow pass over her face. "That's one way of putting it."

Odd response. "A lot of people in town were grateful that the project didn't happen," I said. "Including the environmental crew."

"Yeah. Well, it's not over yet."

I decided to leave that statement alone—people in this town could debate that bridge project forever. "Aside from that, is there something in particular that's bothering you?"

Nicole laughed, but the sound was harsh. "Got a few hours?"

I reached out and put my hand on her arm. "Why don't you just sit for a minute and let me tune in," I said.

"Go on," Ginny urged, giving her a gentle shove toward me.

I watched Nicole fight her knee-jerk reaction to pull her arm away until she finally relented. "Fine," she said. "I guess I could use some help with relationships. Ending one, to be clear."

I smiled encouragingly. "Okay." I pointed to the chair. She sat, a ball of tension, arms wrapped around herself. I pulled up my own chair so I faced her. Ginny wandered away to browse, probably relieved that her friend had stopped fighting me.

"Close your eyes," I said. "I'm just going to hold your hands. You don't need to say or do anything."

Nicole frowned, but finally obliged. I took her hands and held them. Her hands were cool and smooth to the touch. I could feel nervous energy literally flowing through her fingers. At first she was tense, but after a few minutes her hands relaxed into mine. I kept my eyes focused just above her head, tuning into her aura with more intentionality. The message was the same.

Just as I was about to close my eyes, I saw something else in her auric field. A shadow, moving around her, black as a moonless night. I focused on it, trying to identify what it was and why I felt so . . . suffocated all of a sudden. The feeling grew stronger until it literally took my breath away. I tried to block it out but it kept spreading, invading her entire auric field until I had to break the connection. I swallowed my gasp and opened my eyes.

There was nothing there—just the regular colors I'd expect to see in someone's aura. They hadn't changed, but if anything, the dark blue had gotten stronger and spread more around her whole being.

"Everything okay?" Nicole asked, opening her eyes too.

"Perfect," I said, forcing a smile into my voice. "Just relax. Almost done." I closed my eyes again and tried to refocus. Despite my distraction, I got the message loud and clear—Nicole needed some major fear blockers before we could do anything else for her. And protection. A lot of protection. The heavy black shadow had been menacing—there was no sugarcoating it. Protection crystals were essential.

After a few more seconds I squeezed her hands, let go, and got up to make my selections. All the black ones: Black tourmaline in a palm stone. A labradorite tumbled stone. An obsidian sphere. And since she'd mentioned relationships, I picked a rose quartz angel. If anything, it would help her heart heal from whatever had happened. I spent a couple minutes with the stones, using a silent invocation I'd read in Grandma Abby's book that she had noted strengthened the already potent powers of the crystals, then I brought them over to her.

Ginny came over and peered over Nicole's shoulder as I placed the stones on the counter in front of her.

"Oooh," Ginny said reverently. "So pretty!"

"They are beautiful, aren't they?" I turned to Nicole. "Set an intention for each of them to help you with whatever it is you're afraid of. I would recommend carrying the smaller ones during the day, preferably on your person, but if not then in your purse. And put them under your pillow at night."

She gazed at the stones, then looked at me. "That's it?" she asked. "And then I'll be cured?"

I picked up on the sarcasm—it was slight, but it was there. "They will help. You have to believe in them, though. Here, let me wrap them for you." I brought the stones to the counter, wrapped them in tissue paper, then placed them in a velvet pouch with a moon on it—my new signature crystal bags—then handed it to her.

Nicole hesitated for a second, then took it. "Thank you. How much do I owe you?"

I rang up her purchase, then handed her my card. "The obsidian sphere is on me. Feel free to call if you have questions," I said. "And if you feel like you need something else, or it isn't working, please come back."

She nodded and offered me a tiny smile. "Thank you. Ready, Ginny?'

Ginny blew me a kiss. "Thanks, Vi. See you at the bar later?"

I worked to keep the smile in place. My boyfriend, Todd, and I weren't on the greatest terms lately, and I wasn't totally sure that I wanted to hang out his bar tonight. "That's a definite maybe. Thanks for coming in!" I watched them walk out of the store and pause on the sidewalk. Ginny said something to her friend and gave her a hug. Nicole turned away and hunched into her coat, pulling the hood over her head as if she hoped it would make her invisible.

# CHAPTER THREE

The rest of the day flew by and before I knew it, it was five o'clock and time to close. I'd had consults every hour and a ton of walk-in traffic, which made for a busy day. I'd sent Syd home an hour earlier, knowing she needed to get back to her daughter, Presley. The afternoon had quieted down after the lunch crowd thinned, probably because the temperatures had been dropping steadily all day. Winter in New England. It was a crapshoot, for sure. I was as desperate for spring as Sydney, but we were barely into March.

And now I needed to meet my mother for dinner. She'd called me earlier and asked me to come, and I'd learned that when Fiona summoned, you pretty much just went. If you didn't she'd simply beam you to where she wanted you anyway. I switched my sign to *Closed*, locked the front door, shut off all the lights, and went out back. I grabbed my bag and tugged on my moonstone necklace. That crazy feeling of free falling hit me like the rush you get on a roller coaster. A moment later I landed on the porch steps of my old house—my Grandma Abby's house, where I'd lived for most of my life after we left New York City when I was a child—pushed the front door open and stepped inside.

And stopped. Stared. I almost went back out to check if I had the right house, but the one thing of my grand-mother's that remained, her favorite chair and cozy fleece blanket, was still visible in the corner of the living room. I could just see it from where I stood and although it looked incredibly out of place given the new . . . decor, it still gave me peace. I sat in it every time I came over here. It let me feel like Grandma Abby was still with me.

But the rest of this place . . . I could feel her turning over in her grave.

"Problems, darling?"

I whirled around. I hated when Fiona snuck up on me like that.

"No problems," I said. "Just looking at what you've done with the place. It looks, uh, different than last time I was here."

Fiona Ravenstar—my mother—placed her hands on her hips and gave me her best stare, the one that dared anyone to challenge her. "You told us we could live here, Violet. You said we could make changes to the house. Have you changed your mind?" She towered over me in her black platform boots, and the red velvet cloak she'd wrapped herself in made me think of the devil witch costume I'd convinced my dad to buy me when I was thirteen. All she needed were the horns.

She was exceptionally beautiful, though, with her flawless skin, elegant high cheekbones, and today, hair that was blond and turned wine-colored at the ends. It was a different color every time I saw her. She'd also been experimenting with length and right now was wearing it long, halfway down her back. Her presence loomed larger than anything else in her energy field.

Which was also a lot to get used to.

"No," I said. "I haven't changed my mind. I just need to digest the new look and feel of the house. It's a lot different than when Grandma Abby lived here."

Fiona looked around as if seeing the room for the first time, smiling a bit. I knew she was enjoying this. When she turned back to me, she had a twinkle in her eye. "Abigail always had . . . antiquated tastes. You know that's not my style."

"Oh, I knew that in the first five minutes of our reunion," I said, smiling back sweetly.

It had taken me a while to believe Fiona was really my mother, the woman I hadn't seen since I was five years old. I'd pretty much written her off years ago, although I was smart enough to know I'd never fully healed the wound she'd left when she vanished one day. But I'd always wrestled with myself about it, with thoughts ranging from *Why would I want to meet her anyway? What kind of mother willingly abandons her child?* to *I wish she would just come home.*

Then she had shown up, seemingly out of the blue, during a major life crisis moment. With a half-sister I never knew I had and a wild story about how I was three-quarters witch and belonged to the two most powerful families in the witches' realm.

Did I mention it took a while for me to buy into that?

But as crazy as it sounded at the time, it was all true—and instead of being Violet Mooney, as I'd always believed, I was really Violet Raven Moonstone. My grandma Abby had been the matriarch witch of the Moonstone family, and my mother's family, the Ravenstars, were apparently also a very big deal. Which meant I had powers of my own. Big ones, if she was to be believed.

Apparently not big enough to keep my mother in check, though.

"I meant, like, move the furniture around. Get new beds. I didn't think. . . . Grandma Abby's house was . . . a little more soft and comforting," I said, glancing around at the purple metallic paint that now covered the living room walls, which had previously been a soft green. Ravens—fake ones, at least I hoped—perched on every available surface. The new artwork on the walls was all silver, metal, sharp edges. When I'd told Fiona she and my half-sister Zoe could move into Grandma Abby's house since they wanted to be close to me—and in Zoe's case, experience the mortal world for the first time—I didn't think she'd completely redecorate the entire place.

I guess it didn't really surprise me though. Fiona wasn't an ask-for-permission type of woman. This had been evident from day one, when she'd showed up and decided to move Sydney out of her apartment across the hall from me and move in there herself. She'd returned that situation to rights, though, and luckily Sydney had no memory of the brief move.

"That's what I said. Antiquated. Yes, well. It's a new era." Fiona swept over and kissed my cheeks. "Dinner?"

"Sure."

"What would you like?"

I thought about that. I hadn't eaten much today, between Nicole and how busy I'd been. But any time I'd had a moment to breathe I wasn't thinking about food, but rather about my troubled customer. The deep fear I'd felt emanating off her worried me, and I couldn't shake the feeling of that suffocating shadow.

And I wasn't sure she would do more with her crystals than toss them on her kitchen counter, or if I was lucky, in her purse.

So I'd forgotten to eat. "Something quick," I said. "I don't want you to go to a lot of trouble."

Fiona arched a perfectly shaped eyebrow at me, then lifted her hand over her head, snapping her fingers. Little sparks of glitter shot from her long fingernails, and as I watched, the dining room table was suddenly filled with food. A platter of sushi. Pad Thai and drunken noodles. A vegetable lasagna. Even two pizzas, one loaded with veggies and one plain cheese. The cheese was still bubbling. A giant salad. French fries.

My gaze slid from the table to Fiona. She blinked innocently at me. "Zoe," she called. "Dinner."

I knew better than to say anything. I plucked a spicy tuna roll off of the platter and popped it into my mouth. "All my favorites," I said with a smile.

My sister Zoe swept down the stairs. She looked like any other normal twenty-something in her yoga pants, sweatshirt, and ever-present Converse. Today's pair was covered in sparkles. Her waist-length, jet-black hair was down today, sporting fresh purple streaks. She took one look at the table and laughed out loud. "Let me guess. Vi didn't want you to make anything special for dinner?"

"Eventually I'll stop being at the center of all your jokes. Until then, I'm going to enjoy the food." I slid into my chair and spooned some drunken noodles onto my plate. She'd remembered I liked them with tofu, I noticed with a little twinge of glee. I guess I had some unfulfilled need for my mother to feed me. And to remember what I liked.

"Zoe. Whip us up some drinks, dear." Fiona sat and focused on me. "So, Violet. There's something I wanted to talk to you about," she said.

I glanced up, chewing. "Okay," I said once I'd swallowed.

"It's about the Magickal Council. You need to get up to speed pretty quickly. Things are going to be moving fast, with everything that's going on."

"I know," I said. "I'm working on it." When my Grandma Abby died, her seat on the Magickal Council went to me. Which was one of the reasons Fiona was so adamant about me believing her story about my heritage. If I didn't take the seat, it would've been opened up to a public vote for a new member. And some of the people who planned to run were, apparently, not very desirable members of the witch society.

Fiona nodded. "I know you are. And you're a fast learner. I also want you to understand the world itself, not just the logistics of how we operate."

Zoe plunked three glasses of ice water in front of us.

"Did you actually get those by hand?" Fiona asked, rolling her eyes.

Zoe frowned. "I'm trying to remember where I am and do things the way people here do them."

"Oh, darling. Don't be predictable," Fiona said. "You have powers for a reason. Use them." She turned back to me. "I have someone who's going to help you."

"Help me?" I took a sip of water. "Help me do what?"

"Fine," Zoe said. She pointed at the glass of water

Fiona had just raised to her lips, and it vanished, leaving Fiona with a surprised look.

"Well played," Fiona said.

"Thank you. I think we need iced tea," Zoe decided. She closed her eyes, reached up and touched a necklace with a giant raw lapis stone in the middle. A pitcher of iced tea with lemons floating in it appeared on the table.

"Very nice," Fiona said before she turned back to answer my question. "Help you navigate the council, and the rest of the world. He's very smart, well-respected, and he just happens to be our new general counsel." She sat back with a satisfied smile. "And he can't wait to meet you."

# CHAPTER FOUR

Warning bells were already going off. I didn't love the sound of this. "A lawyer?" I asked doubtfully.

"Yes, a lawyer," Fiona said.

I frowned. "Why do I need a lawyer?"

"I'm not saying you need a lawyer. I'm saying you need a resource and the best resource happens to *be* a lawyer. Keep up, dear."

I bit back a groan. I knew already that there was no changing Fiona's mind when she got like this. "Who is this guy?" I asked. "Is he some stuffy old man who's going to quote me all kinds of ancient texts or something?"

Fiona laughed. The sound washed over me, bringing me back to bits and pieces of a childhood I barely remembered. "Hardly. His name is Blake Alexander."

Now Zoe glanced up, her spoon suspended from its prior job of adding something from every dish to her plate. "Really? He's going to work with Violet? Man, I'm jealous."

"Blake Alexander?" I repeated, unable to hide my smirk. "What, did he walk off the set of a soap opera? *As the Witch Turns*, maybe?"

"You think you're joking, but he's definitely hot enough," Zoe said to me. "I wouldn't be surprised if he was some kind of actor or model or something in another life."

Fiona sighed.

"What? I'm just saying." Zoe grabbed a piece of pizza with her free hand and bit into it. I watched the cheese stretch before it finally gave in and broke. "If you've got to have someone helping you, I'd vote for him." She winked. "Especially if you can get some one-on-one time."

"Hot, huh?" I was still skeptical. "Hot how?"

Zoe dropped her spoon, picked up her phone, and flicked a finger at it before turning it around to show me.

"Oh. Well. Yeah, he is kind of hot." I took the phone so I could hold it closer. He didn't look much like a lawyer, at least not how I expected a lawyer to look. Maybe in the witch world it was different. But Blake Alexander had the kind of smoldering good looks that did make him look like a movie star—wavy black hair, five o'clock shadow, espresso-brown eyes. Which is totally a compliment since I love coffee.

"Kind of?" Zoe snorted.

I pointed at my mother. "You. Is this on purpose because you don't like Todd?" I asked, then turned to Zoe. "Is she trying to set me up with a lawyer?"

"I have no idea," Zoe said around a mouthful of cheese. "But you gotta admit—he's hotter than Todd. I mean, Todd's cute but . . ."

"Shut up, Zoe," I muttered. I was well aware of the shortcomings in my relationship and didn't need my sister—or my mother—pouring fuel on the fire. Plus Todd was the polar opposite of Blake, with his reddish blond hair and innocent good looks. There was nothing smoldering about him, and I couldn't deny the smoldering thing was appealing.

My mother rapped her knuckles on the table, shutting us both up. "I'm not trying to set you up with anyone. Your romance choices—poor as they are—are not my concern. I'm simply giving you a resource that you desperately need. And you *will* use him," Fiona added. "Am I clear?"

I hesitated. I still wasn't so sure I wanted to commit to something Fiona suggested without knowing the details.

Zoe watched us, eyes flicking back and forth between our stare down. Finally she said to me, "Go for it, Vi. I mean, I wouldn't mind hanging with him."

"Well, if you weren't dating a mortal," Fiona said pointedly.

Zoe made a face. "I don't mean I'm interested in him or anything. Just saying, he's hot. And Gabe is a great guy, so you can think what you want."

Zoe had recently started dating one of our local cops, Gabe Merlino. He *was* a good guy. And I had visions of that turning out very, very badly—mostly because he had no idea he was dating a witch, and I assumed when he found out it might be unexpected and potentially unwelcome.

Plus, my mother was not a fan of witches dating mortals. My dad had been half mortal, and look how that had turned out, as she would say.

"Mmhmm," Fiona said. "They're all great." She turned back to me. "I've already worked this out with Blake. Is there a problem?"

There were a lot of problems, but they didn't necessarily have anything to do with Blake. "I guess not," I said. "If you really think he can help me."

"I do," Fiona said, nodding with satisfaction. "He is just what you need."

"Is that really his name? Because it really does sound like a name on a soap. Do you have those?" I asked.

"Do I have what?" Fiona snapped.

"Soap operas. You know, like with witch actors?" I blinked innocently at her.

"Totally," Zoe said. "But it's not just limited to witches. We have all kinds of creatures in our world, you know."

My ears perked up. "Really? Like what?"

Zoe shrugged. "Vampires, unicorns, mermaids. My favorite is *Oceans of Magic*. It has mermaids and mermen and also Minotaurs. Their world is underwater. Want to see?" She grabbed her phone.

"No she doesn't want to see! The two of you, honestly," Fiona muttered. "This is serious business and you"—here she jabbed a long purple glitter-covered fingernail at me—"need to start paying attention and taking it as such. The Mazzy Diamond situation is making life very complicated right now, and you, my darling daughter, are right in the thick of that one."

That was enough to yank me out of my joking mood.

"Fine. I am taking it seriously. Jeez." I frowned and sank lower in my chair, images of pink unicorns and mermaids fading away. I hated being reminded of Mazzy.

Ever since someone had turned her into a puddle of slime—known in witch terms as being "genied"—in my shop, she'd been haunting me. I'd met Mazzy about a month ago when she showed up at my shop as an undercover reporter doing an exposé on fraudulent psychic practitioners. She was trying to prove that my crystals weren't really able to heal people. We had violently disagreed on that point and she'd finally come to see it my way—but unfortunately she'd gotten someone else angry along the way. Angry enough to commit one of the worst witch felonies possible.

I had learned that when someone was genied they were basically doomed—unless the exact person who'd done the deed confessed. And this had to happen before three full moons passed—otherwise, the person was locked in that bottle forever, their soul in a tortured place of limbo.

It sounded awful. Also, I wasn't sure if Zoe was messing with me about the mermaids and other creatures.

"Blake will be at the meeting tomorrow. I'll introduce you formally then. He's very excited about working with you," Fiona said.

"I'm sure he is. Can't wait," I said. I was being a little sarcastic. I still wasn't sure what to expect from Fiona, but I was kind of enjoying having them around, truth be told, which hadn't been the case just a few weeks ago. Fiona was a little intense, and I had some reservations about this council business, but aside from that it was nice to have a family again. It had been lonely after Grandma Abby died. My dad had been gone for five years, and she had been all I had left. I really hadn't ever let myself consider life without her.

Now I had a whole new life, and if nothing else, it was certainly getting interesting.

# Chapter Five

After dinner I said goodbye to my mother and sister, stepped onto the porch, and with a tug on my scarf, focused on my living room. Seconds later, there I was, standing in the middle of my apartment. My landings were much more graceful now, and I was getting just the right amount of glitter worked into my entrances. Glitter was my mother's trademark, but I was a big glitter girl myself and I'd adopted it as my own.

I'd been practicing teleporting and honestly, it was cool. When I'd first experienced it, I wasn't sure how I felt. It made me dizzy and I always worried I'd think of the wrong place while I was in transit, or worse, do it wrong and get sucked into a black hole or something. But so far so good, and it definitely saved me time. And gas money.

Monty, my orange cat—who was not in the least bit magickal—wasn't so sure of my new exit and entrance practices though. I think it scared him. He had stopped hiding under the bed, but he still looked at me suspiciously whenever I magically appeared. Who could blame him? Xander, on the other hand, didn't blink an eye. Which contributed to my general feeling that he wasn't really a cat. Especially since he was here in my apartment, and last I'd seen him was in my shop earlier. Since he had no thumbs to open doors—or a key—I figured something else was at play here. But I'd given up on trying to figure out Xander's ability to get around and finally decided to just accept it.

I fed the cats, changed into some yoga pants and a sweatshirt, and climbed into my bed with my grandmother's spell book, pausing to run my fingers over the cover, the words in that old school script feeling somehow familiar under my fingers.

I'd found the book in my old closet in Grandma Abby's house when I'd gone there searching for comfort during the chaotic weeks after Fiona came to town. But it had been only more recently that I'd been able to use it. I'd had to embrace my witch heritage in order to get access to the teachings. And the more that I understood and learned, the more information was becoming available to me in the book. It was the wildest thing. Every time I opened it there were new pages added. At first I'd thought I was going crazy when I kept discovering new pages after I was sure I'd gone through the whole thing with a fine-tooth comb. Then I started to catch on.

This world was both fascinating and baffling to me. But exciting at the same time.

And tonight, I was on a mission. I couldn't get Nicole St. James and that crazy shadow out of my mind. I wanted to help her—anyone living with that much fear deserved to feel better. And if anyone could help me help her, my grandmother could.

If there was something in the book that could tell me what that shadow might be, maybe I could find the right protection against it. I had thought about asking Fiona, but I wanted to try to figure it out myself. I'd recently felt like I'd started getting the hang of this witch stuff, and I wanted to keep improving.

Who knew—maybe I wouldn't need Blake Alexander for much after all.

I took a moment to tune in and really let the feeling of connecting with Grandma Abby's wisdom wash over me. It had been hard those first months without her, but after finding the book and letting this part of her life also become part of mine, I'd started feeling close to her again. Like she really was around me, guiding me and protecting me, the way I'd always felt when she was alive. I reached up and touched my topaz moon necklace. She'd given it to me when I was a child and instructed me never to take it off. When it had broken in an unfortunate accident last month, I'd learned that she'd infused the necklace with a spell to keep my mother away, per my father's wishes. When the spell had been broken, Fiona had been able to find me.

I'd wrestled with the feeling that I'd betrayed my grandmother when I broke the necklace, even though it was an accident. But I'd later realized that a lot of things had changed in the twenty-seven years my mother had been gone, and I truly felt that Grandma Abby would be okay with her being back in my life now. It was one of the reasons why I'd let Fiona move into my grandma's house. And she'd fixed the necklace for me.

I slowly flipped pages, pausing to let my gaze roam over the calligraphy text. My grandmother had been inputting entries into the book for a long time, it seemed. They ranged from spells about love to tips on everything from protection to positive thinking to all the different ways to use crystals to enhance your life. I'd never realized my interest in crystals had come from Grandma Abby. I'd just assumed it was something I'd discovered on my own and developed a knack for. But it turned out my grandmother had done a stellar job of keeping her own witchy stuff from me. She'd been a crystal enthusiast all along, and if I really let myself remember, it had always been her or her friends who had introduced me to one stone or another when I was young.

The only problem with the book was finding what I actually needed. Nothing seemed to be in any sort of order. I'd started simply envisioning what I needed and letting my gut guide me. I usually got where I needed to go—even if it didn't make sense right away. So I closed my eyes, willed the book to help me, and focused on how to conquer fears.

When I opened my eyes, the book was open to a spell. Not surprisingly, it involved crystals. I was pleased to see black tourmaline was the main component—it was one of the stones I'd picked for Nicole. I got up and gathered the other materials: sage, Himalayan salt, a crystal grid cloth, and clear quartz, labradorite, and selenite, the three other crystals called for. At some point Xander had leapt onto the bed and curled up by my side, and now Monty sauntered over and jumped up too, curiosity finally getting the better of him. He wasn't all that enthralled with Xander yet, but tonight he didn't let that stop him. I wondered if he was taking an interest in spell casting.

With my two babies by my side, I lit the sage stick, set the crystals in the grid, and concentrated, closing my eyes and focusing all the attention in my heart space toward Nicole to send love and peace to the places that were so overcome with fear. I held the vision of her safe, happy, and free in my mind until I could almost see it, like joyful colors in a rainbow swirling together after a storm.

I settled into the vision, completely letting go and allowing the peaceful feeling to wash over me, losing myself in the colors. I was in a trancelike state, only vaguely aware of my surroundings.

But then, something shifted. Black edges started to appear around the frame of my joyful space. I tried to focus more deeply on the colors, the peace I'd been feeling, but the black was invasive, creeping in and strangling the light. I could almost feel fingers snaking around my throat, closing around it and slowly cutting off my air. I wanted desperately to open my eyes and shake it off, but I couldn't. It was like one of those awful nightmares that you couldn't claw your way out of, stuck between the fog of sleep and the mobility of being awake, aware but completely helpless.

I tried to reach up and pull the fingers off my throat but my hands wouldn't even move. Just as I started to move into full-blown panic, a being swam into my view. I recognized the platinum blond hair streaked with metallic purples, greens, and blues—otherwise, her face was so contorted with fear I never would've known her at all.

It was Mazzy. And from the looks of it, her prison was just as bad as I'd envisioned. As I watched, she opened her mouth but nothing came out and she was frozen there, in front of me, her face captured in a soundless cry of terror as the blackness continued to seep in around us, trapping us both.

I felt a scream bubbling up but had no voice. I felt like I was truly drowning, and paralyzed from helping myself at all.

Then I felt something soft rubbing against my face, and the swish of a tail wrapping around my head. A soft purr against my ear.

And the blackness began to recede. Mazzy's face faded, and the peace and calm I'd initially found started to return. Instinctively I tried to move my hands and legs, and they worked. I forced my eyes open and found Xander sitting next to me, watching me intently.

I reached for him, nuzzling him close. "Thank you," I whispered. I couldn't help but feel like he'd just saved me from being sucked into some frightening prison. Icy fear swept over me. Had someone—some *being*—invaded my vision? Was it the same shadow that had come to Nicole today?

Goosebumps broke out on my flesh as I considered another option—what if I had been about to be genied like Mazzy?

And now I had no idea if I'd tuned into Nicole at all, or just Mazzy. Frustrated, I reached for my blue calcite angel stone, rubbing it between my fingers. I needed the soothing properties of calcite right now—it was one of my favorite calming stones. I sat with it for a few minutes, letting it do its work. When I felt better I put it next to my bed and rubbed my eyes, feeling calmer.

But I could really use some chocolate.

There was only one problem with that craving. Fiona was dead-set against chocolate. Zoe had told me it was because chocolate weakens a witch's power. And Fiona had removed every bit of it from my apartment. Even worse, anytime I tried to replace it, it magically disappeared.

I wasn't sure I believed this story. It seemed like a really dirty trick. Some witch, somewhere, should be able to use her powers to reverse it. But Zoe swore it was true and had been for centuries.

That didn't mean I couldn't eat any sweets, like, say, cheesecake. Unfortunately, I didn't have any. I supposed I could conjure some up, but that could be dangerous. Instead I went through my cabinets to see if there was anything of any value there. Nothing except some stale sugar cookies left over from the holidays. I tossed those with a sigh and double-checked my freezer for any remaining ice cream. Nothing.

Sometimes being a witch wasn't all it was cracked up to be. Especially when I was banned from my favorite treats.

# CHAPTER SIX

Later that night Fiona stood in her room—Abigail's old room—waiting for the disturbing vision to subside. She'd been just about to go up to the woods to sit under the nearly full moon, where she did her best thinking and planning, when it hit her.

There was a dark force hovering around her daughter.

Worse, she couldn't be sure what it was. But it confirmed her suspicions that everything beginning with Abigail's death was no coincidence. Something—someone—was plaguing their family.

She stalked the room, although it wasn't big enough for the type of stalking she was used to doing. Figured. Abigail had always been understated. She thought it gave her more credibility. Whereas Fiona wanted people to know her, to see her, to understand who she was and what she was capable of.

If you put it out there properly, there should be no confusion.

She paused and put her hands to her temples, focusing on Blake Alexander. "I need to talk to you," she murmured. "Now."

A moment later, the air crackled and he appeared, framed by his signature colored smoke. She would never entertain Zoe by agreeing with her, but her daughter was right—he was definitely hot.

Too bad he could've been her son. Besides, she had other plans for him.

"Fiona. You summoned?" Blake asked with a tiny smile, which faded when he saw her face. "What's wrong?" Then he looked around. "Nice place. It was Abigail's right?"

Fiona nodded. "I had to redecorate."

Blake took a moment to survey the room. She allowed him; he'd been close to Abigail. More than his own family. When she died, he'd been inconsolable. Which was why he was the perfect person to help uncover the truth about her death.

Finally he focused on her. "You know she's still here, right?" he said. "I can feel her. She wants to help."

Fiona did know. And although she didn't like to be reminded of it, she'd accepted that it needed to be so if she wanted to get close to her firstborn. She supposed it was some sort of karmic repayment for her part in the whole family debacle that had resulted in their twenty-seven-year separation.

"Yes, yes," she said impatiently. "But that's not why I called you here."

"Right. So what's up?"

"It's Violet. I'm worried."

Blake frowned. "What happened?"

"I can feel when she's in trouble. It's how I found her when Abigail's spell was broken—I had a vision. And I had another one earlier. There are dark forces circling her. They've tried to block themselves from being detected but I can see them. I just can't see who and what their intent is."

"So what do you think this is about? Mazzy Diamond?" Blake asked.

"It's bigger than that," Fiona said quietly. "It always has been. But yes, Mazzy is part of it. And I need to find out how. And why." She sat on the bed. "I'm hiring Mac."

Blake raised his eyebrows. "Finnegan?"

Fiona nodded. "I want the Diamond case solved and he's the only one I trust. I want to know who did this. And that's where we have to start." What she didn't tell Blake was that Abigail had hired Mac to investigate people too. She'd found an agreement between them in the house, in a secret compartment in Abigail's desk. Unfortunately, she had no details. One of the leprechauns' greatest traits was their ability to keep secrets. Whatever Mac and Abigail had been working on, Mac wouldn't tell her. Which made Fiona crazy.

So she figured if she put Mac on the case, eventually the two investigations would collide.

Blake sat in the chair next to the window, taking this all in. "Mac and his team are no joke, Fiona. They'll leave no stone unturned. No matter who it hurts."

"That's exactly why I want them."

Blake held her gaze. "Even if it's related to Abigail."

"Well of course," Fiona said, her tone matter-of-fact. "We all want to know what truly happened to her."

Blake took that in. "What about the fact that you and Josie took care of Mazzy's cleanup and didn't tell anyone?"

"We'll deal with it. I'm not worried about it. We did nothing wrong."

Blake narrowed his eyes. "Except not alert the highest law enforcement in the land that a crime had occurred. A genieing, of all things."

Fiona shrugged. "We did. Just not in the moment."

Blake held up his hands as if to say, *I can't argue this point with you.*

"They can't touch me. I'm not worried. But there is one other thing," Fiona said.

"What is it?"

"Violet has this boyfriend. Todd Langston." She said the name like it was a foul word. "There's something off about him but I can't put my finger on it."

"Mortal?" Blake asked.

"That's the question," Fiona said. "There is something very familiar about him but I can't quite grasp it. I want to know if there's anything I should be aware of. My daughter . . . isn't well-versed in these types of things."

"Well, how could she be? She's been a witch for five minutes." Blake sighed and ran a hand over his hair. "What are you thinking? A shapeshifter? A demon? A . . . genie?"

Fiona shook her head slowly. "A Sageblood."

Blake's eyebrows shot up. He rose slowly to his feet. "Come again?"

She nodded slowly. "Yes. A relative of yours."

"Careful," Blake said, his tone dangerously soft. "You know how I feel about my family."

"I do. That's why I'm counting on you."

"Counting on me to do what?"

"To find out who he really is. And what he wants with my daughter." Fiona smiled, but there was no warmth. "Before I have to have him taken care of."

Blake looked like he might argue, but decided not to. Instead he said, "Fine. I'll see what I can do."

"Brilliant," Fiona said. "I'll let you know when I've spoken with Mac."

Blake saluted her, then vanished from the room. Fiona opened the window to clear the smoke he'd left behind and ended up sitting there for a long time, staring out into the mortal night.

# CHAPTER SEVEN

*Sunday*

I kept shorter hours at my shop on Sundays—opened at ten, closed at four—which allowed me to have some extra time to myself in the morning. Sometimes I spent it on self-care—yoga or a workout or even just coffee at Pete's, or some extra time in bed lounging with the cats. Others I took the quiet time in my shop to change my displays or unpack new shipments. Today I chose a combination of both. I'd woken earlier than I wanted to and meditated, then hung out in bed and pulled oracle cards with the cats. Monty usually picked his own. Xander, well, he didn't really need them.

But I couldn't concentrate. My crazy experience with the crystal and Mazzy last night had completely thrown me off and was probably why I'd been awake with my mind racing so early. I got to the shop around eight. As soon as I stepped inside, the energy of the place grounded me. I took a moment to savor it, then got to work unpacking and settled into a rhythm where I didn't have to think too much.

I'd been working for an hour or so when I heard a key in the front door and the bell jangling. I looked up and smiled when I saw Josie.

"Hey. What are you doing here so early?" I asked, going over to give her a hug. She was so tall I barely reached her shoulders. "I missed you yesterday."

"Me too." Josie squeezed me back. "I had a couple things I needed to do so I figured I'd stop by now. You know I'm an early bird." She grinned, brushing her bangs out of her eyes.

Josie Cook had been my mentor in many ways over the years, from crystals to just plain life. I'd met her in high school when I started haunting local crystals shops. She'd worked in one that was now defunct. I'd started spending a lot of time in there—so much so that eventually she'd gotten me a part-time job. She'd taught me everything I knew about crystals and gave me enough confidence to open my own shop a few years back. Now she worked here.

But I'd recently discovered Josie and I had another connection. She was also a witch, and she'd known my family forever. So in retrospect, I assumed that me "bumping into her" was more by design than by chance.

Either way I was grateful for it, although I had to admit learning that had been even more shocking than seeing my mother again.

"I wanted to make sure the new order had everything. We had a bunch of requests last week, you know? I like keeping our customers happy." She studied me. "Everything okay?"

I turned to go back to my boxes so I didn't have to meet her eyes. "Just woke up early. Didn't want to waste time, you know?"

"Mmm," Josie said, but she didn't push. "Well, since we have some time, you want to grab some breakfast?"

I thought about that. I hadn't been hungry this morning, but that would likely change soon and then I'd regret not eating. And I could probably use some protein. "Sure," I said.

"Great. Let me just put my stuff down. We'll go to the diner. I can do the order when we come back." She went behind the counter to drop her stuff.

"Sounds good." I put the crystal I'd been about to unwrap back in the box and grabbed my coat. While I waited for Josie, I wandered around, checking out my displays and straightening things. There were a couple of holes that needed to be filled after people had purchased stones so I rearranged a few things. In doing so, I noticed that the green opal that Nicole St. James had been looking at yesterday was out of place. I reached over to straighten it out.

And seared my fingers on it.

Gasping, I pulled my hand back. What in the Goddess? There were stones that heated up in direct sunlight—clear quartz could actually start a fire if it sat in bright sunlight for too long—but today was overcast and cold, just like most winter days around here.

"What's wrong?" Josie asked as she came back into the shop.

I glanced up at her. "This opal . . ." I rubbed my fingers together. They still stung. "It burned my hand."

Josie raised her eyebrows. "You don't say?" She came over to inspect it.

"Don't—" I began as she reached for it, but she plucked it off the shelf and held it.

"It feels cool to me." She closed her eyes and put it close to her heart.

I watched her. Was I crazy? I'd been asking myself that a lot over the past month. Thank goodness the answer was still no to the best of my knowledge, but there was a first time for everything.

Josie opened her eyes and shook her head. "I'm not getting any weird vibe from it. We should cleanse it with selenite."

I nodded, reaching to take it from her.

And it happened again.

I snatched my hand away. "Ow! What the heck? Jose, what does that mean?"

"I don't know," Josie admitted. She studied the stone. "Where did it come from?"

"My Massachusetts supplier. My best one. But that's not the point. It's been here for a while. I moved it yesterday." I was starting to get a bad feeling. "Stones capture people's energies, right? So what does that mean if now it's burning people?" I couldn't shake the vision of Nicole St. James holding it, and that shadow surrounding her like a cloak.

"They're fiery?" Josie grinned, but her smile faded when she saw the look on my face. "I don't know, Vi. I'm not getting heat from it."

"So why am I picking it up? Is it like a message?" Josie had to know.

But she looked as stumped as I felt. "Honestly Vi, that's never happened to me." Josie placed it back in its spot. "Let's clear it." She went over and grabbed a selenite plate from another table and placed the opal on it. Selenite cleared stones of any built-up energy or gunk they'd collected when they were used for healing. "We'll see what happens when we get back. Come on, we should go. I think you need some food."

"I hope that's it." I followed her out, pausing to lock the door behind me. Hot to the touch could mean a few things if it truly was related to Nicole: That she had a fiery temper, or she was in a place that was about to catch on fire. Heck, maybe she was about to meet a fire-breathing dragon.

I gave the door one last, frustrated tug to make sure it was shut. As I did, a phrase floated almost unbidden into my mind: *Playing with fire.*

But who? Nicole? Or me?

# CHAPTER EIGHT

Josie and I slid into a booth in the back of the diner. I didn't see Ginny, though I knew she usually worked Sundays. Bummer, because I wanted to ask how Nicole was. Maybe she had the day off, or maybe she was coming in later. There were only a few other customers—the typical Sunday morning crowd. Families with small children and bleary-eyed parents clearly hoping some waffles would entertain their kids for a while. A young couple, newly in love, holding hands and gazing at each other with goofy looks. I watched them for a moment too long. When I glanced back at Josie she was watching me.

"How's things with Todd?" she asked pointedly.

Great. First Zoe and my mother—with the whole Blake Alexander business thrown in for good measure—and now Josie. I didn't constantly need to be reminded how un-awesome things were with my boyfriend. Aside from the fact that his bar was basically his life, he'd kind of betrayed me with a potential business deal he'd been involved in. It hadn't come to fruition, but he hadn't been honest with me and it hadn't sat well. We'd been on rocky terms ever since. Between that and me finding out I was a witch and not really knowing how to explain that—so I hadn't—I'd been pretty certain I was going to break up with him. But Todd Langston was nothing if not charming, and he'd talked me out of it every time I'd headed there. I simply hadn't had the energy to fight it. So I'd shelved the idea because I was tired of having the conversation. But I found myself avoiding him more and more.

"Fine," was all I said to Josie. I didn't want to get into it. Josie had never loved Todd. She thought he didn't treat me as well as he should. Honestly, none of my friends were that enthusiastic about him, although they didn't outright trash him to my face.

"Hmm," Josie said, but she let it go.

The waitress came over. I was suddenly starving and ordered a veggie omelet with extra hash browns. Josie got eggs Benedict. And lots of coffee.

"Hey. You know a guy named Blake Alexander?" I asked Josie when the waitress left.

"Blake?" I swear she almost swooned. "I do. Why?"

"Jeez," I said. "Got a little crush there, do you?" What was it with this guy? Now I was curious.

"Oh, Violet. Don't be silly." She waved me off but I swore her cheeks were red. "Blake is a little young for me. Why do you ask?"

I shrugged. "Zoe thinks he's hot too."

"No! I mean, why are you asking if I know him?"

"Because my mother informed me that he's going to

be my witch tutor from now on, or something like that." I wrinkled my nose. "Do I really need a tutor?"

"A tutor?" Josie asked skeptically. "Do you mean like a coach or something?"

"You mean there are life coaches in the witch world?" I laughed out loud, then lowered my voice when one of the other patrons glanced over at me curiously. "Seriously though, I thought that was only for us weirdo mortals."

"I'm sure that's not your mother's intent," Josie said. "Blake is a lawyer, for one thing. He's very well versed in the ways of witches and our whole world. He's been advocating for the rights of beings who've found themselves with fewer rights than the witch population for many years."

"Really? What kind of beings?"

"Oh, trust me. There are plenty of others who are supposed to be equal citizens, but they find themselves experiencing all kinds of prejudice because they aren't witches, or are only partial witches. When the reality is, there are tons of different beings that make up our world, and our world is way better because of it. In my opinion."

"Hmm." That, at least, sounded interesting. And like there were a lot of parallels to the mortal world.

"Yeah. He's a good guy. Very smart." She was swooning again.

"How do you know him?" I asked.

Josie shrugged. "Lots of people who've been involved in any kind of political or advocacy work know him. He's always involved in something that makes things better for someone." She smiled. "I think he'll be a big help to you."

I still felt skeptical. "Fiona was pretty vague, but she said she didn't want me to just understand the council logistics. That there were things about the world I needed to learn fast."

The waitress approached. Josie waited until she'd dropped off the coffees. "Because it's just like this world, Vi. You're not born knowing things. You have to learn. And there are laws and rules and social etiquette just like here. And you're going to be on the council so it's really important that you know what you're doing. You don't want to make any major faux pas. And this thing with Mazzy . . ." she trailed off, shaking her head.

I didn't want to think about Mazzy right now, or her fate. "So why can't you and Fiona teach me?"

Josie laughed. "Because you're not so great at taking what your mother says at face value. And I don't know nearly enough. Listen. Blake is the perfect guy to do it. He understands the council, he knows the law, and he loves to teach. Plus he's an objective third party, something your mother and I most certainly are not."

Before I could ask her anything else, the door to the diner opened and, as if we'd conjured him up from our earlier conversation, Todd walked in. I was surprised to see him—it was early for him, especially after a late night at the bar. He glanced around the diner, then his eyes fell on me. We both froze for a second, then I lifted my hand and waved.

"Who're you waving to?" Josie turned, looking around, then saw him making his way over. "Oh."

"Hey." Todd stopped next to our booth and bent to brush my lips with his, pausing to nod at Josie. He smiled the boyish smile that had captured my attention and, for a long time, my heart, a lock of hair falling impishly over his eye. "Morning, babe. Haven't heard from you since yesterday morning."

"Sorry. Was out and about early," I said.

"How are you, Todd?" Josie asked.

"Good. You?"

"I'm fine," she said.

"You're up early," I said when they both lapsed into silence.

"Yeah, lots to do today." He stood next to our booth, a bit awkwardly.

"You're getting breakfast?" I asked.

He nodded.

I motioned for him to sit. "We already ordered, but you can eat with us." I scooted over so he could sit next to me.

He slid into the booth and placed his hand over mine.

I extracted my hand and picked up my coffee, relieved to see the waitress arrive with our food.

She placed our plates on the table then smiled at Todd. "What can I get you?"

He ordered some bacon and eggs, then turned back to me. "Want to do something tonight?"

I attacked my omelet, both because I was hungry and also because I didn't want to answer right away. "I'm not sure I can," I said, once I'd swallowed. "I have a big day tomorrow."

I regretted the comment as soon as I said it. I had the Magickal Council meeting tomorrow night, but I couldn't very well tell Todd about that. The whole idea of telling him anything about my newfound heritage made me squirm. And the more time that passed, the harder it was to imagine it. How do you start that conversation? *Hey, by the way, I'm a witch.* Todd was pretty normal—wrapped up in running his bar and, well, all things mortal. He had no time to play Darrin to my Samantha. And I'm pretty sure he wouldn't want to. And if I was honest, I wasn't sure I wanted him to. When I thought about my new life I definitely didn't have the whole picture yet, but from what I could see Todd wasn't playing a huge role in it.

"Really? What's going on?" he asked.

I took another giant bite of food, acutely aware that Josie watched the whole exchange through narrowed eyes. "Back-to-back consults, and training Syd, and I have to have dinner with Fiona tomorrow night."

Josie kept eating, not saying a word. I wished she'd hurry up.

"Oh," Todd said, looking deflated. "I miss you, Vi."

I took one more bite of hash browns, feeling like I was in a speed-eating contest, and glanced at Josie, hoping she was almost done. "I miss you too. But we'll find some time soon."

"Sure." He didn't look convinced. He opened his mouth to say something else, then changed his mind.

The waitress must've put a rush on his food because she brought it over shortly after. We all ate in relative silence. I finished first. And probably had given myself indigestion. But Josie followed suit a minute later.

I looked pointedly at my watch. "Gotta get going. I'll call you tomorrow, okay?" I said to Todd.

"Yeah. Sure. We could always get coffee in the morning," he suggested.

"I'll text you. Not sure if I'm going to yoga." I smiled, a little too brightly, then turned to Josie. "Ready?"

He made no move to let me out. I was suddenly overcome by the urge to snap my bracelet and teleport myself home so I didn't have to deal with all this. But that would cause quite a stir.

Josie drained her cup too, tossed a twenty on the table and nodded. "Ready." She looked pointedly at Todd. "That means you have to get up."

Todd wouldn't cross Josie. He reluctantly slid out of the booth. I gave him a quick kiss, our lips barely touching, then pulled on my coat and followed Josie out.

"Things seem to be going well with you two," she remarked dryly as we stepped out into the night air.

I ignored her comment. "So back to Blake," I said, annoyed that our conversation had been interrupted. "Do you think he can he help me make my powers work better?"

"I don't know that he's going to be that kind of teacher, Vi. I think your mother wants to make sure you know the rules of the road. That's all. But," she said, her eyes twinkling mischievously, "maybe you can get him to bend the rules a little bit. I've heard he's good at that too."

# CHAPTER NINE

*Monday*

"Fiona, doll, you gonna call this meetin' to order?"

I watched, fascinated, as the woman with glittering orange hair and shrill voice who chewed gum like a Valley girl directed this question to my mother and wondered how fast my mother would turn her into some kind of small animal. Or if they really did those sorts of things here in witch land.

Although they had plenty of animals already present. Apparently the council members often brought their familiars to the meetings, a small detail my mother hadn't mentioned to me. I knew she wasn't big on familiars—at least that's what she'd told me—but I would've loved to have brought Xander for the festivities. Although I supposed if Xander wanted to come, he would've just showed up.

Regardless, he would have been enamored with the falcon sitting on Vivienne Dandy's shoulder. At least, I thought it was a falcon. I'd never actually seen one up close and personal before. There was also a bunny curled up next to Posey, Fiona's niece, which I guess made her my cousin, and a ferret next to Gordon Magnum. He was adorable—the ferret, not Gordon—and I really wanted to play with him.

Judging from the look on Fiona's face as she observed the orange-haired woman, though, the small animal spell was still a possibility. "My dear Theodora. I'm well aware of what time it is," Fiona said. "We're waiting for one more attendee." Her eyes swept the council chambers one more time, looking, I assumed, for the elusive Blake Alexander, who had yet to show up for his first meeting as our esteemed legal counsel. And my esteemed tutor, or coach, or whatever he was doing. I assumed this because his seat with his gold-plated name on the table in front of it was the only empty seat left.

I wasn't really sure what to expect at this Magickal Council meeting. I knew Mazzy was on the agenda, and that made me nervous. But Fiona seemed very blasé about the whole thing. She had escorted me here tonight, which meant she'd grabbed my hand and I'd barely had a chance to blink before . . . poof! We were sitting at this table, in this giant room with cathedral ceilings and crazy cool etchings from floor to ceiling. The setup was similar to other councils I'd seen, like in North Harbor where city council members sat on an elevated platform behind a big fancy table with fancy chairs, although that was nothing compared to this place. The chair I sat in was made from lush leather and the heavy mahogany table could've been something out of the Royal Family's meeting room.

The council members, however, would probably not be the types of people who would hang out in the Queen's presence. There were four men and seven women besides me and Fiona, and they ranged from kind of normal to straight out of a TV show in appearance. They weren't wearing pointy hats or anything, but still—you had Theodora and her giant orange hair crusted with gold sparkles, and Christobel with her long, ivory lace dress, Goth make-up, and killer boots with the five-inch heels. Ember, with a short, platinum bob who wore all white, from her dress to her shoes. Alan, with long, thick black hair that women must envy. Gordon, the professorial type with his gray ponytail and what looked like a raven feather tucked into it. Vivienne, who seemed grandmotherly but had a sharp streak in her. And Jet, the quietest member—aside from me—a skinny guy with short hair, glasses, and a nose piercing that connected to an earring.

I'd been part of two other council meetings so far—the first, my swearing in, which had been purely ceremonial, and one other, which I'd spent worrying that I would have to talk. Like when you went to a new school and had to stand up and tell the class something about yourself. God, I hated those moments. I'd always wanted to vanish into my desk. I'd worried this would be worse, but they'd gone surprisingly easy on me. I figured it had something to do with Fiona.

What was even more fascinating to me was that I was actually related to some of these people. Fiona had promised that as soon as I got settled, she'd have a party for me here in this realm with my other family and some close friends. It was kind of mind boggling to me. I'd had such a tiny little family for so long, and it had whittled down to no one after Grandma Abby died. And now it seemed like I had a huge family to whom I needed to get acclimated. For example, Fiona had four sisters—so I had a lot of aunts. I could hardly wrap my mind around it.

I figured they felt the same way about me. Like Posey— my cousin—and her rabbit sat across the table from me but she had barely looked at me. Posey had more of a librarian vibe than a witch vibe, maybe because she hadn't looked up from her book since I'd been here. She had the same red hair as I did, but it hung flat and limp. She wore a simple black dress, no jewelry, and seemed perfectly comfortable being alone in this crowd of people. I wanted to talk to her but she didn't seem all that friendly. Christobel, however, had been super friendly from the start. I also knew she was a distant relative on my Grandma Abby's side.

I spent some time trying to tune into auras, but there were too many of them and it was overwhelming. I abandoned my efforts and sipped my coffee, which Pete had given me before I'd "left" for the meeting—the teleporting aspect of this whole new life was still so weird to me—with a promise that he'd done a little something to it so it stayed hot all the way to the bottom of the cup, for which I was grateful. There was not much worse than your coffee going cold halfway through. And I was exhausted. I'd gone to yoga this morning after all, so I hadn't had a chance to meet Todd, and the shop had been busy all day so I hadn't even spoken to him. We'd exchanged casual texts, but that was it. Josie had pointed out to me— again—that I needed to address the situation.

I would. Eventually.

The door to the council chambers crashed open and a man strode in. He had the hurried gait of someone running late, but he didn't look rushed or frazzled. Instead, he flashed a lazy smile at the group gathered around the table as he took his seat at the end, tossing his too-long black curls out of his eyes, which settled on me as they passed over the crowd. He wore jeans and a button-down shirt with a casual jacket, and he hadn't shaved. He looked just like the picture Zoe had showed me. He took a seat at the council table in the one empty chair.

Blake Alexander. In the flesh.

Damn, was my first thought. Everyone was right—he *was* hot. It was even more apparent in person. But he also looked like he was confident in his hotness. He probably didn't hesitate to use it to his advantage.

"My apologies," he said, his gaze traveling over the council members. "I had a leprechaun consult that ran over."

Unfortunately, I'd just taken a sip of my coffee, because I promptly choked on it. Leprechaun consult? Was he kidding? What in the . . .

Fiona shot me a look. Blake's amused grin settled back on my face. I could read the curiosity in his eyes.

"Darlin', you can be late anytime you want," Theodora murmured, completely unfazed by the leprechaun reference. "Just walk a little slower on your way over to your seat, 'kay?"

Fiona shot her a look and rapped her gavel against the table a bit harder than necessary. "This meeting of the Magickal Council will come to order. Roll call please, Serenity."

Once Serenity went through the names of all the members, she paused and looked at Blake, then at my mother.

Fiona sighed. "Do you need me to introduce Blake, Serenity?"

"Well, yes, please," Serenity stammered a bit. "Since you're the chairwoman."

"Fine. Council, please welcome Blake Alexander. He is our new legal counsel and will replace Manfred Wooley as our representative. Any questions?"

No one had questions, but most of them welcomed Blake, except for Oscar Sageblood, the one member of the council who seemed to outwardly hate me. Oscar sneered at him a little.

"Great. Let's get to the agenda." Fiona paused and flicked a finger at the screen on the wall. A scroll appeared with the agenda on it. It had one topic: *Mariza Diamond.*

I shivered a little. I'd known it was coming, of course, but just thinking about the day I'd found Mazzy in my shop, nothing more than a puddle of slime, made me feel sick.

"So." Fiona looked around the room. "We're all aware of what happened to Ms. Diamond. As you all know, we haven't had a genie incident in nearly fifty years. This is a very brazen, disturbing act that has our community quite unsettled. And it's up to us to take further action and get to the bottom of this. And ultimately, we have the power to free Ms. Diamond if we put our resources and our heads together to uncover who did this. Which would also help us prevent future attacks. Because as you all know, if they get away with it once, it becomes easier to do it again, and again." She sat back. "So who wants to start?"

"Well," said Oscar, "why don't we start with your daughter, Fiona? After all, this happened at her mortal place of business, right? Timely, given her grand reentrance into our world."

All eyes in the room turned to me. I froze, feeling my face turn as red as my hair, not sure what I was supposed to say. Here I was the newest member of the council, placed here as the heir apparent to my Grandma Abby, and I couldn't seem to string a sentence together. I hope she wasn't watching this from afar and wishing her seat had just gone to a vote.

"Oscar, you're so predictable," Fiona said with a sigh. "As you all know, my daughter had just been introduced to her heritage and her powers at the time of the attack. She didn't even know what it meant to be genied. So it's a good try, but I'm afraid accusing her of something has no basis in reality."

"She'll still have to give a report to our police," Oscar said. "She's a witness, if nothing else."

I didn't like his suggestion. Actually, I didn't much like *him* at this point.

"Leave her alone," Ember chimed in. "She's not the issue here. Mariza is where we should focus—whatever she was involved in could give us a clue. She was a reporter, after all. Which meant she could have been looking into something that someone didn't like."

"Excellent point, Ember," Hattie Blandon said, winking at me. I liked Hattie—she came off as a little flaky, but I could see by the way she watched people that she was no dummy. I sensed she preferred it that way so she always had the upper hand. "Has anyone spoken to her newspaper colleagues? Have the police been looking into this?" She looked at Fiona.

"Of course, Hattie," Fiona said, a little impatiently.

"I'm sorry Fiona, but if this was a random attack, why

was the location of the act at this particular store?" Oscar asked pointedly, ignoring Hattie's attempt to take the conversation in a different direction.

I didn't like the way he spoke about me as if I wasn't there. I also didn't like the fact that he still hadn't made eye contact with me once. I was a peer now. I was on this council, and I deserved to be treated with some respect.

"I didn't say it was random, if you were listening," Fiona said. Her voice reminded me of a freshly sharpened knife, gleaming and ready to take on its victim.

Before she could go any further, Blake cut in.

"May I make a suggestion?" he asked. When Oscar opened his mouth, presumably to protest, Blake ignored him and went on. "We need to appoint a subcommittee with members from this council, along with members of our police force, to plan for a deeper look into this. I don't think it makes sense for the whole council to dedicate their time to it. The council should be here to discuss findings and make decisions on next steps. If everyone agrees, I'll take the lead in organizing that subcommittee."

"Fabulous idea," Theodora said, batting her spiderweb eyelashes at him. "I'll volunteer!"

Blake returned her smile, though his own held a twinge of amusement. "Thank you, Theodora. I think we'll limit this to four from this group, just so we make sure we keep everything flexible and fast-moving. I'd like to recommend Fiona as chairperson, as well as Ember, and Alan. Violet will, of course, be there in an advisory capacity due to her proximity to the issue."

"Blake's proposal makes sense to me," Fiona said, before anyone could chime in. "All in favor?" She raised her gavel—which was covered in glitter—and looked expectantly around the table.

Oscar gave a derisive snort, demonstrating that he was clearly not in favor. The rest of the committee looked at each other, then almost in unison raised their hands—with the exception of Serenity. She and Oscar were the only naysayers.

"Approved." Fiona banged her gavel, then looked expectantly at Blake. "Can you work with the police force for their representation and set up our first meeting? Time is of the essence."

"Done," Blake said smoothly.

Fiona nodded and then moved on, opening the floor for a roundtable. Blake caught my eye and winked. I felt my face turn red and looked away.

# CHAPTER TEN

After the meeting, Fiona motioned for me to wait. I knew she wanted to formally introduce me and Blake and send us off on our way so he could teach me everything I needed to know about being a witch with a seat on the Magickal Council. It took the rest of the group a while to clear out of the chambers—aside from Oscar, who'd made a beeline for the door as soon as the meeting was over, clearly disgruntled about the way the meeting had gone.

Vivienne made her way over to me, leaning in for a hug. "How are you doing, sweetheart?"

"I'm fine," I said. "Just trying to learn everyone and everything. It's a little . . ."

"Overwhelming?" Vivienne laughed. "I'm sure. You

have a lot of catching up to do. Don't let that buffoon Oscar get to you. You're a natural. I can see it in you. How can you not be, with the Ravenstars in your lineage? And the great Abigail Moonstone, while we're being honest."

Hearing my grandmother's name made me sad. "I'm certainly not going to be able to fill my grandmother's shoes any time soon," I said.

"Honey," Vivienne said. "She wouldn't want you to fill her shoes. She'd want you to buy your own shoes." Then with a wink and a tug on the chain holding her eyeglasses, she was gone.

I remembered as a kid watching *The Wizard of Oz* with my dad and grandma and how fascinated Dorothy had been with the way the magickal people appeared and disappeared. *My, people come and go so quickly around here*, she'd said. I kind of felt like Dorothy these days.

After Vivienne left I waited while Blake, Fiona, Ember, and Alan finished having a conversation, then Fiona finally brought Blake over to where I was sitting, still sipping the coffee Pete had made me—which was totally still hot. Gotta love that power. I put that on my mental list of powers I needed to learn.

"Blake, I'd like you to meet my daughter, Violet," Fiona said, presenting me with a flourish.

I stood up and offered my hand. "Nice to meet you."

"Same here," Blake said. He looked amused by the handshake. Come to think of it, he looked like he was amused by most things. His hand was soft and cool and he hung on a second too long. "Welcome to your life. What do you think of it so far?"

I glanced at Fiona. "It's . . . interesting."

"Well, it's gonna get even more interesting, so hang on," Blake advised. "Speaking of which. Your mother tells me you need some help."

"She certainly seems to think so," I said.

"Darling," Fiona cut in. "You *do* need help. I told you, you have to get up to speed quickly, remember?" She pretended to smile at me, but really she was gritting her teeth pretty hard. I could almost read her mind: *Don't embarrass me!*

"It's okay to admit you need help, you know," Blake said, that amused smirk still playing at the corner of his pouty mouth.

I couldn't tell if he was teasing or not, but either way I kind of hated feeling like I was a hundred steps behind everyone else.

"I'm getting there," I said hating the defensive sound in my own voice. "I'm a fast learner. I can teleport really well. And I'm getting even better at my auric and crystal work. I've been reading my grandmother's book."

A heavy sadness flashed across Blake's face, so fast I thought I'd imagined it. Had he and Grandma Abby been close?

"Her book, huh?" Blake said. "What book is this?"

"A book of her knowledge. Spells and stuff. She did a lot with crystals and the moon."

"I see. Did her book tell you what to do if another type of being tries to harm a witch?"

I frowned. "Another type of being? I don't think so. Although pages keep appearing so I guess it means that I'm learning more when that happens?" I looked at Fiona for encouragement, but she didn't say anything. She looked annoyed to be discussing Grandma Abby's book at all.

Blake ignored me. "Does it tell you how to handle a situation where a witch commits a forbidden act against a member of his or her own family? Or what a forbidden act even is?"

I shook my head, feeling my jaw clench of its own accord.

"Did it tell you which members of the council you can trust, and which ones you can't? Did it tell you about the centuries-old resentments that have been festering in this community for years and have started to come to the surface? Does it tell you what could happen if a witch was found guilty of negating another witch's power by using black magic?"

I got the sense he could go on like this for a while. "No," I snapped. "She wasn't a judge or a lawyer. She was collecting spells and passing along her knowledge in case I ever came back into this life. I get it—I don't know anything compared to you. I'm sure no one does."

"I beg your pardon," Fiona said, drawing herself up even taller on her platform shoes.

I ignored her. "So whatever you have to teach me, let's just get it over with, okay?" I picked up my coffee cup and pitched it toward the trash. I missed, hitting the rim of the can, and the small bit of remaining coffee splattered onto the floor. Without even thinking about it I snapped my fingers and made a lifting motion with my hand. The liquid poured upward back into the cup and finished its journey into the trash can.

Behind me, Blake applauded. "Nice work."

"Oh, save it," I muttered. I hated condescending men who thought they were smarter than any woman they met. He might be hot, but he was just as annoying as the rest of them.

Although I knew it wasn't really him I was mad at. I hated the huge learning curve ahead of me. I wished I could just figure out a way to infuse the knowledge I needed into my brain. I mean, there had to be a way, right? We were witches.

But everything he'd just said had sounded so daunting.

"Violet." Fiona's voice cut through my mental rant, and she didn't sound pleased. "Stop acting like a child. Blake is here to help you. And I expect that you'll take his knowledge and expertise and get the full benefit of it. He's being generous with his time."

Before I could even turn and acknowledge what she'd said, I heard the air crackle, which meant she'd taken leave of us. When I spun around, all that was left was her usual pile of glitter. This time, it was multicolored.

Blake chuckled. "Your mom always knew how to make an exit. And an entrance, for that matter."

I sniffed.

"Listen, Violet. I'm not trying to be a know-it-all hot-shot lawyer guy. Because I know that's what you're thinking. Isn't it?"

"Yeah, actually it is. Because that's what you sound like."

He nodded. "Fair enough. But this Mazzy Diamond thing? It's pretty crazy. And what your mother is worried about is exactly where Oscar the Great started going today. Right at you. And if you don't know how to navigate what's coming, you could be in big trouble."

I studied him, trying to see if I could energetically feel his aura and figure out if he was telling the truth. It wasn't hard to tune in to him. And the color that came through loud and clear was blue. Vibrant blue, not murky or dark. Blue definitely meant balance—someone who was cool, calm, and collected. And confident. But I could see that before I even thought of checking his aura. What I didn't get was any kind of negative color. I'd almost expected red, which wasn't necessarily negative, but could indicate an overwhelming personality. None of that came to me.

He watched me watch him for a minute, then he smiled. "Get what you need?"

I was a little taken aback, but tried to cover it up. "What do you mean?"

"You're trying to see who I am. I get it. I would do the same if I was you."

I narrowed my eyes at him. "You read minds or something?"

Blake grinned. "I can't give away all my secrets right off the bat, can I?"

I wondered if he could actually see what I was doing, and if he could influence how I saw him. I had no idea what kind of powers this guy had, and even though my mother seemed to trust him implicitly, I wasn't as quick to jump on the bandwagon. I didn't say anything.

"So when are you free to meet?" he asked. "I get the sense Fiona wants us to start getting together soon."

"You think?" I sighed. "How about tomorrow?"

He nodded. "I can be free tomorrow. Where do you want to meet?"

I had no idea. The only places I'd been in this new realm were the council chambers and a gemstone store Zoe had taken me to with charmed stones. I'd loved it and definitely wanted to go back, but hadn't had a chance yet. I had no idea if it was appropriate to invite Blake to North Harbor, but Josie knew him so maybe Pete did too. We could meet at Pete's, but then that might raise questions that I didn't want to answer. How would I explain my clandestine meeting with a guy who, while annoying, was pretty hot, to Todd?

"Violet. That wasn't a hard question," Blake said, but he sounded more curious than annoyed.

"I don't really know anywhere," I said. "To your earlier point about how clueless I am. But I like coffee."

He sighed. "I did not say you were clueless. I think you're very brave and I can tell you're smart. So listen. Why don't we meet at Potions Cafe right around the corner on Amethyst Street? I think you'll like it."

I smirked. "As in witches' potions?"

He grinned. "You'll have to wait and see."

"What the heck," I said. "At least I'll get to people watch."

# CHAPTER ELEVEN

*Tuesday*

"**A**re you going to the meeting tonight?" Sydney asked.

We were in my shop the next day eating a quick lunch in the back room while Josie manned the floor. It had been busy—we hadn't stopped since we unlocked the door at nine. I'd finally noticed around two that we hadn't eaten anything and called over to the sushi place to save us.

Sydney had been working here for nearly a month now. I liked having her around. She brought a different energy to the shop—enthusiastic newbie. If anyone had told me she would ever be working at my store, I would've laughed. Syd was not very woo-woo. She hadn't even been inside my store until recently, and we'd been friends ever since she'd moved to town two years ago. It wasn't that she wasn't supportive. More like she had trouble believing in anything she couldn't see. But she'd recently started to come around after encountering some challenges in her own life.

And she was having trouble with her shop, Yesterday. Not the business itself—people loved the wide selection of vintage clothing and other wares she sold—but there were certain members of the town government who didn't like that she had parked the tiny house that housed her business in Charlie Klein's parking lot. Mostly they didn't like that she wasn't paying taxes thanks to this setup. So Charlie had gotten notice that he'd be paying the taxes if she didn't move the house. While he'd vowed to help her fight it, Syd had focused most of her operations online and moved the shop to Grandma Abby's driveway until she figured things out.

Which also gave me heartburn, because Goddess only knew what she might see hanging out over there.

Josie and I also needed more help because The Full Moon was busy. Which made me happy, but was also causing me some stress lately given all my new responsibilities. With Syd here it took some of the pressure off so I could deal with Fiona, and Blake, and everything else I seemed to have gotten myself into. Plus since she ran her own business she already knew that whole side of it, so all I really had to teach her about were the crystals.

I selected another piece of sushi and popped it in my mouth as I considered her question, trying to figure out what she was talking about. "Which meeting?" For a second I thought she meant my meeting later with Blake, but she couldn't possibly have known about it. That was just my guilt at hiding my newfound powers from one of my best friends.

"The town meeting. Remember, it's the special meeting to talk about next steps for the railroad bridge?" Syd ate the last veggie spring roll dripping with soy sauce, eyeing me while she chewed.

"Oh crap, that's tonight." I'd completely forgotten about it, and I did want to go. Partly because I cared about my town and partly because I was hoping to see Nicole St. James there, given her involvement in the project. Although I wasn't sure if she was still involved since she had changed jobs, but it was worth a shot. I wanted to see if the crystals were working for her. She hadn't been back to tell me and Ginny hadn't spoken to her, so if there was a chance I could bump into her, all the better. "What time?"

"Starts at six thirty. I have a sitter for Presley. Josie is going too. It's important, Vi."

I knew it was important. We all knew it wasn't over after the proposal had been shot down at referendum last month, but no one thought it would be back on the docket so fast. The people pushing for it were raising the alarm bells that the old tracks were getting more dangerous by the moment, and we needed to come together on a solution. It was especially important to Sydney and mirrored a contentious time in her own life. Her daughter Presley's father had been involved in the fight against the bridge, and although he'd left town, I think part of her wanted to carry on with it.

My meeting with Blake wasn't until eight, so I could probably make it work. "Yes, I'm coming," I said.

"Thanks," Syd said, her face crinkling into a relieved smile.

"Have you heard from Presley's dad?" I asked.

She shook her head. "Aside from the checks, no." She

pasted on a smile, but I could see the disappointment behind it. "It's okay. He told me not to expect much from him. The money is helping."

"But it doesn't take the place of a dad for Presley. I get it."

Syd jerked her shoulder in a shrug. "Whatever. He's probably not the best dad I could've picked for her."

I didn't know how to make her feel better, so I reached over and squeezed her hand. It made me think of my dad, who had fought so fiercely for what he believed to be right for me that it had changed the whole trajectory of my life. But still, I'd ended up exactly where he hadn't wanted me—a practicing witch living two lives. Was it better or worse that he had simply delayed the whole thing? I wasn't sure. I just had to believe that everything had worked out exactly as it was supposed to.

I still missed him terribly. My mother wouldn't discuss him, and since Grandma Abby was gone, I had no one to talk to about him. I certainly had no one to help me unpack his decisions about renouncing his powers and trying to make sure mine stayed dormant. I knew he'd done it only to protect me, but it was still hard to understand given what I knew now.

*Ask Blake.* The thought came so unbidden into my mind, as if someone had whispered it in my ear, that it startled me. What would Blake know about my dad? He'd seemed to have known my grandma, but that didn't surprise me—Grandma Abby had been active on the council until the day she died. My dad hadn't been part of this world since my mother had left us twenty-seven years ago. Unlike my grandma Abby, who had also seemingly been living two lives, my dad wanted nothing to do with this side of his family and she had respected his wishes.

"What?" Syd asked.

"Hmm? Nothing. Just thinking." I picked at the last couple pieces of sushi in my tray, then pushed them away. "I've gotta get back out front. I have a one-on-one consult in a few minutes."

"Okay. I'll finish this for you if you're done." Syd winked at me. Eating was her favorite thing.

"Help yourself." I headed out into the shop, grabbing a selenite palm stone out of my little basket behind my counter for my pocket. I hoped it would clear out some of these thoughts so I could focus on the job at hand.

# CHAPTER TWELVE

Josie, Syd, and I closed up at six and piled into Syd's little red Honda CRV to head to town hall. I wondered how this meeting would go. The divide among the townspeople over this project hadn't had enough time to dissipate yet, so I didn't see how we would get much done with emotions still running so high. I wondered if the rush was truly about the welfare of the community or about someone's pockets. While I hoped it was the former, I had a sneaking suspicion it was the latter.

We arrived fifteen minutes early, but the council chamber was already packed. I thought back to last night's closed-door Magickal Council meeting. It felt a lot different than this one. Contention would still abound, but at least I wasn't at the center of it.

I scanned the room for familiar faces and saw a few.

Charlie Klein was here. Charlie was one of our town's most colorful residents, in my opinion. He'd lived in North Harbor forever and owned a barbershop one street over from my shop—with the infamous parking lot that had been causing so much controversy. Charlie lifted his hand in a wave when he saw us, then returned to his conversation with the man sitting beside him.

At six twenty-nine, the council members filed through the door in the back and onto the dais to take their seats. There had been an emergency election to fill Carla Fernandez's seat last month after her unfortunate death. Krista Carmichael, who owned the delightful Hubert's Candy Store, had won the election by a landslide. Her opponent had been a lot like Carla and it seemed people were ready for a change. Also, Krista was a witch, the second witch I knew on the council. Frank Mercury, president pro tempore, was a witch as well. I wanted to ask Blake about that—was that a common practice? Did it only happen in communities that had a lot of witches?— unless it would make his head bigger.

Krista, for her part, looked delighted to be there. She waved at the crowd like a celebrity taking the stage.

I'd learned that there was a lot more to my local friends than met the eye. Once I'd been indoctrinated into the witch world, I'd discovered that more and more people who lived in my town shared my secret. One fun fact I'd learned: witch-owned or witch-friendly businesses kept mason jars filled with twinkling white lights in their windows as a safe-space signal to others. Pete had them. I'd thought for years that he was just a thoughtful decorator.

The mayor, Simon Birch, banged the gavel at exactly six thirty and thanked everyone for coming. "As many of you know, we recently saw the original bridge project proposal defeated at referendum," he said. "Since then, we have been asked to bring another proposal to the town for public comment. At this time I'd like to ask the engineering firm the city retained to summarize their report. Donald?"

The lead engineer stepped up to the mic at the front of the room and started talking about infrastructure, basic design, and a bunch of other engineering jargon that made my mind wander. I took another look around the room for Nicole St. James, but didn't see her. I tried not to read too much into it. It was, after all, a whole new case. And she had switched jobs, so maybe this was all in the past. Or maybe she simply couldn't make it.

After the engineers spoke, Birch glanced at his agenda. "I also have a law firm representative who would like to make a statement. Nicole St. James, from Townsend and Hammerstein, if you could come up?"

I sat straight up in my seat. Apparently she was still involved, even at her new job. I looked around, but didn't see her anywhere. Nor did she get up to take the podium.

Impatience twisted Birch's face. "Nicole St. James," he repeated.

I heard some whispers in the crowd, then a woman with fiery, orange-red hair standing out in corkscrew curls stood up and strode to the podium, straightening her suit jacket as she walked. I wondered if her hair was naturally that color.

"I'm afraid she isn't present," she said. "I'm Sylvia Townsend. I'll make the statement."

Townsend. She must own the firm, or be related to someone who owned the firm. I studied her, trying to gauge how old she was, as if that would give me a clue. I couldn't tell, but she certainly seemed poised and confident and as if she'd been around the legal block a few times. She had an iPad with her, but barely glanced at it as she told the room why she and her firm were working with the town on an ongoing basis to move the bridge project forward.

I leaned over to Josie. "Did she say her firm is working *for* the project?"

Josie nodded.

I wondered if that was weird, that Nicole had been on one side at her last job and now found herself squarely on the other. I leaned forward, listening more intently as Sylvia spoke about how the railroad bridge unequivocally needed to be repaired or replaced, and the town and its residents must come together in a thoughtful manner to get that done with minimal disruption to the town's economy.

Once she finished and went back to her seat, Birch opened up the floor for public comment. The first person to stand up and ask to be recognized was a man dressed in an expensive suit. He looked like he was in his late forties, with dark hair slicked back and one of those trendy scruffy beards. He strode over to the microphone in the center of the hall like he owned the place. As I watched, his gaze lingered on Sylvia Townsend for a minute longer than anyone else. She stared back at him, unflinching.

"Ladies and gentlemen of the council, and of North Harbor, thank you for recognizing me," he said with a nod. "I'm Jackson Bogart, 75 Tucson Lane, and owner of the building at 800 Main Street, which the town is proposing to take by eminent domain to redirect the railroad tracks. I understand the need to ensure our railroad continues to bring prosperity to the region in a safe and sound manner, especially since we're a commuter town and many of our residents work in New York City. However, I need to ask that we also be sensitive to the needs of our own community. I built that building fifteen years ago, and it has since been an economic driver in town, housing a number of productive and revenue-driving businesses."

Bogart went on for another few minutes about how many businesses thrived in the building and how many workers would be displaced. He stressed that he wasn't opposed to redirecting the tracks but asked that the engineers find a different route that would be less disruptive to the city—and offered up financial resources to do a study on what it would take to repair the current tracks. Which brought the environmentalists off the sidelines, who had a lot of arguments about why that would disrupt the river's ecosystem.

We sat through an hour and a half of residents from both sides of the tracks—no pun intended—verbalizing their opinions on why the project should or should not go forward. A lot of it was reiteration from the last couple of months, arguments I could repeat in my sleep. Some of the people who spoke up offered alternate plans, which others pooh-poohed and said they had no basis in reality or engineering. Finally, just as I was about to slip out to make my meeting with Blake, the line of residents ceased and the council declared the meeting was over.

I leaned over to Josie and Syd. "I have to go," I said. "I have an appointment."

"With who?" Syd asked automatically.

I hesitated. Since she didn't know I was a witch, it made it a little hard to tell her about my meeting with a fellow witch attorney who was going to help educate me on the rules of the Magickal Council. "My mother," I said.

Josie hid a smile. Syd gave me a skeptical look. "You need to make an appointment with your mother? Don't you need a ride?"

"She's very formal. No, I'm going to walk back for my car. I'll see you tomorrow," I said, and hurried out before she could ask anything else.

As I merged with the crowd of people making their way for the door, my brain was working overtime. I wondered why Nicole hadn't showed up tonight. I truly hoped she was okay. I had a nagging feeling in the pit of my stomach but I wasn't sure if that was a true intuitive feeling about her, or stress about the council meeting and Mazzy, or a combination. I wondered if Ginny had been in touch with her yet. I glanced at my watch. She was probably at Todd's. Even if I'd wanted to go—which I didn't—I had to go meet Blake.

It would have to wait until tomorrow.

# CHAPTER THIRTEEN

I left City Hall, went behind the building into a small alley, and tugged on my earring, intent on landing at the Potions cafe. I had no idea where it was and hoped that my intention was enough to get me there. I did love the name of the cafe and couldn't wait to check it out.

When I opened my eyes, I was definitely not in North Harbor anymore. And I was pleased to find myself standing in an adorable little alleyway right in front of the place I'd been seeking. I took a moment to look around. This street reminded me of some little gems I'd found in London the time I'd visited with Grandma Abby, right after my dad died. She'd taken me to get our minds off our sadness and we'd had a lovely time exploring the city. And every so often we'd find a little cobblestone street down which cars couldn't even fit, tucked away like our own little secret. Usually those were the places with the best shops.

I still had no idea where I actually was. I'd held a picture in my mind of Blake and the cafe, and to my great relief had gotten myself here. If I had to figure out the "normal" way to get around in this new world on my own, I seriously hoped there was a witchy GPS that could assist me.

I pushed open the door and stepped inside, not sure what to expect. I sort of thought it would be like Pete's place, since he was a witch and all, and at first glance it was. Patrons crowded the tables and the little bar facing the street, and if I didn't know where I was, I wouldn't think any of them were witches. Plus it was the same type of setup you'd expect for a coffee shop, with a barista bar and a menu written in chalk hanging behind the counter. I focused on the menu, curious about whether the coffee would be similar to what I would get at Pete's. But after looking at it, I was surprised to see the menu was changing every few seconds. And not like a digital sign changes based on the computer to which it's connected. The chalk writing was erasing and rewriting every so often, showing first a coffee menu, a "potions" menu, and then a food specials menu.

The counter display, where Pete's might be full of pastries or sandwiches or snacks, offered interestingly shaped bottles full of colorful liquids that reminded me of science experiments. I wondered if it was just a fancy way to display milk. I ventured closer to the counter and realized the coffee machines were running themselves. There were some baristas behind the counter, but they were not physically making the coffees. The machines were humming along, making the concoctions and then, as I continued to stare in fascination, the cups and plates were delivering themselves to the patrons.

I didn't realize I was smiling like a fool until Blake appeared at my elbow. "Having a good time without me?" he asked, that teasing lilt in his voice.

I cleared my throat. "I love coffee shops," I said, forcing my face back into a serious look.

"Well, good. Then I'm glad I suggested we come here. Although it's a little more than coffee. Come on." He took my arm and led me to the counter. The girl at the register with two hoops through her left nostril turned to greet us, giving Blake a google-eyed look. Then she turned to me and her eyes widened.

"Are you . . . Violet Moonstone?" she asked, a touch of awe in her voice.

I stared at her, trying to think if I'd met her somewhere already. I'd barely spent any time in my new world, and she didn't look familiar at all. "I am," I said uncertainly.

"Ohmigod." The girl clasped her hands together in front of her face. "You guys," she called over her shoulder. "It's Violet Moonstone! Like, *the* Violet Moonstone!"

Blake glanced at me. "Wow. Either you're a celeb or your reputation precedes you," he said under his breath as the other counter people crowded around, all of them staring at me unabashedly like I was a zoo animal who was there for their pleasure and scrutiny.

"Wow, it really is her," the older of the women said, tilting her head to examine me from all angles. Her metallic silver hair swung in a short bob around her chin. "Welcome home, sweetheart! You are the spittin' image of that mommy of yours. Except for that red hair!" She reached over, delicately, and threaded her fingers through a chunk of my hair. "It's gawgeous!"

"You're, like, a legend around here," the nose-pierced girl said. "I heard you have the powers to, like, see into people's souls. What is that even *like*? I mean, people claim they can do that on the Wicked Web and stuff, but I didn't think anyone really could."

I hadn't heard that myself, and had no clue what she was talking about. I looked at Blake, silently asking for help.

"You have no idea what she can do," he said smoothly. "But we actually have a meeting, so you'll have to chat about it with her some other time, okay?"

They all nodded. "What potion do you want?" the older woman asked.

"You mean coffee?" I asked.

She cocked her head at me. "You've got some things to learn, don't ya? Coffee's the add-on, baby. This here's a potions cafe. You come here to get the pick-me-up you need in your life. You in the mood for confidence, peace, strength? Or . . ." she inclined her head toward Blake, a small smile playing around her lips. "Love?"

For some reason that made my face heat up. I avoided looking at Blake, but had no idea how to answer.

Luckily, he jumped in. "We'll have two of your wisdom and confidence mixes with espressos," he said smoothly, then steered me to a table.

"Potions?" I said once we were seated. "Like, real witchy potions you make in a cauldron?"

Blake tipped his head back and burst out laughing. He had a nice laugh. "I have no idea how Maisie Chabert cooks her potions, but she's one of the most famous witches you'll ever hear about," he said. "She's been bottling and selling her potions for hundreds of years. Her daughters mostly run the business now. They have cafes in every major city in our world. I told you it was a potions cafe."

Maisie Chabert. I filed the name away in my mind for some research later. Clearly there *was* a lot I needed to learn. But something he'd said caught my attention. "Hundreds of years?"

He nodded.

"So how do you know who gets to live hundreds of years? And is that relative? Like, is it not a big thing here, but if they live mostly in the mortal world, it's more apparent that they're older and they might die younger?"

Blake's expression sobered. He was quick—I could tell he knew exactly why I was asking.

My Grandma Abby, by everyone's account—even Fiona's, and she'd had some fundamental differences with my grandma—had been one of the most powerful witches ever. So when she'd died, it had raised my mother's suspicions that some deeper conspiracy was happening.

Because it seemed she wasn't supposed to be able to die—at least that's the sense I was getting from a lot of these conversations. I knew my mother was trying to downplay it for my benefit, but I could tell how serious it was.

But Blake gave me a straight answer, which made me respect him. "Mortal world life doesn't matter," he said. "Most witches have no time limits on their lives unless they choose to have them. And for extremely powerful witches, it's even more true."

I frowned, still trying to make this all make sense. "So you don't age?"

"It's not really about aging," he said. "Most witches who are present in the mortal world can change their appearance to reflect the ages society thinks they should be"—he used air quotes around the word *should*—"but aging and appearance and mortality aren't the same here."

I glanced down at my own thirty-two-year-old skin, wondering why my mother had never taken the time to tell me about this over the past month. She'd been so ready with other helpful hints, like how chocolate diminishes a witch's power and how you should avoid being genied at all costs, but this whole conversation had never come up. "So . . . I'm not really this age?"

"What, you worried you're going to need wrinkle cream?"

I rolled my eyes. "Never mind."

"Violet." He reached over and laid a hand on my arm. "I'm teasing. Look, like I said, there are a million things you need to know and you're not going to figure it all out in one hour-long conversation with me. And right now, we have more pressing things to talk about."

More pressing than why my grandmother died? I disagreed, but kept my mouth shut for the moment. "Fine. But what did that girl mean, I could see into people's souls? Can I do that?"

Blake sighed. "There's a lot of rumors out there about how powerful you are. I would ignore most of them and figure out your own stuff. Okay?"

"One more question," I said.

I could tell he wanted me to shut up, but to his credit he motioned me to go ahead.

"What's the Wicked Web?"

"It's like the dark web for witches," he said. "Nothing

you need to be worried about. Now can we focus on business?"

"Fine. Where do we start?"

"We start," he said, "with the Magickal Council. What it is, who's on it, and why you shouldn't trust the majority of the council members."

# CHAPTER FOURTEEN

Our drinks landed on the table in front of us—a tray for each of us with beautiful steaming bottles, each bubbling and gurgling in its own special way, along with a mug full of our espressos. I needed a moment to process what he'd just said, so I examined the bottle. "What do we do, just add it to the coffee?"

Blake nodded.

"What if it tastes weird? What does it taste like?"

"It doesn't. Trust me. Remember, she's been doing this for hundreds of years."

The feeling that I'd gotten when Fiona and Zoe first showed up in my life—like I'd fallen down some wacky rabbit hole—was back and in full force. I lifted the pink, twisted bottle with the steam coming out and tentatively sniffed. It smelled pleasant enough. I'd expected something floral but it wasn't, and I couldn't quite put my finger on what, exactly, it was, but it seemed okay. I watched Blake, trying not to make it obvious that I didn't know what I was doing. He poured enough into the mug to fill it, so I followed suit.

"So this is really going to make me smarter and more confident?" I asked. I was kind of joking, but he nodded.

"Absolutely. And the best part of all, the base recipe is the same but it's crafted to react to the person's individual genetics. So it will give you exactly what you need. And the taste is different for everyone too." Blake lifted his cup and sipped. "There are a lot of witches who are way better witches thanks to Maisie."

Sounded good to me. Seems like I needed all the express help I could get being a better witch. I sipped my own and my eyes widened. It tasted amazing. A little sweet, but I could still make out the coffee flavors, along with chocolate and caramel and maybe marshmallow? I felt like I was having a candy bar or the best cup of cocoa I'd ever tasted. "This is delicious." I might not miss chocolate if I could have these.

"You think I would steer you wrong?" Blake took another sip, then set his cup down. "Okay. Back to business. The council members."

"Right. The council members." I sipped more, reluctant to put my cup down. "I thought this council were the people who held witches to their highest standards? Why wouldn't I be able to trust them? Well, aside from Oscar." I wrinkled my nose at the memory of his blustering remarks at the meeting.

Blake rolled his eyes. "Really? Do you feel that way about the government down in your other world?"

I thought about that. "Federal or local?"

"Does it matter?"

"Sometimes." Then I sighed. "No, not really. Okay, I get it. They're political and out for themselves." Then I frowned. "Do you mean my mother too?"

"If you're asking if I'm saying your mother is crooked, absolutely not. Everyone has their own motives and agenda though, right? Your mother's is to fiercely defend the witch world as we know it. As the Ravenstar and Moonstone ancestors said it should be. Violet, you do realize you are part of two of the most powerful families in our world?"

I was getting a little tired of hearing that. It seemed like a lot of pressure. "Yeah, so I've heard. My mother told me," I said. "Many times."

Blake shook his head impatiently. "I don't mean did someone tell you and you nodded and smiled. I mean, do you really understand what that means?"

I shrugged. "Yeah. I mean, I guess so. It means they had everything to do with this world as you know it." I waved my hand vaguely around me, trying to encompass the magnitude of where I was. I was failing too. He was right. I had no clue.

Blake watched me for a second through the steam from his mug. "You should read up on it."

"Where would I do that? I doubt my local library has the history of the Moonstone and Ravenstar witches." I was being sarcastic again but Blake shook his head.

"Not your local library, but there are plenty of libraries and the historical center here," he said. "All you have to do is ask for the information."

He had a point. I'd seen firsthand how available information was when Josie had shown me a video on her "mortal" cell phone of me and my mother when we were kids. I had to stop thinking of this like my other world. Which was easier said than done.

"Okay. I get it. So who should I not trust?"

"I'll restate the obvious, but Oscar for one."

"Noted. And I didn't even need your help on that one." I sipped my drink again. "I think the way he tried to get me blamed for Mazzy's . . . situation tipped me off there. Any other helpful hints?"

"Oscar is more dangerous than you think," Blake said quietly. "Don't turn your back on him. There are grave penalties for consorting with genies for nefarious reasons, and that's exactly where he's trying to steer things."

Despite the warmth of my drink, I felt a shiver of foreboding. "You mean he's trying to set me up?"

"I don't know what his intentions are, but he doesn't like you."

"He doesn't even know me," I protested.

Blake shook his head. "Doesn't matter. He's a Sage-blood. Most of them hate the Ravenstars and the Moonstones, so you have a double black mark. They think your families have been in power way too long and are prohibiting advancements."

I thought about this. "What kind of advancements?"

Blake smiled wryly. "Not the kind of advancements anyone with any sense would want. Really they just want to be in power."

"They sound charming," I muttered.

"Like I said, most of them. Not all. Also, your cousin Posey. Watch out for her."

I thought of my quiet cousin sitting with her book and her rabbit. "Why? She's related to me."

"Doesn't matter. She's jealous of you and your mother. She thinks her mother—Fiona's sister Winifred—should have more of a standing in the community so she can have more power. She really resents the fact that you swooped in and are kind of a celebrity."

Again with that word. "What is it about me that makes anyone think celebrity?" I asked, exasperated. "I'm probably the most clueless person sitting here in this realm right now."

"Yeah but your . . . past is kind of legendary around here. You saw how the girls at the counter treated you," Blake pointed out. "You think that doesn't carry over to things like the council?"

Legendary? I was having a hard time processing all of this, especially the idea that people didn't like me or were jealous. These were supposed to be my people who would rally around me. At least that was the message I'd gotten from Fiona when she'd been trying to convince me to come to the "other side."

"That's ridiculous," I said, trying to sound confident. "Everyone on the council has the same standing. But if anything, I'd be lower than everyone else because I'm so new. And clearly don't know anything."

Blake leaned back in his chair and cocked his head at me, drumming his fingers on the table. "Are you this naive in your other life?" he asked finally.

"What do you mean, naive? I'm not naive!"

"Violet. In what reality is everyone of equal standing in any political environment?"

"Well, in my world—my other world—there's Democrats and Republicans," I began, thinking he was asking me a serious question. But he laughed out loud, cutting me off.

"I wasn't asking you for a civics lesson in mortal terms. I was making a point. Yes, you have Democrats and Re-

publicans over there. But up here, you have families. And
legacies. And long-standing resentments and people who
feel they've been sidelined. That there's a system in place
that doesn't reflect the idea that times are changing and
that the same people have been in power way too long.
And really, all of that isn't much different than what
you're experiencing over there. It's just manifesting differently, because, well, we're witches and they're mortals."

I pulled my chair in closer. "Tell me the real story
about being genied."

His eyes got very dark. "What do you mean, the real
story? You saw it with your own eyes."

"I mean, there's got to be a reason why it's such an
awful crime, right?"

"Again," Blake said, "you saw it with your own eyes.
Being stuck in a bottle for eternity doesn't seem awful to
you?"

I glared at him. "Don't get flip with me. You know
what I mean."

"Violet. We're not here to talk about that. We're here
to talk about the council."

"And since that's a huge focus for the council right
now, don't you think I have the right to know?" I folded
my arms over my chest and locked eyes with him.

He stared me down. "Look. Sometime I'll tell you
about the history there, but now is not the time."

"But why not? Don't we want to save her?"

"Of course we want to save her."

"Well, the clock's ticking." I tapped my watch for em-
phasis. "Three full moons, right? We've already had one
and the next one is in three days. That means—"

"I know what it means," he cut in, his voice terse. "And I'm telling you to leave it alone."

"But I can help! I'm getting better at figuring out my powers." I leaned forward earnestly and dropped my voice. "I even think I've seen her. In various forms. When I'm using my crystals. There's colors and shapes and I've seen her actual face—"

"Enough." His tone was harsh enough that it shut me up abruptly. "Stay away from this, Violet. I'm telling you, this is not something you want to be involved in any more than you have to be. Do you understand me?"

# CHAPTER FIFTEEN

*Wednesday*

The next morning I woke up in a bad mood. I wasn't going to yoga today, even though it would probably make me feel better. Instead, I wanted to get my coffee and a giant, feeling-sorry-for-myself muffin at Pete's, then go to the shop and immerse myself in my work. I was totally letting all the stuff Blake had told me last night get to me.

When I'd landed back in my apartment after our meeting, I was exhausted. And overwhelmed. I hated to admit it, but Blake was right. I didn't know anything about what I was involved in. And yet I was supposed to be one of the people making decisions, while protecting myself against the people who hated me because of my family and some who wanted to set me up to take the fall for Mazzy's situation. And, if I had my way, finding a way to get Mazzy out of her prison despite the fact that everyone wanted me to stay out of it.

It felt like a lot.

I had a flash of anger at Fiona. One, because she had glossed over a lot of this stuff, assuring me life would be grand once I accepted my lineage and stepped up to my responsibilities. Two, because she'd made sure any and all of my chocolate was removed from my home and I desperately wanted a piece right now, even though it was only seven in the morning.

"So much for the confidence potion," I said to Monty, who lounged at the foot of my bed, his tail twitching.

I debated how long I could lie in bed. I hadn't thought I'd feel this hopeless this soon. I mean, I wasn't expecting all rainbows and unicorns (no pun intended given Zoe's claims that there were, actually, unicorns in my new world) over in my mother's hood, but I definitely wasn't expecting feuds and revenge and evil plots. Especially not ones that I was in the middle of just because of who I was and the seat I held.

Plus, Blake had made me mad last night. After he'd basically shut me down about Mazzy, we'd spent another tense half hour together while I silently fumed at him. Which I suspected he knew.

Of course, I was supposed to see him again in the very near future for my next "lesson." At this point I thought I'd just rather have it out with Oscar Sageblood.

Maybe I'd talk to Josie about some of the stuff I'd learned last night.

I didn't like to think that our relationship had changed at all after my mother came to town, but when I'd learned that not only had Josie known all this time about what had happened in my family but that she was also in contact with my mother, it really bothered me. She'd known how much my mother leaving weighed on my mind my entire life and had never even given a hint that she knew anything.

In fairness, I was sure Grandma Abby had forbidden it. She and Josie both probably knew I'd have stormed right to my grandmother and dad and demanded answers for why they had banished my mother from my life.

I threw off my covers and got out of bed, about to head into the kitchen to get coffee when the now-familiar static that signaled a witch was nearby tingled in the air. A second later my mother appeared in front of me. Dressed to the nines, as usual, even at this time of morning.

"Good morning, darling," she said, flashing me a smile and flicking some glitter at me for good measure.

"Do you really need to do that?" I asked, aware that I sounded cranky. "I do have a door, you know."

Fiona smiled wickedly. "So you'd rather me show up in the hallway this way?"

She had a point. "What do you need? I have to get to work."

"I wanted to drop by and tell you our first subcommittee meeting is tomorrow morning. Nine o'clock."

"Meeting?" I repeated.

"Yes, darling. The subcommittee we formed the other night. Don't you remember?"

Truthfully, I'd tried to put it out of my mind, but it looked like I couldn't avoid it. "Yeah. I remember. Where do I need to go?"

"I'll pick you up," she said with a wink. "Be ready." She tapped her giant ring and vanished.

I brushed the glitter out of my hair, then focused on a

cup of coffee. And smiled with satisfaction once it landed in my hand, bold and steaming.

I took a few minutes to enjoy my coffee, then showered, got dressed, and paused to examine myself critically in the mirror. I had black circles under my eyes. I concentrated really hard, running my finger under my eyes like I had a concealer stick. I was delighted to see the black disappear. I tried it on my hair to give it more lift and was pleased when that worked just as well. While I was at it, the color could use a sprucing up as well. I ran a hand over my hair, keeping my intention focused on a brighter, sharper shade of red. When I was done I stepped back and studied myself approvingly.

At least I was pretty good at this part.

I fed the cats, threw my phone into my bag, and headed downstairs. I stepped out onto the street and pulled my scarf up around my face as the first blast of cold air hit me. I hadn't brought gloves so I stuck my hands deep in my pockets and hurried down the street.

If I hadn't looked up to wave to Charlie Klein when he called to me from across the street, I would have missed the poster stuck to one of the telephone poles near the street corner. As it was, it barely registered.

But then I looked again. And my eyes widened.

It was a "Missing" poster. It wasn't for a dog or a cat—which relieved me at first because those things tore my heart out whenever I saw one—but for a person. When I realized which person, my heart plummeted into the depths of my stomach.

The face staring back at me was Nicole St. James.

I stood there for a moment, staring at the telephone pole while the morning went on around me. I could feel people walking by. I'm sure some of them stopped to send curious glances my way, but I didn't even notice. Nicole looked happier in the photo than she had in person. She was hiking somewhere and had turned to smile at the camera. Her blond hair was longer in the photo and hung loose around her shoulders. She wore a smile that, again unlike when I'd met her, this time reached her eyes. I'd never gotten someone's aura from a photo before, but I was confident that this version of Nicole had a completely different read than the woman I'd met.

I had no idea how long I stood there before I felt someone come up behind me and I heard a voice.

"So sad, right?"

I turned to find Anna Montgomery, owner of the art shop and paint bar The Muse, standing behind me. "Yeah," I said, trying to force my voice to normal. "It is. Do you know anything about this? When did she go missing?"

Anna shrugged. "Not much. Just what I've heard around town. Of course it's big news this morning because Ginny has been passing out posters. I guess she hasn't shown up for work in a couple of days. But I heard the cops didn't jump on it because her car is gone. You know, grown woman and all, they figure she probably took off on her own." She shook her head, still gazing at the photo.

Ginny. I'd meant to call her first thing this morning to ask about Nicole's absence last night from the meeting. I guess this explained it. "Do you know Nicole?" I asked.

Anna nodded, shifting her eyes to me. "A bit. Her mother is an art teacher and she gets all her supplies from my shop. She was so proud of Nicole for being a successful lawyer."

"Do you think it's true? That she took off?" I asked.

Anna shook her head. "I don't. Her whole family is here. They're pretty close. I can't imagine what they're going through. So sad," she repeated. "I guess you can't be too careful." She squeezed my arm and walked away.

"Yeah," I murmured. "I guess not."

I forced my feet to move and pulled open the door to The Friendly Bean a few minutes later. As I came in Pete glanced up from making a coffee and waved.

I waved back and joined the line, still trying to reconcile what I'd seen. Nicole was missing. I felt sick. Like a complete failure. Maybe Blake Alexander was right and I needed to check myself thinking I was good at being a witch. So far the only thing I seemed to be good at was teleporting and pouring coffee because I certainly hadn't gotten a good handle on Nicole even using my crystals, no matter how hard I'd tried. Instead I kept seeing Mazzy everywhere.

Another horrible thought seized my mind. Did that mean something equally as terrible as what had happened to Mazzy had happened to Nicole, just on the human plane?

By the time I reached the counter I was well and truly freaked. I ordered a latte and the most decadent muffin on the menu and stepped to the side to wait for it, my mind in overdrive.

Pete leaned over and placed a couple of drinks on the bar, shouting for someone named Jessie, then focused on me. "What's up?" he asked.

"Nothing," I said.

He gave me a *Seriously?* look. "Whatever nothing is, it's all over your face," he said.

I sighed. "The missing woman. Nicole St. James."

He nodded. "I've been hearing bits and pieces. You know her?"

"Not really. But she came into my store the other day. She was a mess. I really wanted to help her but I guess I couldn't."

"Vi. You aren't a miracle worker. Maybe it's true that she really did take off on her own."

"Maybe." I didn't really believe it. "I get that some people can pick up and go somewhere with a completely blank slate, but most people can't. Especially when they have family they're close to." I shook my head, frustrated. "But some people don't like their families, I guess." And sometimes the happy family pretense was just that, a pretense. I thought of Fiona and then immediately pushed the thought away. My mother hadn't left me because she wanted to, after all. It had been proven and verified by all kinds of sources now.

Pete turned back to the espresso machine, keeping one eye on me. "You can only do so much for people, Vi. Don't beat yourself up. And listen. I'm here if you want to talk. About anything. You got me?"

"Yeah, Pete. I got you." I picked up my breakfast. "And I'll probably take you up on that."

# CHAPTER SIXTEEN

I knew Pete was right about there being limits to the help I could give, but it didn't make me feel much better. Although now that I thought about it, he would be the perfect witch to talk to about a lot of this other stuff. I trusted Pete implicitly. We'd hit it off the first time we'd met and over the years he'd become a good friend. I knew I could count on him to be straight up with me.

I walked slowly to my shop with my muffin and coffee, but I didn't have much appetite. All the telephone poles along the way had the same photo. I wondered if Ginny had done it on her own, or if Nicole's family had helped. Or were they willing to believe that she'd just up and left a life that had become overwhelming?

I needed to talk to Ginny. I'd get the shop opened up and once Syd or Josie came in, I'd go to the deli and find her. I'd just flipped the sign to open when I heard the bell on my shop door jangle. Figuring it was one of them, I offered a greeting without turning around. "Morning."

"Vi. I need your help. Did you hear?"

Not Syd or Josie. I turned and saw Ginny standing there. She looked like crap, like she'd been up all night. I felt sorry for her. She'd been through enough lately. Mazzy had been one of her friends too, and I knew she'd taken that whole thing pretty hard. To now have another friend go missing . . . I nodded. "Nicole. Yes, I saw the poster. I was coming to see you as soon as someone got here to take over."

She came over and flung her arms around me, burying her face in my shoulder. "Can you help find her?"

I wished I knew how. I patted her back awkwardly. "What happened?" I asked. "When did you find out she was missing?"

"Her mother called me yesterday. But I was already worried. We talked to the cops yesterday afternoon." She swiped furiously at her eyes. "Then she was supposed to be at the council meeting last night. I heard she didn't make it. That was the final straw for me. There's nothing that would've kept her from that—unless something really is wrong. Nicole took her job really seriously."

I nodded. "I was there. Sylvia Townsend covered for her. Who is that?"

"Her new boss. But they've known each other for a long time. I guess her mother called the office yesterday and talked to Sylvia. Sylvia said she hadn't been in since last week so her mother called me. I talked to her early Monday, but that was the last time. And no one in her family has talked to her since then either. That's not like her." Ginny turned back to me, and her eyes were wide and wet with tears. "The cops aren't taking this seriously and I'm so frustrated. Something's wrong. We have to do something!"

I grabbed her hand and led her over to my chair that I used for consults. "Okay. Calm down and come sit. She mentioned she was ending a relationship. Had she done it yet, or was that still in process?"

Ginny made a face. "It was done. She's been trying to break up with him for ages and she finally did it a few weeks ago. He didn't take it well. Vi, he's . . . not a nice person. But she didn't tell a lot of people. Definitely not her family. You understand?"

I understood. No wonder I'd gotten such a strong sense of fear emanating off of her. Nicole had just left an abusive relationship. Without a lot of support. "Would she have just taken off to get away from him?"

Ginny shook her head emphatically. "She would've told me, at least. And called in sick to work or explained or something. She was happy to get that new job. She wouldn't have just stopped showing up after a few weeks." She held up a hand and ticked off points on her fingers. "Her phone is shut off. She never shuts her phone off. I have a key to her place, so I went over there yesterday. Roxie, her cat, was there alone. She'd never leave without Roxie. And she'd never just leave her without food. Her bowl was empty!"

I understood that. Monty was my whole life. Everything I did was with him in mind. And now I had two babies to care for, although Xander seemed a bit more . . . self-sufficient than Monty. I asked the only question that made sense while I processed all this. "Where's Roxie now?"

"I took her home. But all Nicole's stuff was at her

place. Phone charger, her purse, her favorite jacket. I'm telling you, Vi, something bad happened. And I feel like it has to do with *him*."

"Does 'he' have a name?" I asked.

"Chris Strand. He lives in town too. He runs a contracting firm."

A lawyer and a contractor? Seemed like an odd match. "So what did the cops say?"

"Her mother and I talked to them. It was one guy, actually, and he didn't seem that interested. Plus it's hard because her parents . . . liked Chris. They didn't know. And she didn't want to tell them what he was really like. She thought it would make her look weak if they knew. And stupid. She was a lawyer, you know? Those things don't happen to lawyers."

"Oh, Ginny." I sank down next to her. "How dangerous was this guy? Was he violent? Did he threaten her?"

"He wouldn't leave her alone. She stopped talking about it a while ago. Said she was trying to put it all behind her. I don't know if he was still bothering her, honestly. I told the cop about her place, though. That all her stuff was there. The cop actually said, 'Don't you girls change purses all the time?' I wanted to punch him in the face."

"What was his name?"

"I don't even know. Older white guy."

So not Gabe Merlino. That, at least, was a relief. Gabe was a good cop, and I was already thinking about calling him. "Did you at least give him Chris's name?"

She nodded. "And then Nicole's mother started talking about how upset he'll be when he finds out. That she tried to call him too but hadn't been able to get a hold of him. She actually agreed with the cop that they might be together. It's like she's almost willing to accept the story that Nicole took off so she doesn't have to think of . . . the alternative."

I studied Ginny. She looked incredibly distraught. "Ginny. You said she had a lot going on, just started a new job, broke up with someone she'd been with for—how long?"

Ginny wrinkled her nose. "Too long. Three years."

"Okay. So that's stressful even if she was the one who initiated it, and especially if he was making it hard for her. Do you think maybe she did just go away? Even for a short vacation? And maybe the pet sitter was late?"

"No." She said it so emphatically it startled me. Glancing around, she leaned in closer and said, "When I went to her house I got a bad feeling."

"Bad like what?"

"I touched her purse and got a . . . vision."

There it was—the elephant in the room. My room, at least. Ginny was a witch and had powers too. So why wasn't she taking advantage of that? "So what did you see? Did you get a vision of Chris? Like, doing something to her? Is that what your powers are—you can see the future? Or is it the past?" I was still so curious about how all this worked. I'd wondered why she hadn't used *her* powers to help Nicole. Why did she need my crystals in the first place?

But I wasn't sure who had what kind of powers. Like, did everyone get the same basic ones and then develop special skillsets from there? Was it like college—you decided what you were interested in and chose a major? Another thing I should've asked Blake, but he'd been too busy lecturing me.

That made me feel cranky again so I pushed the thought away.

Meantime, Ginny was clearly trying to figure out how to explain what she'd seen, squirming in her seat a bit. "It wasn't like that. I only wish I could . . ." she trailed off. "Anyway, it was like this weird vibe of . . . sorrow or something. I didn't see pictures, or faces. So maybe vision wasn't the right word?"

"Sorrow," I repeated. "Like Nicole's sorrow?"

She lifted her shoulders, looking at me helplessly. "I guess. Who else's would it be? I was at her place, touching her stuff. But was it sorrow because she wasn't there, or sorrow because she was in trouble, or what?"

"I don't know. Can you use your powers to find out?" I asked pointedly.

She frowned. "Can't you?"

"I'm trying! But in case you haven't noticed, I'm kind of brand new at this." I got up and paced the room, nervous energy getting the better of me. "I don't know what the heck I'm doing. I want to help her. All I've been thinking about is helping her. But I'm failing miserably." I turned back to her. "So really. Tell me about your powers. Maybe we can put our heads together. You know, like that old cartoon, *Wonder Twin powers, activate!*?"

Clearly she didn't know that one because she stared blankly at me. "It's not that easy for me," she said. "I haven't used my powers in a while so I don't know if they're any good anymore. I've been . . . living here for a long time and my mom isn't a witch. She doesn't like to talk about that part of our family. My dad is part witch and tries to plug me in where he can but she hates it. He was the one who got me the job doing the . . . specialized maid service."

The witchy cleanups. Josie had mentioned that Ginny would've been her pick to clean up the Mazzy mess in my store, if it hadn't been her friend. Not that I understood what any of that entailed. And it didn't sound like it would help much here, unless someone had kidnapped Nicole and was making her clean their house.

"Okay," I said, trying to muster up all the patience I could. "So what do you want to do?"

"We have to find her, of course," she said, like I was an idiot to whom she had to speak slowly.

"Okay," I said again. "Any suggestions on how to do that without the benefit of . . . added insight? I think the cops are our best bet here. We need to get them to take it seriously."

"How? We tried that." She crossed her arms over her chest. "They don't want to help. And if they won't help then we need to figure out something else."

"Before we go there, I'm going to try Sergeant Merlino. See if he can help."

Ginny sniffed. "You trust him to care?"

"I do."

"Fine, then. What else?"

"What do you mean, what else?"

"What else can you do?"

I frowned. "Not following."

She leaned forward in her chair. "Come on, Vi. I know that you have pretty cool powers. That's why I brought her to you in the first place."

The girl at the Potions Cafe counter flashed in my mind. *I heard you have the powers to, like, see into people's souls.* "Ginny, I just told you—"

The door to the shop banged open and Syd charged in, out of breath. "Sorry I'm late, Vi. Presley was giving me a hard time this morning and . . . oh, hello. I'm sorry to interrupt," she said when she saw Ginny. "I'll be right out," she said to me, then hurried out back.

"We'll have to talk about this later," I said to Ginny. I didn't really want to talk about this with Syd around.

Ginny stood, looking so sad and lost that I felt even more guilty. "Sure. I'm sorry. I just . . . want to help my friend."

I squeezed her hand. "I know. Don't worry about it. I'll do everything I can, okay? Please let me know if you hear from her."

Ginny nodded. "Thanks." She turned to go, but I called her back and pressed a stone into her hand—a blue calcite. Like the one that had helped me the other night.

"Take this," I said. "You'll feel better."

She examined it, then closed her fist around it. "Thanks, Vi." She looked up at me, and I could see tears in her eyes. "I'm scared."

I gave her a hug. I didn't know what to say, because I was too.

# CHAPTER SEVENTEEN

After Ginny left, I stood at the window watching people hurrying by on their way to work, or breakfast, or wherever they spent their days. A lot of people were out walking their dogs today, and I allowed myself a few minutes to revel in the cuteness trotting past the shop. I'd always wanted a dog, but Monty had not been supportive of that plan.

I had to call Gabe. This Nicole thing sounded serious, although I wasn't actually surprised a seasoned cop wasn't running off to try to track down a woman who hadn't called her friends or gone to work in a couple of days. She was an adult; her life seemed to be kind of crappy at the moment; she pulled a Houdini. But the fact that she'd left her purse and her cat bothered me.

And of course, there was that black shadow that I couldn't really mention to anyone.

I pulled out my phone and texted Gabe.

*Are you working?*

Gray dots appeared immediately, indicating he was typing.

*Not yet. Stopped by your sister's with coffee. What's up?*

*I need to talk to you.*

*Come by,* he replied immediately.

Not really the place I wanted to have that conversation, but I needed his help. I thought about just appearing in their house, but appearing out of thin air in front of him might raise some questions.

I guess I had to drive over there like the mere moral that I'd been until a few weeks ago. Who had time for that?

I called out back to Syd. When she poked her head out I told her I needed to run a quick errand and I'd be back soon, then I raced down the street to where I parked my car.

It took me about ten minutes to get there. I parked and headed up to the door.

Zoe pulled it open before I could knock. "Hey, sis. What's up?" As usual, she looked like a cross between an Amy Brown fairy and a punk rocker with her long black lace skirt, red Converse, and violet-black hair pulled up in pigtails.

"Hey. I need to talk to Gabe and he told me to come by here."

Zoe swung the door open. "Come on in."

Gabe was at the kitchen table drinking coffee. He looked up and waved when I came in. "Hey, Vi."

"Hi. Sorry to interrupt your morning." I glanced at Zoe but of course she ignored the cue.

"No worries. What's going on? Everything okay?" Gabe asked.

I took a breath. "I don't think so. It's about Nicole St. James. The missing girl."

He frowned. "What missing girl?"

"That's the thing. The cop that her family spoke with won't declare her missing officially even though her friends and family haven't seen her. They think she left on her own." I filled him in on what Ginny had told me and added a little color about Nicole's current situation. "So she could really be in trouble," I finished.

Gabe had listened intently. Now he sat back in his chair and drummed his fingertips on the table. "When was the last time she was seen?"

"I don't know for sure, but according to Ginny the last time anyone heard from her was on Monday. Ginny is one of her best friends," I said by way of explanation. "Not sure if anyone else spoke to her. I know she hasn't been to work and that's apparently very unlike her."

"Do you know which cop she spoke to?" Gabe asked.

"She couldn't remember his name but said he was an 'old white guy.'"

"Figures," Zoe muttered.

I had to agree with her. "I met her last week and she was definitely worried about something. She's been having trouble with a boyfriend too. They recently broke up but it sounds like he was abusive. And her mother can't locate him either. Gabe, if she needs help . . . I don't want it to be too late before she gets it."

Gabe nodded. "I understand."

"So you can help?"

"I can talk to her family if they're willing to talk to me," Gabe said. "For sure."

"Awesome. You can start with Ginny. She's really upset," I said. "Let's go."

"Now?" Gabe glanced at Zoe.

"Well, you can finish your coffee first," I said impatiently. "But I don't think we should waste any time, do you?"

"She's right," Zoe said. "You should go."

"I'll text her," I said, pulling out my phone to text Ginny.

*Meet me at Pete's in fifteen. It's about Nicole.*

# CHAPTER EIGHTEEN

Gabe and I got to Pete's before Ginny. I grabbed coffees for all three of us while Gabe commandeered a booth in the back away from the few other patrons. Pete worked the counter.

"Back so soon? What's up?" he asked when he saw me, nodding in Gabe's direction.

"I can't get into it now, but it's about Nicole. Can I get three coffees?"

He nodded. "Nothing fancy?"

"Not right now. I'm not feeling very fancy," I said with a sigh.

He poured the coffees and patted my hand. "Let me know what I can do."

I took the coffees and headed to Gabe, sliding into the

seat across from him. "I think she's upset at the police in general, so don't take it personally if she isn't super friendly," I said.

Gabe smiled wryly. "Don't worry, I'm used to it," he said.

I nodded to the door. "Here she comes."

Ginny had her head down against the wind as she pulled the door open. She took a minute to catch her breath, then spotted me and came over, taking the chair next to me.

"Thanks for coming so quickly. This is Gabe." I pushed her coffee cup in front of her. "We got you coffee."

"Hey, Ginny. I'm sorry you had a bad experience with my department," Gabe said right off the bat. "That shouldn't have happened."

Ginny nodded. "Thank you. I appreciate that." She lapsed into silence, fiddling with her cup.

"So tell me about Nicole," Gabe said. His tone was kind, and he focused all his attention on her as she began to talk, and pretty soon Ginny was relaxed and speaking openly about her friend.

She told him about Chris Strand and the volatile end to that relationship, how Nicole's family loved the guy, and her recent job change. "I know how it sounds," she said when she finished. "Believe me, I thought about it too. But she would never leave Roxie, like I told Vi. Even if she took off, she would've taken her. That's the one thing I'm sure of."

"Do you think she could have reached out to a domestic violence help center?" Gabe asked carefully. "Given what you've told me about her boyfriend. Maybe they counseled her that she had to leave without Roxie to get help?"

Ginny shook her head. "No matter what she would've made arrangements for Roxie. Even if it was just texting me to go get her and keep her for a while. But even that . . . she loves that cat. She wouldn't go without her. She's in trouble. I can feel it. And so can Violet." She turned to me, her face earnest. "Tell him, Vi."

Gabe looked at me. I shifted uncomfortably in my seat. "She came into my shop, like I said. I got a . . . vibe that things were worse than she was letting on. And she's been on my mind a lot." I didn't really know how to express this to him without sounding like some kind of woo-woo weirdo, so I stopped there.

He didn't look all that impressed with my revelation. He turned back to Ginny. "What about her family or other friends? I know you already told my colleague this," he said, reading the look on her face. "I just need to be sure I've covered my bases so when I raise this, I don't get questioned."

She looked at me. I nodded. "I was with Nicole's mother when we spoke to the other officer. No one's spoken with her since Monday morning. And she didn't go to work Monday or yesterday, or the council meeting last night, which she was supposed to speak at. Which is so not like her in normal times, but with a new job it's definitely not like her."

Gabe took notes on all that. "What's Chris Strand's address?" he asked without looking up from his scribbling.

"I don't think I have the exact address, but he lives in

that new apartment complex over by the water." Ginny pointed vaguely outside and to the left. "The fancy one."

"I know it. Anything else strike you as odd when you went to her place?"

She nodded. "Her purse, phone, and coat were all still there. And Roxie, like I said. She had no food or water. I took her home with me until we find Nicole."

Gabe scribbled a few more words, then closed his notebook and folded his hands over it, his face carefully blank. "Okay. I'm going to go talk to my lieutenant. I will recommend we revisit this and log it as a missing person."

"Does that mean you'll look for her?" Ginny's eyes shined with hope for the first time.

Gabe nodded. "Absolutely. So if you can give me a list of names and numbers of the people I need to talk to, that would help me get started. Especially Strand."

Ginny gave him as much as she could from her phone to start with, and he promised to be in touch. After he left, Ginny gave me a hug. "Thank you. So much. I can't believe he took me seriously."

"Why? Not all cops are jerks," I said. "Gabe was really good to me when I had my . . . situation. You're in good hands."

"I hope he finds her. I'm so worried."

"Keep me posted," I told her.

She promised, then left. I had to get to the shop, but needed more fuel. Food probably, but coffee too. At the risk of sending myself into a caffeine coma, I made my way back to the counter.

Pete glanced at me as I approached. "Do I need to cut you off?"

I smiled. "I was actually looking for food, so it's okay."

"So you going to tell me what's going on?" he asked, dropping his voice.

"I wish I knew." I sighed. "The cops—well, one cop—refused to call Nicole St. James a missing person. Ginny was super upset. So I asked Gabe to step in." I glanced over my shoulder to make sure we were alone. There was no one behind me in line, and there were only two other people sitting at a nearby table, a young couple with their heads bent over some hefty textbooks.

Even so, I dropped my voice. "I'm not sure what kind of powers you have, but do you have . . . anything that might help? I'm sorry, I don't know the politically correct term yet," I added with a grimace.

Pete laughed. "I don't think there is a politically correct term." His smile vanished. "You really think she's missing?"

I thought of the black shadow I'd seen around Nicole and inadvertently shivered. "I think something's wrong, yes."

Pete nodded. "Let me poke around a bit."

I wasn't quite sure what that meant, but was too tired to get into it. "Hey, do you know Blake Alexander?" I asked instead.

Pete nodded. "Yeah. We hang out every now and again. Catch some Banish Ball. It's a sport," he said at my blank look. "Anyway, he's a cool guy. Why?"

"My mother asked him to 'mentor' me. Or coach me. And I'm not sure I'm happy about it."

"Ah." Pete leaned against the counter, watching me

with an amused expression. "She wants you up to speed pretty quickly, being on the council and all. Blake won't steer you wrong, if that's what you're asking. He's a smart guy. He'll take good care of you. And you can always come to me with anything that you're not sure of. Okay?"

That made me feel better. "Thanks, Pete."

I turned to go, but he called me back. "Hey, Vi? There was something I wanted to ask you." He rubbed at an imaginary spot on the counter with his rag.

"Yeah?"

"I know it's not the best time with all this other stuff going on, but I've been waiting a while and figured I just need to do it."

I waited. It wasn't like Pete to be at a loss for words. "Do what?" I prompted when he trailed off.

He met my eyes. "I want to ask Sydney out. Do you think she'll say yes?"

I stared at him, a smile spreading across my face. "Yes! It's about time!" I clapped my hands together excitedly, wondering how he'd react if I jumped over the counter and hugged him. "I think she'll be thrilled."

"You think? Or you know?" He watched me intently. "I really don't want to make a fool of myself."

"Oh please. She totally likes you." I'd thought for a while that Syd and Pete had a thing for each other. Whenever I was with Syd at the cafe they flirted with each other. And Pete always gave Presley something special from his pastry case, which made Syd smile. I felt in my gut they would be good together. "You must really like her, though. I never thought of you as anything other than confident when it came to the ladies." I winked at him.

He reddened, slightly, and turned back to his latte machine. "Please," he muttered.

"I'm teasing you." I glanced at my watch. "I have to get back to the shop. Otherwise she'll never have a chance to come in here so you can ask her out."

# CHAPTER NINETEEN

*Thursday*

The next morning, I woke up early after a crappy night's sleep. I'd spent the rest of yesterday at the shop, trying to tune in to Nicole in my spare time. I wasn't sure if I could actually tune into someone who wasn't in front of me, but I focused on either activating or developing those powers if it could be done.

I hadn't gotten far. Which made me cranky, and I'd gone straight home from work, put my phone on do-not-disturb, and tried to sleep. I saw this morning that Todd had been texting me. I shot him a text back saying I'd gone to sleep early, figuring he wouldn't believe me, but I couldn't handle that right now. I needed to focus on the bigger problems at hand: Nicole St. James. And Mazzy. I felt like a ticking clock was hovering over my shoulder, reminding me that time wasn't something I had a lot of.

But I still pulled the pillow over my head, intending to lie there just a minute longer. I must have fallen asleep again, because next thing I knew I was jolted awake by a loud crackle. I sat up to find Fiona standing next to my bed, which was now covered with glitter, as was I.

"You are an artist's nightmare," I muttered, brushing glitter out of my hair.

"What. Are. You. Doing?" she demanded.

I blinked and sat up. "Getting ready to go to work," I lied.

"Yes, it certainly looks that way. Did you forget what today is?"

I stared blankly at her.

"Our subcommittee meeting on Mazzy Diamond!"

Oh crap. It had completely slipped my mind. "No, of course not," I said, hurriedly flinging the covers off and getting up. "When is it again?"

"It's right now. And I don't have time for this." She pointed at me. Little sparks flew out of her long, blood-red fingernails. I felt the now-familiar crackle in the air all around me, and kind of a weird jolt, like I'd just had a triple espresso. I didn't think I could honestly say I felt better, but I certainly had a flood of energy. I threw the covers off and got out of bed.

And realized I was suddenly dressed. The outfit looked more suited to her than me—long, velvety dress with ginormous-heeled boots—but I didn't have a chance to protest. Another zap and my hair, often unruly in the morning, fell in smooth waves around my face. There was no time to look in the mirror, but I was pretty sure my teeth were brushed and my face was washed and made up. And before I could blink again, I was in a small conference room. Blake, Alan, and Ember from the council, along with three men I didn't recognize, were seated when Fiona and I arrived in a shower of glitter.

"My daughter apologizes for her tardiness," Fiona said, taking a seat.

Blake grinned at me. "No worries. We can move time around as much as we want."

Fiona shot him a look, but it didn't seem to faze him.

Ember regarded all of us, unsmiling, then looked back down at some papers in front of her. She wore all white again. Today that included a white scarf over her hair.

Alan cleared his throat. "Shall we get started?" He turned to me and smiled. I could tell he, like many of the council members, didn't quite know what to do with me. Fiona's doing, I supposed. She was such a strong personality that they either assumed I was like her, or if I wasn't, they didn't want to cross her in any way by handling me wrong. Except for Oscar, who seemed to have no problem trying to throw me under the bus.

"Yes," Fiona said. She looked at the other men, who were both watching me with open curiosity. That familiar feeling of being on display returned. "Violet, this is the chief of Magickal Police, Theonius Bell, and his first deputy, Justin Merriweather. The Magickal Police is the highest level of law enforcement in our world. And this," she indicated the other man, "is Gary Lavender, of the Fourth Domain police. He's been engaged because Ms. Diamond lives in his district."

The first deputy nodded and said hello. He had a nice smile. The Lavender guy said nothing. His face didn't so much have an expression, per se, but it still didn't look very nice. And this whole setup was yet another thing I still didn't understand—the way the witch police worked. I added it to my mental list of questions. I raised my hand in an awkward wave at them all. "Nice to meet you. That sounds like a big job, Chief Bell," I said. "The highest level of law enforcement sounds very important."

Chief Bell puffed out his chest and rose a little higher in his seat. "Why yes indeed, young lady, it certainly is."

I cringed at the term, but kept the smile pasted on. No point making the police angry before we'd even gotten started.

"We have a police force that oversees all the local efforts," Bell continued. "The purpose is to make sure we've got the bigger picture covered for the good of the entire population, while Gary here focuses on his own domain. He's got his work cut out for him," he added. "That Fourth Domain is a difficult place. Although nothing compared to the Second Domain back in your day, Fiona." He winked at her.

My mother gave him a withering look that made him physically shrink in his seat.

Once she seemed certain he was sufficiently in his place, she spread her hands wide in a gesture that included the three of them. "So. Do you want to update us on your investigation to date?"

"Ah, yes." Chief Bell cleared his throat and opened a folder with chunky fingers. "Well, the investigation is still very much ongoing. We have a few leads but we need more definitive evidence before we can take any action."

"So in other words, you have nothing," Ember said, her voice clear and cold.

Chief Bell squirmed a bit. The other two remained perfectly still, as if Fiona might not notice them if they were statues. "We do need something in order to help us move forward," he said.

Fiona's eyes narrowed. "What's that?"

He cleared his throat again and turned to me. "I'm afraid we're going to need you to make a formal statement as a witness. And afford us the opportunity to examine the crime scene."

Examine the crime scene? A month later? He had to be joking. I stared at Blake, trying to drill into his brain with my eyeballs.

I could feel Ember and Alan both watching me, waiting for my reaction.

"She already gave her statement," Fiona said. "And examining the crime scene? Really?"

The Lavender guy turned a steely gaze on her. "Yes, she gave an informal statement. Ms. Ravenstar, I'm sure you understand we need to preserve the integrity of an investigation of this magnitude. So we must do everything by the book. I'm sure as our council leader you understand that. And being able to visit the scene is typical procedure."

Fiona looked like she was about to argue, but Blake held up a hand. "It's fine, Fiona. Violet can give a statement. She has nothing to hide, as we all know. And I'll be present, of course, as the advising attorney for the council. Once the statement has been given, we can arrange a visit to her store."

I opened my mouth to protest, but Blake sent me a look that clearly said it should stay shut. I could tell Fiona was still on the fence too. We all held our breath for a moment, me trying to send her a telepathic message, encouraging her to make a big stink about it and use her influence to get me out of it.

After a moment, Fiona nodded slowly. "Fine, then. She'll speak to you with Blake as acting counsel."

Lavender didn't look like that pleased him given the sour line his mouth settled in, but Chief Bell smiled with apparent relief. "That's wonderful. Thank you, Violet."

"Excellent." Lavender said, sounding like he'd swallowed something distasteful. "When shall we put that on the schedule? How about after this meeting? Would that work for everyone?"

Today? So soon? I glanced at Blake, panicked. "I really can't today. I . . . have work. Can we do it some other time?"

"Ms. Moonstone, this matter is of the utmost importance—" he began, but Blake cut him off.

"I have meetings today as well. But if we're going to put Ms. Moonstone through this hoop, we may as well do this right," he said, snapping his cuffs after glancing at a giant watch on his wrist. "We should do it next week in front of the council. That way, it's officially on the record."

I stared at him. What was he doing? In front of the entire council? I looked at Fiona, but I couldn't read her face either. Nor did she say a word. Neither did Alan or Ember.

Bell pointed a pen at him. "Excellent idea."

The first deputy nodded in agreement. Lavender glowered.

Blake ignored them all. "Great. Fiona will put it on the agenda. Now. Let's get on with today's agenda, shall we? Can we hear your initial report?"

I sank back in my chair, both grateful that I'd gotten a slight reprieve and terrified about the prospect of what would happen at the council meeting. It was stupid. I hadn't done anything, but it still freaked me out. Not because I did anything wrong or had anything to do with it, as

Oscar wanted to believe, but because I was starting to be
suspicious of everyone. I knew enough about conspiracy
theories and dirty cops to know that they could be working with someone like Oscar to get me in trouble. I
started to think I might need Blake after all.

Bell turned to his deputy and motioned for him to
speak. Merriweather smiled reassuringly at me, pulled
out his own folder, and began delivering every excruciat-
ing detail they knew about Mazzy's genieing in my shop.
"Chief Lavender received the anonymous tip about the
event the next day, and reported it to us." Merriweather
flipped the folder closed. "Since Ms. Moonstone wasn't
yet . . . wholly informed of her heritage and the situation,
we did not make contact at that point. A few days later
Fiona alerted us and told us what her daughter had told
her. As Chief Bell mentioned, our next step will be to examine the crime scene ourselves. Which we'd like to do
following Violet's formal statement."

Blake didn't even blink. "Thank you, Deputy. Do you
have any leads on the perpetrator?"

As Merriweather—joined by Lavender—went into a
lot of flowery explanations about why they didn't have
anything substantial about how to find who'd done this to
Mazzy, my mind was circling on what I had just heard.

When I'd discovered the pile of slime also known as
Mazzy, my sister Zoe had been right behind me. While I
hadn't realized what I was seeing, Zoe had—and she'd
summoned Fiona immediately. And Josie had come with
her. After Fiona lectured me about the whole situation,
Josie helped me out by bringing in a special witch cleaning service to get my shop back to normal. I'd just assumed Fiona had immediately called whoever needed to
know these sorts of things, especially since she led the

Magickal Council. And since Fiona had been there, I'd assumed she'd told them that too.

But Merriweather had said the police department had been notified by an anonymous tip and they hadn't heard from Fiona for days.

So who had tipped them off? And why hadn't they seemed to know Fiona had been there?

# CHAPTER TWENTY

The meeting wrapped up shortly after. I couldn't wait to get out of there. The whole thing made me feel like I couldn't breathe. I was the first one out of my seat, not even making eye contact with Fiona as I left. I didn't want her whisking me away somewhere. But I wasn't quick enough. Blake caught up with me as I hurried outside.

"Let's go somewhere we can talk," he said into my ear.

"I can't."

"Right. You have to go to work, you said?"

I nodded. "I have a busy day."

"Look, Violet, we are going to have to work closely on prepping you for this statement. We can't waste any time."

I dug my heels in. "I told you I can't. I have to get to work. And I thought you had a meeting?"

Blake's piercing eyes stared straight into mine. "I can move my schedule around. I didn't want you to be on the spot having to answer their questions, that's all. So if you have to work, that's fine. I'll come with you. I can help. I'm good at setting up displays. Good eye."

Before I could protest, he reached for my hand. The next thing I knew we were in my shop.

Like, in the middle of my shop floor. Luckily, there were no customers. Also no Sydney. Who was minding the store? I rounded on Blake. "What do you think you're doing? This is my shop!"

"I know. It's great." He nodded admiringly, walking around slowly to take everything in. "You said you had to come and do some work, right?"

I stomped my foot. "Of course I did! But I can't have people seeing—"

"Vi?" Sydney came out of the back room, a doughnut in one hand and a cup of coffee in the other. "I didn't hear you come in." She glanced curiously at Blake. "Hi."

"Yeah, uh, hi," I stammered, feeling my face turn red. "I guess I was just quiet. Or the bell is broken or something. Sorry to startle you."

"You didn't. It's been quiet so I figured I'd get some of the new boxes unpacked for you. I'm Sydney," she said to Blake. "I'd shake your hand, but . . ." She indicated her full hands.

Blake smiled at her. "Hi there. Blake Alexander. Corporate counsel for—"

"The shop," I broke in, cutting him off. "Corporate counsel for the shop." I wanted to wipe the amused smirk off Blake's face, but was more concerned with getting him out of Syd's line of interrogation. Which was definitely coming.

My deflection worked. It had certainly distracted her. She spun around to fix a hawklike gaze on me. "Corporate counsel for your shop? You need a lawyer? Why do you need a lawyer?"

"No. I don't *need* a lawyer. What would I need one for? Not right now anyway. I mean, well, you never know, right? Don't want to be caught off guard, so I figured I'd get ahead of things. Can you cover the floor? I need to go over some paperwork with Blake. I think I have an appointment soon. Just come get me." I grabbed Blake's arm and dragged him out back, leaving Sydney staring after us, then rounded on him. "What were you thinking?" I demanded.

He glanced at his watch. "That we need to get started because I do have meetings. And that you don't have great communication with your coworkers."

"No, I mean what were you thinking coming here like this!" I paced around, noticing that Xander had showed up and was lounging on my desk. My door at home was always shut and locked tight. My cat was magic.

I'd really have to process that another day.

"Coming here like this? I followed you here." Blake pulled out my desk chair and sat, reaching over to stroke Xander.

I wanted to smack the amused smile off his face. "That's not what I meant. I meant Syd isn't . . . like us!" I dropped my voice to a harsh whisper. "We could've totally freaked her out."

"Freaked her out? How?" He didn't look concerned, only mildly interested, which infuriated me even more.

"She doesn't know about me!"

"What about you, darlin? Do tell."

I glared at him, feeling stupider as this conversation went on. "That I'm a—"

"Violet!" Syd rushed in, her face flushed the way it always got when she was flustered. "Todd's here." She looked anxiously from Blake to me.

Crap. How was I going to explain Blake? "Tell him I'll be right out."

With one last glance at Blake, Syd hurried out.

Blake smiled at me. "Todd? Who's that?"

I glared at him. "Wait here." I hurried out front. Todd stood in front of my sphere display that I'd worked on yesterday, gazing at the different-sized stones. I didn't think he was actually looking at them. He'd never taken much interest in my business. He thought crystals were "pretty if you went for that sort of thing, but not really useful."

"Hey," I said.

"Hey." He turned around and handed me one of the two coffees he was holding. "Pete's new latte. Matcha something."

"That's really nice. Thank you." I took it awkwardly, sipped, and burned my tongue.

Syd, not one to be discreet, watched us openly until I shot her a look. She turned away and busied herself cleaning one of the cases.

"So. What's going on? I'm actually in the middle of . . . some stuff," I said, jerking my thumb behind me.

"Oh. Sorry. I just wanted to stop by on my way to the bar. I was thinking of taking off early tonight since I have a full staff. Wanted to see if you wanted to get dinner later."

"Tonight? Um . . ."

"Vi—" Todd glanced at Syd, who was clearly still listening while trying to pretend she wasn't. "Can I talk to you outside?"

"Sure." Reluctantly I followed him out onto the sidewalk. It was freezing out, and I wrapped my hands around my cup to try to get some warmth from it.

Once the door had closed behind me I faced Todd and waited.

He shifted from foot to foot, looking awkward. "Vi, I know you're upset with me. That you've been upset with me for weeks now, because of . . . well." He cleared his throat, leaving the sentence unfinished.

*Because you lied to me. Because you went behind my back and were about to strike up a deal with the devil.* I focused on my coffee and said nothing, waiting.

"Well." He cleared his throat. "I need you to forgive me. I want to get back to where we were. And I thought we should start by spending some time together." Todd sent me a pleading look. It was so weird—he wasn't usually like this. Unsure of himself.

"Todd. I appreciate the sentiment. Really I do. And you're right. We need to talk. But this week is a little crazy for me. I'm not sure what time I'm going to get out of here tonight." I hunched my shoulders against the cold.

"When are you going to make time for me then? We've barely seen each other since everything happened and your mother came to town."

"My mother? What does my mother have to do with anything?" I asked.

"I know she doesn't like me. I feel like she's, I don't know, poisoned you against me or something." He held my gaze, his own gaze challenging. "Am I wrong?"

"You are wrong. I haven't even seen that much of my mother. And she's never said she doesn't like you." It was true. She'd said I could do better and he hadn't impressed her, but she hadn't flat out said she didn't like him. A few more minutes with him and she would probably come to that conclusion, but I hadn't been letting them spend any time together. "And quite frankly, if you think I'm that weak that I would take the opinion of a woman I've known for five minutes, then I'm not sure we should be together anyway. Todd, listen. I'm cold and I have to work. I'll call you when I'm done, okay? If you can still get away, we'll go."

He stared at me long enough that it made me uncomfortable. "Yeah. Sure, Violet. Call me when you're done," he said finally, then turned and walked away.

I watched him go. He strode back toward the bar, pausing to chuck his coffee cup in the bin. When he disappeared out of sight around the corner I pulled the door open and hurried inside. Blake had emerged from the back room and stood near the window. I suspected he'd been watching us. "Hey, sorry about that," I said. "Let's get to work."

But he didn't look like he was in a joking mood anymore. "So who's the guy?" he asked.

"Who, Todd?"

"If that's who you were talking to, yes. That's your boyfriend?"

I wasn't sure how to even answer that anymore. I gave a half nod.

"Todd who?"

"Langston. Why?"

"He from around here?"

I nodded. "Born and raised in North Harbor."

"Family around?"

"I know you're a lawyer and all, but this is an odd line of questioning," I said. "Why?"

He looked at me for a long moment. "No reason. Let's get this done." He turned and headed out back.

Syd intercepted me as I tried to follow. "Vi, what the heck is going on? Are you seeing this Blake guy or something? I mean, not like I would blame you or anything. He's hot. No offense to Todd," she added hastily.

I gritted my teeth. Syd and Zoe had apparently compared notes. "I am not seeing him. It's strictly business."

"Well are you still seeing Todd? Because that doesn't look promising."

I crossed my arms over my chest and stared her down.

She threw up her hands. "Fine. Don't tell me."

"Syd, there's nothing to tell. I'm figuring the Todd thing out. Blake is a business associate. End of story. I gotta go deal with him," I said. "Hey, why don't you go grab us some coffee from Pete's? I'll be done soon."

She looked pointedly at the coffee in my hand.

"He got me the wrong kind," I said. It sounded lame, even to me.

"Fine." She tossed her hair. "I'll be back soon."

"Thanks sweetie." I went to give her a hug but she sidestepped me and grabbed her coat.

# CHAPTER TWENTY-ONE

Syd flounced out of the store, clearly displeased with me. I watched her go, then with a sigh headed out back to deal with my other problem.

Blake sat at my desk, holding my clear quartz sphere in one hand, hefting it up and down. Xander sprawled out on the desk in front of him, rubbing his head against Blake's arm. Traitor. "Everything okay?" he asked.

"Great. My best friend is mad at me and I have to . . ." I trailed off. I'd been about to say, I have to dump my boyfriend because we are so totally wrong for each other, but once I verbalized it that would make it real. Plus, the first person I should say that to was definitely *not* Blake Alexander.

"Have to what?"

"Work," I snapped. "Let's go out to the shop so I can unpack some stuff." I grabbed the box Syd had half unpacked and went out front.

He didn't protest. He set the sphere back on its stand and followed me. Xander hopped down as well and trailed along after us.

I set the box down and reached in, pulling out a free-form rose quartz wrapped in bubble wrap. Using my box cutter, I sliced neatly through the wrap and freed the stone. "So what do we need to talk about? I know what happened that day. It's not like you have to coach me."

"Right. But I want you to say as little as possible for this formal statement."

"That shouldn't be hard. I don't know anything except that Mazzy turned up in a puddle of slime in my shop." I set the rose quartz down and pulled out a carnelian flame. I unwrapped it and tilted it into the light, admiring the little caves visible in the shades of brilliant red-orange.

"So you knew Mazzy, right?" Blake asked.

I nodded. "A little. We'd had . . . some encounters."

"Encounters?"

"Yeah. We'd met."

He narrowed his eyes. "When was the last time you saw Mazzy before this happened?"

I placed the stone down and reached for the next. "A day or two. I can't remember exactly." I'd tried to put the events of last month out of my mind as much as possible.

"Where did you see her?"

"At the deli on the outskirts of town. I met her there."

His eyebrows shot up. "You were having lunch or something? I thought you two were at each other's throats?"

I sat back on my heels. "Where did you hear that?" It certainly didn't describe our relationship, if you could call it that, accurately. I didn't have any love lost for her, but she'd righted her wrong against me and I was fine.

"Your mother insinuated that."

"Ah. Of course. Fiona is all knowing." I knew I sounded sour right now but couldn't help it. "It wasn't that we didn't get along. I didn't trust her."

"Why?"

"Because she'd written a crappy article about fake spiritualists and included me in it. I wanted her to retract the part about me." I didn't mention the part about how I thought she and Todd knew each other. They'd bumped into each other at my shop and there had seemed to be recognition there on both sides. He'd denied it. Ginny thought it was because she went into his bar sometimes, which made sense, but he'd still sworn that he had no idea who she was.

Which made me suspicious.

"And did she agree to retract it?"

"She did." I didn't add that I'd had to threaten her future career efforts to get her to do so.

"Just like that." Blake sounded skeptical.

"You doubt me? I can be pretty persuasive when I want to be."

"I don't doubt that at all. So she printed a retraction."

"Sure did. She must've filed it before she . . . before it happened because it came out after."

"So the last time you saw her, you left on good terms."

I shrugged. "Good enough. By the way, do they know my mother was on the scene? After I found Mazzy?" I blinked innocently at him.

I could see a muscle in his jaw jump, though he kept his face blank. "She was?"

"Yeah. Did she forget to mention that?" I remembered

that day vividly. Fiona had been quite upset with me and used the Mazzy debacle to underscore all the reasons why I needed to fall in line and listen to her. After she'd done that, she'd vanished in her typical cloud of glitter and left me and Josie to deal with the slimy aftermath. I decided not to mention Josie yet. I didn't want her to get dragged into this mess, even though she'd organized the cleanup crew.

"She must've," Blake muttered. For the first time since we'd started talking about this, he seemed rattled.

"So does that mean she could get in trouble?"

"Listen to me," Blake said. "You should not mention her being there at all. They're giving you some leeway because you didn't have a clue about anything—"

"Hey!"

He ignored me. "But if they know Fiona was there they could give you a harder time. Got it?"

I frowned. "How would that come back on me? Wouldn't they want to know why she didn't do anything?"

Blake shrugged. "They might. They might even call her position on the council into question. Or they could say that you used your seeming ignorance to get away with something. It might make you look worse."

I tried to digest that. I'd never thought it could get me in more trouble. Or was he messing with me?

But Blake had made his point and now he wanted to move on. "But let's take a step back. When you found Mazzy, did you know what you were seeing?"

I shook my head slowly. "I didn't know she was a witch. She still had some . . . form left when I got here. So I called the cops. I thought she was, you know, a person and something had happened. But then my sister came in. She called my mother."

Blake groaned. "Your sister was here too?"

I nodded.

"Great. A freaking family affair." He stalked around the shop, raking his hand through his curls. "Zoe. She knew exactly what she was seeing?"

"Yes. That's why she called Fiona. Well, summoned her or whatever. Fiona was upset. She'd been telling me that I needed to take all this stuff seriously and she thought I wasn't. So she said . . ." I swallowed. "She said I could be next if I didn't start listening to her."

I could see that answer didn't make Blake happy either.

"And then what? You guys cleaned up the mess? No one called anyone else?"

I shook my head slowly. "I'm not sure. Josie said she'd take care of it. She may have gotten someone to do it."

Blake muttered something I couldn't quite make out. He took one more walk around the shop, then came and stood in front of me. "And what did Fiona mean by telling you that you could be next, exactly? That she thought someone was going to genie you?"

I shrugged. "I guess I was having a little trouble processing all of it. I had no idea if she was even for real at that point. I hadn't seen her in—" I stopped. No need to get into all of this with him. He probably knew all about my screwed-up family history anyway.

But he knelt down so we were at eye level. When he spoke his voice was surprisingly gentle. "Violet, I get it. It was all new and must've seemed really unbelievable. But this is important. Why did Fiona think someone might target you?"

"She didn't say. Are you going to tell Fiona I told you?

Because I feel like she might take away my voice powers or something if she finds out."

One side of Blake's mouth lifted in a hint of a smile. "No. But that's why it's important that you don't mention it when you give your statement. Although we can't take it for granted they don't know."

"Do you trust these cops? Or do you think they're trying to find some way to turn this around on my family? Or let the real perp go?"

He threw back his head and laughed. "You watch a lot of mortal TV, huh?"

I frowned. "No. And how do you know what mortal TV is like if you don't watch it too?"

He tipped an imaginary hat. "Well played. Okay, here's the deal. When you speak to the police, I am advising you to stick to only the following facts." He ticked them off on his fingers. "One, you knew Mazzy Diamond on a very superficial business level. If pressed, you can say that you two had a discussion about the story and agreed on terms, but don't offer it up. Two—and you need to check your timeline—you saw her one or two days before the incident, and left on neutral terms. Three, when you came to your shop and found her in that state, you didn't realize what had happened given your limited knowledge of such things and you cleaned up the mess yourself because you didn't know what you were looking at. You told your mother later, and she called and reported it. Okay?"

I felt like I should be taking notes. "Then how did I come to understand what had happened?"

"You took a picture and showed your mother. She confirmed."

I cocked my head at him. "Are you telling me to lie?"

"No. I'm telling you to save your behind. Let me know if you have any questions." He stood up, tapped his watch, and vanished from sight. A telltale puff of smoke, smelling distinctly like incense, remained in his wake.

Just like him, it was kind of sexy.

# CHAPTER TWENTY-TWO

Fiona slapped the latest edition of the *Magickal Times* closed and picked up her coffee, trying to curb her annoyance. Today's coverage of the Mazzy Diamond genieing entailed a statement by a vampire who claimed to have inside knowledge that Mazzy and Violet were embroiled in a scandal involving a demonic attempt to take over the Magickal Council, and the genies had swooped in to save the day. According to the story, the only reason Violet hadn't been genied too was because of her family, who had scared the genies back to where they belonged—stuck in bottles.

"Since when did this paper become a tabloid?" she asked out loud.

A puff of black smoke appeared in the kitchen, immediately followed by Blake Alexander.

"It's been going downhill for a while," he said, stepping out of the smoke. He took a seat at the table. "What is it today?"

Fiona pushed the paper toward him. "Usual bits of nonsense. This one has Violet and that Diamond girl involved in a demonic scandal. I should turn them all into sniveling worms with no hands so they can't write their insipid stories."

"Not today," Blake said. "We've got enough to deal with. That meeting didn't exactly go as planned."

Fiona laughed. "My dear boy. What does? There are too many variables with that whole incident. Including the fact that my daughter had no idea what she was doing, or seeing, so of course it looks like she did something wrong. Coffee?"

Blake nodded. "Please."

Fiona waved a ring-covered hand and a perfect mug of coffee with cream only appeared in front of Blake. She thought for a moment, then waved her hand again and a plate of scones appeared.

"I'm hungry today," she said. "Chocolate chip and blueberry. Today calls for a decadent lunch, no?"

"Yes. I'm starving. And you're the best." Blake picked up a chocolate chip scone and bit into it. "I just came from Violet's shop. I wanted to make sure she understood how to give this statement next week."

"Excellent," Fiona said with an approving nod. "How did it go?"

Blake grinned. "She's funny. Sassy, like you. I think she'll be fine. Unless they know you were there." He said the last bit so casually Fiona almost didn't catch it.

Then her head snapped up. "What?"

Blake popped more scone into his mouth. "Violet is

smart," he said around a mouthful. "And she's wondering why you never told anyone you were in the shop after Mazzy was genied. Come to think of it, I'm kind of wondering the same thing. I figured you could've at least given me a heads up so I could be prepared."

Fiona sighed. She really hated being lectured by anyone, even Blake, for whom she had a fondness. This time he was right, so she didn't fight him on it. "I was angry that day. I left it to her to deal with. And Josie, I suppose. She happened to be with me when Zoe let us know what had happened. I told Violet what I thought, then Zoe and I left. I really didn't think beyond that." It wasn't completely true, but a girl didn't need to give up all her secrets, did she?

Blake regarded her with those intense eyes. "She's worried about Josie. I think she figures you can take care of yourself," he said with a grin.

Fiona already knew this, and it irked her. Indeed, it seemed Violet was more worried about Josie than she was about anything else at this point, including her own safety. "My daughter is a worrier. She'll be fine."

"We're going to make sure she's fine," Blake said. "But I am concerned she's going to try to do something about this Mazzy situation. She seems awfully adamant about helping her."

"Well, she's a bit of a bleeding heart too. That faulty wiring can be attributed to her father, certainly not me." Fiona despised bleeding hearts. In her world, you took care of your family and yourself, not every sorry being that stumbled across your path. Especially one who had tried to take you down. "Why, has she said something? Is she asking around?"

Blake shook his head. "I don't think she'd tell me even if she was asking around. I'm not sure she trusts me yet."

Fiona smiled. "Of course she doesn't. She still doesn't trust me, and I put you in her path." The fact that her own daughter still had suspicions about her motives, about *her*, ate away at her daily, but she'd never say it. Especially not to Blake.

He gave her an odd look. "You think that will change?"

"I have no idea. She's a bit headstrong. Also like me."

Blake took a long sip of coffee. "This is excellent coffee. You might want to try to speed up that getting-her-to-trust-you process though. I'm worried that she might try to go off and do something on her own. If she trusts you—and by extension, me—she'll maybe ask for help before she does something crazy."

Fiona sent him her best withering stare. "You think I'm not trying my hardest? She trusted me enough to let me move into her precious grandmother's house. That's a decent start, wouldn't you say?"

Blake held up his hands in defense. "I'm just saying. We need to stick together. And she isn't sticking yet."

It didn't matter how fond of him she was. At that moment she wished him gone. Not enough to actually make him disappear, but she didn't want to talk about this with him. Granted, she'd been the one to give him the role of Violet's handler, but him pointing out that she still couldn't get a great read on her own daughter rubbed her wrong.

She'd thought once Violet had begun to absorb the culture and take an interest in learning about her families that things would improve. That Fiona could have those mother-daughter moments with her oldest that she'd always dreamed about, sharing spells and stories about family witches. But now that she had access to the book Abigail had left her, Violet's nose was usually in it—and she hardly ever asked Fiona for her advice.

Truthfully, it was making her crazy enough that she'd thought about closing Abigail's book for good. But that was petty and mean and would probably just push Violet further away, so she didn't do it. She wanted to, though. And living here, where Violet and her grandmother had shared all those memories, wasn't helping.

And now here was Blake, rubbing her face in it.

She knew he didn't mean to. Blake was a good man, and he took his responsibilities very seriously. Violet was his responsibility now. And Fiona was no fool. He liked her daughter already. She'd known it would happen. Hadn't even had to help it along. But he just wanted what was best for her.

As they all did.

"I'm working on it," was all she said to Blake now. "Meanwhile, what are *you* doing about it?"

He gave her an amused look and ignored her question, something that not many people could get away with. He finished his pastry, wiped his mouth, and swallowed the rest of his coffee. "Delicious. Oh, one more thing before I go."

Fiona gave him a go-ahead gesture with her hand while she sipped her coffee with the other.

"Who do you suppose tipped off Bell about Mazzy?"

Fiona set her cup down. That anonymous tip. It had been bothering her too. "I don't know."

"Josie?"

"I doubt it. She would never do anything to put Violet at risk."

"Who would? Or should I say, who could have known about this and had the connections to do it?"

They both watched each other.

"You have an idea," Fiona said.

Blake nodded. "I do. I saw her boyfriend today at her shop." He took a breath.

Fiona got the sense she wasn't going to like what he would say next. She was right.

"He's my father's second cousin's son," Blake said. "He hasn't even lived in our world since he was a kid. I remember him from years ago, mostly because he's a black sheep like me. Him because he has no interest in this life—he completely acclimated to the mortal world. He's got some reason for hanging around her. I don't know what, but I have a strong suspicion he could've been the tipper."

The fury hit her quick and hard—reminiscent of her younger years, the days when she'd fly off the handle without a second thought and all her actions had consequences. Before she even realized it, the coffee mug crashed into the wall. Brown liquid dripped down. She ignored it. "He's a Sageblood."

Blake nodded.

"You're sure about this?"

Blake didn't react to the mug. "I'm sure of who he is. The tip part is just a guess."

"I wasn't paying enough attention," Fiona murmured. "I let her put herself in danger."

"How could you know?" Blake asked. "You can't know everything, Fiona. This guy has been around since before you came back."

Fiona whirled, the sheer power of her anger causing

the lights to flicker around them. "Exactly my point. I should know everything when it comes to my daughter. Especially Violet. She is vulnerable. This is all Abigail's fault." With a snap of her wrist, the coffee poured itself back into the mug, now in one piece, and landed on the table with a crash. "She kept me from my daughter and put her at risk." Another snap, and a glass flew off the counter and into the sink. "I knew I didn't like that insipid boy the first time I saw him."

"Fiona," Blake said quietly. "I get it, but you have to stay calm. Getting mad isn't going to help you, and it's certainly not going to help Violet."

Stupid boy. Of course it could help. She could destroy all of them without a second thought. Stop all this madness. But it wouldn't really stop. There would be someone who would pick up the torch and burn everything down again.

It was all so exhausting.

"Then what do you suggest?" she asked him, her tone dripping ice.

"Let me take care of it," Blake said.

"How?"

"I'm going to find out if it was him first, and what his endgame is. And I'm going to make sure they don't stay together. Just give me some time."

Fiona sent him a skeptical look.

"She's not into him, Fiona. I can tell. That's why I say he has to have some reason for hanging around her. I'm going to find out. And I'm going to put a stop to it. I just have to be careful how I do it."

She watched his face, the way his jaw set, the serious glint in those deep eyes. He cared for her daughter. She'd predicted it, although she hadn't interfered at all despite him being her preferred choice.

Finally, she nodded. "Whatever you need to do, Blake. And remember. I just found my daughter again. Whatever I need to do, I won't lose her. Are we clear?"

"Crystal," Blake said. He tugged his tie and disappeared from the room, leaving only the faint scent of palo santo in his wake.

# CHAPTER TWENTY-THREE

*Friday*
*Full moon in Aries*

I needed to go to yoga.

It felt like forever since I'd gone, although it had probably only been a couple of days. But I needed yoga to keep me sane, and with everything going on in both my worlds I needed it now more than ever.

So I got up early the next morning—the day of the full moon, and the end of the second cycle of Mazzy's limbo—fed the cats, pulled on my favorite glittery, moon-patterned yoga pants, and grabbed my mat. As I headed down the street I saw Mr. Quigley and Charlie Klein huddled in the doorway of the building next door, talking seriously about something. I lifted my hand in a wave, but they were so engrossed neither of them noticed me. I wondered what they were gossiping about. Charlie had more knowledge about what was going on in town than the local news-paper, and Mr. Q spent a lot of time out on the street—some people called him the unofficial mayor of North Harbor—so he also was in the know about most things that went on in town.

I wondered if it had anything to do with Nicole. That would definitely be the big news.

I rounded the corner and approached the door of the yoga studio. The vibe had changed with the ownership. When my friend Natalie Mann became unable to run the studio, her husband had taken on a new partner to keep it open. It was still yoga, but not quite the same. Yogis say that at some point during your practice, you find "your" teacher. Natalie had been that for me. I'd always left her class feeling lighter, free, but super grounded. She always seemed to know exactly what quote to read, or what les-son to teach that ended up being exactly what I needed. I missed her.

Still, I trudged into class, set up my mat in my usual spot in the back, and tried to center myself. Which was easier said than done these days. I could hear the class filling up around me. Then the teacher's voice, quietly asking everyone to come to a comfortable seat. I opened my eyes and peered at her. I didn't know her.

She introduced herself as Brittany, a new teacher. "Any-one have any requests or intentions for the class they want to share?" she asked when everyone had gotten settled.

A man in front whom I vaguely recognized from other classes cleared his throat. "I'd like to ask if we could all keep Nicole St. James in our intentions. She is . . ." his voice broke a bit, "missing."

My heart sped up a bit. Another friend of Nicole's. I needed to talk to him.

Brittany, meanwhile, nodded somberly. "I lit some candles for her," she said, indicating the altar behind her.

No one else could top that intention, so she started class. I could barely keep myself focused on the poses, and when we finally ended I hurried to put my stuff away so I could grab the mystery guy.

I caught up with him outside the studio. He'd hurried down the steps and was about to walk in the opposite direction from me when I called to him. He paused, then walked back over to me. "Yeah?"

"Hi. I'm Violet Mooney. I own the crystal shop over there." I waved vaguely in the direction of Water Street.

He nodded politely, clearly confused about why I felt the need to make him late for wherever he was off to to tell him this. He was around my age. Tall and lean, like someone who not only did a lot of yoga but was also a runner or swimmer or something like that. His hair was cut short, almost buzzed.

I pushed on hurriedly so I didn't lose him. "I'm sorry to bother you, but I heard you mention Nicole St. James. I met her last week. She came into my shop looking for . . . some help."

That caught his interest. His whole body language changed and he took a step closer to me. "She did?"

I nodded. "I felt terrible when I heard she was missing and I couldn't help but wonder how you know her."

"She's a good friend," he said, and I could hear his voice shake. "We worked together for the past six years at the law firm. Well, until she quit last month. I'm so worried about her."

I nodded but stayed silent, hoping he'd continue.

He did. "We were supposed to go out for a drink this week. I've been texting her, but no reply. It's like her

phone is shut off. Then I saw the posters the other day."
He hesitated for a second, then said, "I'm Isaac. Isaac
Brady."

"Nice to meet you," I said. "Her friend Ginny—I'm
sure you know her?" I waited for him to nod, but he just
looked at me blankly. "Anyway she's the one who
brought her to see me. And she put up all the posters."

"I don't know her," he said after a minute. He shook
his head, looking out into the distance. "I guess there
were a lot of things I didn't know."

I wondered what that meant. "Hey. You drink coffee?"
I asked.

He looked at me like that was the stupidest question
he'd ever heard. "Who doesn't?"

"You want to get a cup with me? Compare notes? The
more we can tell the cops, the better chance we have of
them helping her."

He cocked his head, studying me. "Why are you so interested? You said you just met her. Are you one of those
people who likes to get involved in true crime or something?"

"No, I'm not. Honestly. I just . . . I take my job really
seriously, and I wanted to be able to help her. She came to
me for protection and I feel like I failed. So I guess I'm
just taking an interest in trying to figure out what happened. And I know the cop who's looking into it." I
looked down at the pavement and scuffed my toe.

Isaac was quiet for so long I almost wondered if he'd
walked away before I dared look up again. When I finally
lifted my head, I found him watching me intently.

"So they have no idea where she could be? If she's . . ."
he grimaced and shook his head. "I don't want to think
about that."

Whoa. He went right to worst-case scenario. "Not that I've heard about. But if everyone puts their heads to-gether . . ."

Isaac nodded. "Couldn't hurt, right?" He glanced at his watch. "I can talk for a few minutes if that works for you. The Bean?"

I smiled. "Let's go."

A few minutes later we settled at Pete's counter with coffees—a latte for me and a straight-up bold coffee, no milk, no sugar for Isaac. He wasn't very chatty right off the bat, sipping his coffee and staring out the window. I gave him as much space as possible to start, then figured we'd be sitting there all day if I didn't say something. "So you and Nicole are pretty tight?"

Isaac nodded slowly, running his finger around the lid of his cup. "She was my work wife." He smiled a little. "Our offices were right next to each other at the firm. She spent more time in my office than her own."

"Until she left," I said.

He nodded. "Until she left." His eyes shifted away from mine.

"Why did she leave?" I asked.

He went back to staring out the window. "Honestly? I don't know. She was tight-lipped about it. Told me like, the day before her last day." He shook his head, lips pursed. "It was weird. Especially since I know they of-fered her a promotion at our place."

A promotion? "That doesn't sound like a good reason to leave. She wasn't happy there?"

Isaac shrugged. "I always thought she was, but some-thing changed recently. She never really said what."

"Recently like when?"

He thought for a minute. "Maybe two months ago?"

"You think it had something to do with her work? Or did she not get along with her boss?"

"She loved working with Tim Steele. That was the partner she worked under. They got along great. She always got good cases too. Like the bridge project."

"Yeah, she won that, didn't she?"

Isaac nodded. "I think that's what got her the promotion. Our client who was against it was real serious about that project going away, or at least getting revised so it didn't involve taking down his building."

"Which client?"

"Jackson Bogart. He owns the building they wanted to tear down."

I called up a picture of Bogart in my mind from the council meeting the other night. The fancy suit guy. "So why would she have left if that was coming back around?"

"I guess she just got a better offer," Isaac said with a shrug. "Although she never really said to me what it was about the new job that she found so appealing. The firm is smaller and their cases aren't very high profile. And that woman . . ." he wrinkled his nose. "Sylvia Townsend? She's a piece of work. Ruthless, I've heard."

"Aren't all lawyers?" I said with a smile.

Isaac didn't return my smile. Guess they didn't have much of a sense of humor either.

"Does Sylvia own the firm?"

He nodded. "She and her husband used to run it together, but when they split she got the business. So it's Townsend and Hammerstein, but there's no more Hammerstein."

"They knew each other already though, right? Maybe Nicole wanted to help her build the firm up? An opportunity for her to make partner quicker?" I didn't know a lot about law firms, but it seemed that on all the TV shows everyone was all about getting to partner. I figured that had to hold some water in real life too.

Isaac picked up his cup and tilted it back and forth. "They knew each other?"

"That's what Ginny said."

"Huh. Maybe that makes sense then," he said listlessly. "She was on the other side of the bridge project. I figured she poached Nicole so if it came back around she'd have a chance of winning."

I remembered being surprised about that at the council meeting. "Was someone bothering her at your office? Harassing her, maybe?" It was worth asking, I figured. "Or did she change her mind about her stance on the bridge?"

"The only person harassing her was that piece of crap she was dating," Isaac said bitterly. "The partners wooed her to stay. Heck, even Bogart sent her a giant box of fancy chocolates and a personal plea to stay on his case. But she wouldn't budge. I have no idea about her stance on the bridge. It was always just a case for us, you know? We didn't talk about our personal feelings about it."

So Isaac knew about the boyfriend troubles. Which made sense, if they were so close. "Nicole mentioned that she was having a lot of issues with her relationship. She told you about it?"

Something I couldn't quite read passed over his face. "Of course. She was having a really rough time with that guy. I tried to help her as much as I could, but she was adamant about dealing with it herself. Said she didn't want to get anyone else involved."

"Because he was dangerous?" I asked.

He turned to me, eyes narrowed. "She tell you all that?"

"She alluded to it. Ginny told me a bit more."

"So you know he'd been stalking her? Showing up at the office? That he broke into her place once and threatened her cat?"

"You're kidding." For as mad as I was about what had happened to Nicole, this generated a different kind of mad. Scumbags who hurt animals, or even threatened to hurt them, should be locked up forever. In my opinion.

"No, I'm not kidding. Her cat is safe, right? She loves Roxie so much." His eyes got all watery. I could feel the intense sadness emanating off him. And something else. Jealousy, maybe. I wondered if there was something more to his relationship with Nicole.

Up until now, I'd resisted tuning in to his aura. I didn't want to invade his privacy like that, especially since he was doing me a favor by talking with me. But now my hackles were up. I fixed a smile on my face. "Yes. Ginny has her. So did Nicole ever report this to the police? Or get a restraining order on him?"

While I waited for him to answer, I focused just above the crown of his head and to the left. Oranges and yellows warred for attention. I wasn't surprised. The harshness of the orange told me he tended toward the obsessive, while the paler yellow signified jealousy.

Isaac shook his head. "She didn't report it. She was too afraid. And I hope they have the good sense to start with him."

I understood that, even though I found it infuriating that in this present day, women still felt like they wouldn't get enough protection if they reported an abusive partner. "They are," I assured him. "Ginny gave Sergeant Merlino his name. Do you know if she had been seeing anyone else?" I watched him closely. He kept looking out the window, but I saw his jaw clench and unclench.

"I don't know," he said flatly. "She didn't tell me if she was. But I guess she could have been, right? Especially since she keeps blowing me off when I try to see her lately." He shredded his napkin meticulously, bunching all the pieces together in front of him.

"So you didn't see her much after she took the new job?"

"Not as much as before, no."

"Did you ask if she was seeing someone else?"

Isaac shook his head. "I didn't want to pry. She wasn't herself, you know? And I wanted to respect her privacy. But now I regret it." He looked at me, and this time he didn't even try to hide the tears. "Maybe I could've protected her if I knew how bad things were. But now it could be too late."

# CHAPTER TWENTY-FOUR

After I left Isaac and the Bean I headed to my shop, closing and locking the door behind me. I still had time before I had to open and I needed to think.

Isaac had tried to be casual, but his aura had told me everything I needed to know. He wanted to be more than friends with Nicole. And he definitely didn't like Chris Strand. I wondered if Isaac had tried to date her, or if he'd suffered in silence. If he had tried, maybe she'd been freaked out about it—either because she was afraid of what Chris would do, or because she wasn't into him as more than a friend. Either of those reasons would've made for a difficult conversation and a strained friendship.

I also got the sense that he wasn't a fan of Sylvia Townsend, although that could've just been because

Nicole had left him—as he probably thought of it—to go work for her and it sounded like they hadn't been as close since that happened.

I pulled my phone out of my bag and called Gabe. "I just met a friend of Nicole's at yoga," I said without preamble.

"Yeah? And?" I could hear a lot of noise behind him, like he was in the station with cops all around him.

"And I'm wondering if there was something between them. They worked together at the firm she recently left."

"Name?" Gabe asked. He was all business today.

I gave him Isaac's name. "You'll check him out?"

"I will."

"Any other news?"

"Nope. I gotta run, Violet. Thanks for the info." And he disconnected.

"You're welcome," I said to the empty line, then sighed and tossed my phone onto my desk. I surveyed my store, not exactly sure what I was looking for. Then my eyes landed on my giant crystal quartz sphere. I kept it in the store, but it wasn't for sale. I loved it and used it to help me tune up my aura-sensing powers. I went over to pick it up now but was distracted by something on the counter next to it. A perfectly smooth, flat, circular black stone on an ornate brass stand.

I picked up the stone and studied it. I knew exactly what it was—an obsidian scrying mirror—but what I didn't know was how it had gotten into my shop. I'd never ordered one. It was something I wanted to explore but I hadn't felt equipped to do it yet.

Scrying mirrors had a lot of history and beliefs attached to them. People in ancient Mexico were said to have used them for black magic. I'd heard it referred to as "seeing into darkness." Once the scryer reached a higher level of concentration, visions would appear. Some said that it was more than a powerful psychic tool, and was actually a portal into the astral plane. Others said it was simply another crystal that could be used as a charging plate for other stones.

I believed a little bit of all of it. And I wondered again how it had gotten here.

I glanced around, but I was still alone in the shop, although I suddenly felt a presence. "Is someone there?" I asked.

Nothing. Not that I'd expected an answer. But I couldn't shake the feeling I was being watched.

I snatched up the mirror and held it close to my chest. A warm feeling flooded my body. I closed my eyes and set an intention, asking my angels and guides of the highest truth and protection to keep any dark forces away and help me find what I needed to know, then picked up the stand and headed out back, drawing the curtain. When I reached my desk, I wasn't surprised at all to find Xander sitting there, tail swishing, regarding me with those all-knowing eyes. I had expected as much. Maybe he was the presence I'd felt.

"You here to help?" I asked.

He blinked.

"Okay then. Let's do it. We need to figure out where this woman is." I sat down, placed the mirror on its stand, and eyed it. I was a little nervous about this—between the stone itself, and what I was attempting to do. Fiona had said many times that there was a line that should never be crossed when it came to witches interfering in mortal world happenings. I wasn't sure what that line was. Maybe this was okay.

If it wasn't, I wondered what would happen.

"Well, guess we're going to find out," I said to Xander.

He slunk over and laid down, wrapping his body around the mirror. I wondered if that was his way of helping.

I closed my eyes and focused on Nicole's face, like I'd read in my grandmother's book. When I had a vision of her in full view, I called in images of Isaac and Sylvia. I had Googled Chris Strand and found one grainy picture of him online, but it was enough to call that in also. Then I opened my eyes and focused on the black depths of the mirror. I could almost see myself staring back at me, the stone was so smooth and shiny.

I must've fallen into a meditative state because I lost track of time as I sat and held the space, hoping for something to show up. I sat for what felt like a long time, staring into the black, but nothing appeared. No images of someone kidnapping Nicole. No picture of one of my suspects with a guilty sign flashing across their forehead in neon.

I muttered a curse, blinking my eyes to clear them. Xander opened one eye—guess he'd been napping—and looked at me, then closed it again.

"Well, that was useless," I said. Just as I started to stand up, an image appeared in the mirror. An outline of something cylindrical . . . a bottle, I realized as the image filled in. Fascinated, I sat back in my seat as Xander also sat up, snapping to attention.

As I watched, the colors in the bottle turned pink, then green, then faded into a rainbow of purples, greens, and blues that reminded me of . . .

Mazzy's hair. I jumped back in my chair, startled. Xander's gaze was fixed on the mirror too, which made me think it wasn't just me. I stared at the stone as the colors continued to morph together, fading into black again. But now I could see a face in the midst of the blackness. Mazzy. I felt it with absolute certainty. But then her face faded and another took its place—Nicole's, I realized. It stared back at me, but something about her eyes . . . the picture shifted again and there was a building, with large, arched windows. I knew I'd seen it before but couldn't place it. Why was I seeing this? I stared, unable to look away, as that same feeling of claustrophobia that had squeezed me when I was doing Nicole's reading creeped in, holding me in place. I literally couldn't look away. The shadow was moving through the mirror, obscuring the building, and I felt fear.

Only this time, I couldn't tell if it was mine or someone else's.

*Someone else's.* The thought came to me unbidden, as I realized I didn't feel like I was even in my body anymore. I could feel a scream bubbling up in my throat but nothing was coming out when I opened my mouth. I raised my hands to my throat, an unconscious effort to remove whatever chokehold was on me, but nothing was there.

But I couldn't breathe.

I actually thought I might pass out.

And then, suddenly, the mirror disappeared from in front of me. I heard a crash, felt Xander scrambling to hide, and then I was jolted back to the present moment, to my own body, to find Blake standing in front of me.

# CHAPTER TWENTY-FIVE

Blake's dark eyes were twin storm clouds. "What in the name of the Goddess do you think you're doing?" he demanded, his hand coming up and at me.

I flinched, not sure what he was doing, but he sounded angry enough that I thought he might hit me. Then I felt his hand on my cheek, his touch surprisingly gentle.

"Are you okay, Violet?" he asked. His voice was still sharp but concern tinged the edges.

I nodded, and concentrated on slowing my heartbeat, flexing my fingers to work some circulation back into them, breathing. "Yeah. Did you break that mirror?"

"Damn straight I broke the mirror. What were you doing with that thing? Do you know how dangerous that is for someone like you?"

I stared at him. "What do you mean?"

He buried both his hands in his hair, pulling at it like he was trying to rip it out. "Where did you get that?"

"I . . . I'm not sure. It was in my shop."

Blake turned and stared at me. "But you didn't put it there."

I shook my head.

"And you don't know who did."

"Had to have been Josie or Syd," I said, trying to convince myself as much as him. "Who else could it have been?"

"That's a good question," he said quietly. "Vi, scrying mirrors can be dangerous for people who have powers like you. You can see things about people. That can enhance your power tenfold. And put you at risk."

"At risk for what?"

"For dark forces to take over."

I frowned. This was all starting to sound a little too Hollywood witch for me, black shadows aside. I got up from my chair, thankful my legs were working. I didn't want to show weakness in front of Blake. "That sounds a little far-fetched," I said, trying to sound more confident than I felt. "And I always put out the intention for protection when I work with crystals in that way."

But I'd never worked with an obsidian scrying mirror before. I had no idea what I was doing. I also knew the full moon amplified clairsentient powers. And since there was only one more moon cycle before Mazzy was stuck in that bottle forever, maybe she'd come to me to ask for help.

"Violet!"

Blake's voice jolted me back to reality.

"What?"

"I said, what did you see? You looked pretty disturbed

when I came in. Like you couldn't actually move away from it if you wanted to."

My eyes immediately went to the pieces of the mirror scattered on my floor. Was it my imagination, or did I see a glint of rainbow colors again?

"I don't know. Mazzy, I think. And one of my clients. And some building." I tried to bring that picture back into my field of vision, but no matter how much I reached for it, it wasn't coming. "A shadow. It was squeezing my throat. I felt . . . like I couldn't breathe." My hand went to my throat instinctively.

"And you felt like you couldn't move?"

I nodded. "I think so. I don't know. What are you doing here, anyway?" I asked, frustrated.

"I came to see if you wanted to go through your statement before Monday."

"Didn't we already do that?"

"We didn't do a dry run," he said.

I rolled my eyes. "So you're going to play Chief Bell? Thanks, but I'm good. I need to open my store." I glanced at my watch, shocked to realize it was almost ten. I'd been looking at that mirror for more than an hour. What on earth?

Then my phone started to ring. Before I even picked it up to see who it was, I got a bad feeling.

Something was wrong.

And when I reached for it and saw Gabe's name, that feeling intensified.

I wondered if it was Zoe. Had something happened to my sister? I mean, I still wasn't totally sure how I felt about Zoe as an only child who'd just had this sprung on her, but I reserved the right to figure it out. Plus, I was probably being silly. Zoe was a witch, after all. The chances of something bad happening to her were probably zero.

Although, my mother had thought that about my Grandma Abby too.

Hand shaking, I answered. "Hey. What's up?"

"Vi." Gabe sounded far away, like he was outside. There was a lot of commotion around him. "I need to talk to you. I have some bad news and I didn't want you to hear it somewhere else."

My heart plummeted again. "What? It's not Zoe, is it?"

"No. Your sister is fine." He paused. "It's Nicole St. James. We found her."

I paused, waiting for him to add *in Chicago,* or *at the airport*, or *back home after she'd gone away for a few days to clear her head*. But he didn't say any of those things. "Okay," I said, and my voice sounded hoarse to my own ears. "Where? Is she okay?"

It was his turn to pause, and in that black hole of silence I instinctively knew the answer.

"No. She's not. We found her at Wildflower Park. She's dead, Vi. Someone killed her."

# Chapter Twenty-six

I heard Gabe say a few more things, like he'd tried to reach Ginny but couldn't get her, but soon I stopped listening. I remember letting the phone fall away from my ear, and Blake coming over to take it from my hand.

"Violet. What is it?" he asked. "What happened?"

I stared blankly at him. I wasn't sure what to tell him. Not that he would care about some mortal woman who'd gotten killed. But I found the words spilling out anyway.

"Nicole. My customer," I said. My voice shook. I could hear it and I hated it. "She's dead."

He frowned. "Dead? Someone from . . . here, you mean?"

I nodded. "She was missing. They just found her." I waved vaguely at the phone. "Gabe. And the other cops. Or maybe someone's dog. Isn't that how they find a lot of bodies? When dogs sniff them out?" I was babbling and probably hysterical, but I couldn't help it. I wondered if Ginny knew. I had to talk to her. It was probably irrational, but I figured she would blame me.

And I couldn't help but think that she would be right to.

I looked at Blake. "How bad is it to get involved in mortal stuff . . . like this? Like trying to find out what happened to her?"

Something moved across Blake's face that could have been a smile. "Your mother was right. You are a bleeding heart."

"What? What does that mean? Someone is *dead*!"

"I know. I'm sorry, Violet. You're having a rough week, aren't you?"

I nodded. He moved over to me and next thing I knew, his arms were around me and my face was buried in his chest. I tensed, ready to pull away, then realized it felt good and snuggled in.

I don't know how long I held on for, but Blake made no effort to let go. Finally I came to my senses, took a deep breath, and stepped back. "I'm sorry. Thank you," I said, aware that I sounded like an idiot.

"You don't need to be sorry, and you certainly don't need to thank me," he said. "Are you okay?"

"Yeah. But I have to go." I had no idea where Josie or Syd were, but I needed to go see Ginny. I turned away, my eyes falling on the pieces of mirror on the ground. "I have to clean up this mess before the cat cuts his foot, though."

"I got it." Blake said. He made a circular motion with his hand and the shards vanished. "If you see anything like that again, leave it alone and call me. You hear?"

I stared at the place where they had been, then nodded. No worries there. I'd had enough of being a witch today.

\*   \*   \*

I grabbed my coat and walked out front, still in a daze. I stood for a moment, thinking, then went to one of my counters and selected three stones: A chrysoprase, an Apache tear, and a rose quartz. All good for grief.

Ginny would need them.

But as I pulled my door open, I felt the familiar crackle of static and my sister appeared behind me in a lovely cloud of pink.

"Hey," she said. "Are you okay?"

I shut the door again and leaned against it. "Yeah. No. What are you doing here?"

"I heard what happened. Vi. I know what you're thinking right now."

"You do?" I found that hard to believe. I liked my sister well enough, but we weren't that close yet that she'd be privy to my inner thoughts and feelings. Although truth be told, I didn't have a full picture of her powers.

"I do. You feel guilty."

I leaned against the door, suddenly feeling exhausted. "How do you know that?"

"Because I've heard you talk about this woman. And you came to see Gabe because you were worried about her. It's kind of obvious. Look." She grasped my arm. "Just because she came to you for help—for crystals—doesn't mean you had the ability to stop what happened."

"I don't even know what happened," I said. "I mean, I know Gabe said someone killed her, but he didn't tell me anything else. Or did he? Did I somehow tune him out?"

"I don't know what he told you, but yes, she was murdered."

I winced at hearing it out loud. "Did he say how?"

Zoe shook her head. "I can find out."

I narrowed my eyes. "How?"

"I can tune into him pretty well." She closed her eyes.

I grabbed her arm. "No! I mean, I don't want to be responsible for you poking around in Gabe's head. He'll tell me what he can tell me. I'll talk to him when things calm down."

Zoe opened one eye and cocked her head at me. "Seriously, Vi? When are you going to embrace the fact that we can make our lives easier with our powers?"

"And when are you going to embrace the fact that we don't use our powers to meddle in the daily affairs of mortals?" Fiona's voice inquired from behind me.

We both whirled around to find our mother standing there. She looked like something out of a movie, standing in the middle of a floor that looked like the art supply fairy had gotten drunk in my store and spilled the contents of her glitter jar, surrounded by sparkling crystals. Her hair was in an updo today, which made her look even more elegant and in control than usual.

Fiona glided over to stand in front of us. "I warned you, Zoe. You cannot use your powers in a way that interferes with the mortals' way of doing things. There are certain times when we can and should step in, but using your power to infiltrate a police investigation isn't appropriate."

"He's my boyfriend," Zoe protested.

"Even worse, then. Have I taught you nothing?" Fiona snapped.

Zoe crossed her arms defiantly over her chest. She looked like she wanted to argue the point but in the end decided not to.

Fiona turned to me. "I heard some of that. Why do you feel responsible for this person's death?"

"I don't feel responsible, I just feel like I could've done more to help her. I tried. Honestly I did. I used my crystals the way Grandma Abby outlined in her book. Then today I used that stupid mirror I found—"

"Mirror?" Fiona's voice was sharp. "What mirror?"

"There was an obsidian scrying mirror here. Josie probably bought it and forgot to tell me. Anyhow, I used it and I saw . . ." I trailed off. I wasn't sure if I should bring Mazzy up right now.

But Fiona was sharp. "You saw what?"

"Mazzy," I muttered. "And I think Nicole too. But I couldn't tell what it all meant."

Apparently Mazzy's name got her attention. "You saw Mazzy? How? Violet," she said urgently, "it's very important that you tell me exactly what you saw."

I sighed. "It wasn't the first time. I see her with a bottle around her. Which shouldn't be surprising given what happened, right? It's usually her hair—she had crazy-colored hair. But this time it faded into black. Then I saw Nicole, and then some building, but that was it." I shook my head, frustrated. "They found Nicole at a park, so I'm not sure what the building has to do with—"

"*What else?*" Fiona's voice was urgent.

"Jeez. I didn't see anything else. It was more like a . . . feeling. Like something suffocating. A dark shadow. I thought I was feeling what Mazzy felt. Is that possible?"

"Where is this mirror?"

"Uh. Blake . . . smashed it."

She stared at me. "Excuse me?"

"Blake. He showed up while I was using it. He smashed it and made the pieces vanish."

"Well," Fiona said with a small smile. "How about that." Then the smile faded. "I don't want you using anything like that again. Do you hear me? And I especially don't want you using them to try and get a read on that Diamond woman. This is dangerous, Violet. And it's high time you listened when people told you that."

And with a flick of her scarf, she was gone.

# CHAPTER TWENTY-SEVEN

"Where did she go?" I asked Zoe, bewildered.

Zoe, too, looked like she had no idea what had just occurred. "Not a clue. That was weird. Even for Mother." She grabbed my arm. "Forget her. Let's go talk to Ginny."

"You're coming?" I asked as she pushed me to the door.

"Of course I am. You need support. And I want to help."

"Wait. I need to figure out where she is." I picked up my phone to text her, but suddenly an image of her waiting tables, smiling, appeared in front of me. Was this right? Was she at the diner working? That would mean she hadn't heard yet.

And why was I suddenly getting visions?

No time to question it now. "The diner," I said to Zoe. "Let's go."

Honestly, I was glad Zoe was there. If she hadn't been, I probably would've just sat there in shock. But at least we were doing something.

When we stepped inside and scanned the tables, I saw Ginny right away. She was taking an order from an elderly couple. When she stuffed her pad in her pocket and headed back to the counter, Zoe and I intercepted.

She glanced up, smiling when she saw me, then her gaze shifted to Zoe, curious. "Hey, Vi. What's going on?" She nodded at Zoe.

"You, uh, met my sister?" I asked.

Ginny and Zoe both nodded. "We know each other," Ginny said.

Zoe said nothing.

I'd worry about that later. "Do you have a minute?" I asked Ginny.

She glanced at the clock on the wall. "I have a break in about fifteen."

"Can you take it now? It's important," I said when she hesitated.

She studied me for a moment, then nodded. "One second." She disappeared out back, then returned minus her apron, shrugging into her coat. "Let's go outside," she said, motioning to the side door that led out into an alley. One of the cooks stood against the side of the building, smoking. He glanced at us, nodded at Ginny, then flicked his butt on the ground, crushed it with his heel, and went back inside.

Once he was gone she looked from me to Zoe and back again, her eyes bright with curiosity. "So what is it?"

Zoe shifted uncomfortably from one foot to the other, waiting for me to speak.

I hated this with every fiber of my being. But I wanted her to hear it from me, not some news article or town gossip. I was actually surprised that she hadn't heard yet in this place. I took a breath. "It's Nicole," I said.

Ginny's entire face crumbled and she reached for the wall behind her. "What? Did they . . . find her?"

I nodded, swallowing against the lump in my throat. "Gabe called me. He tried to call you. I'm so sorry."

"She's . . . she's dead?" Ginny could barely get the word out.

I nodded. The grief on her face wrecked me and I pulled her into a hug, looking helplessly at Zoe over Ginny's head as she cried ugly tears.

Zoe clearly didn't like tears. She gave it about ten more seconds, then muttered something and pointed at Ginny's eyes.

Abruptly, Ginny stopped crying and stood back, looking like she wasn't exactly sure what was happening.

I frowned at Zoe, then looked at Ginny. "You okay?" I knew it was a stupid question but I didn't know what else to say.

She shook her head. "What happened to her?"

"I'm not sure. We'll need to talk to Gabe."

"Where did they find her?"

"At the park," I said. "I don't know any more than that."

"Are they . . . sure?"

"Gabe sounded pretty sure."

Ginny sagged back against the wall. "It was him, wasn't it?"

"Who?"

"Chris."

"I have no idea," I said. "We don't know what happened. Well, maybe Gabe does, but he didn't tell me if he did." I was babbling. "Listen, Ginny. I met Nicole's friend today. Isaac?"

I could see her brain working to process the name. "Who?"

"Isaac Brady. Nicole's friend? From work?"

The blank look remained. "I don't think I know him."

He hadn't known her either. Either Nicole was extremely compartmentalized, or she and Isaac weren't as tight as he had indicated.

"I met him at yoga. It sounded like they were close, I guess. He might have even liked her. Or dated her. Would she tell you if she was seeing someone else?"

Ginny closed her eyes and rubbed her temples. She sank so low against the wall that she was almost on the ground. "Yes. She would've told me." Ginny thrust her chin up, eyes defiant. "We were best friends."

I could hear the slight hitch in her voice and understood that she had about as much confidence in that statement as I did at the moment—which wasn't much. "Okay. But I think he might have had a thing for her, even if she didn't for him."

"So what does that mean?" Ginny asked, her voice full of despair. "Is he, like, a bad guy or something? Are you telling me she had two crazy guys after her?"

"I don't know," I said. "You didn't mention Chris stalked her at work and broke into her place and threatened her cat."

"What?" Now she jumped up. "I didn't know that. Are you sure?"

I was starting to get a clearer picture of Nicole as a

woman who completely compartmentalized her life so that one piece barely touched another. It reminded me of one of my childhood friends who used to keep every food item on her plate spaced out enough so that nothing touched anything else. And if it did, she had to throw the whole thing away and start over again. "I'm telling you what he told me. That's all."

"Okay, so, we have to tell Gabe. This just confirms it. He killed her!" Her voice rose a couple of notches to hysterical.

"Shhh. Calm down," I said as someone walking by the alley glanced curiously at us.

"I can't calm down. We have to help them get him. He killed her. He killed my best friend." Ginny started to sob again.

"Seriously?" Zoe muttered. She went to do her stop-Ginny-from-crying move when suddenly Ginny turned to her, bringing her hand up in a defensive posture. Zoe jumped like something had hit her. "What the . . . ?"

"What, do you think I'm going to let you put spells on me all day so you don't have to feel uncomfortable? That's just like you. I can see you haven't changed."

"Hey. What's that supposed to mean?" Zoe took a step forward, challenging.

"Stop it," I interrupted, moving between them. "Really guys? And how did you do that?" I asked Ginny. "I thought you were kind of paused on powers."

Ginny shifted uncomfortably from foot to foot. "I was working on it. Getting some help."

"From who?" For a split second I had a jealous moment thinking that Blake had been helping Ginny too.

She looked at me, then her eyes slid away. "Mazzy."

My mouth dropped open. "Mazzy? How come you never mentioned that to me before?"

Ginny jerked her shoulder in a shrug. "I don't know. Because you didn't like her. And she's gone anyway." Her eyes filled with tears again. "Both my best friends are gone. And there's not a thing I can do about it."

# CHAPTER TWENTY-EIGHT

*Saturday*

Zoe called me the next morning. "Gabe and I are going to Pete's for coffee. Meet us there. I told him you wanted to talk more about that woman."

I sighed, rubbing the sleep out of my eyes. Yesterday had passed in a blur after we found out about Nicole. I'd closed up early and gone home to be alone. Which meant crawling into bed at eight o'clock. "Zoe, he probably can't talk about it."

"He'll talk," she assured me. "Half an hour?"

I guessed it couldn't hurt. "Fine. Sure."

"Jeez. You're welcome." She hung up.

I groaned and rolled out of bed to get ready. I had a splitting headache and felt like someone had beaten me with a bat.

I couldn't imagine how Ginny felt. She'd left the diner

in a daze after telling them she needed the rest of the day off. I hadn't talked to her since. She was probably holed up with Roxie. They would both be mourning.

Tears stung my own eyes and I angrily wiped them away, glaring at myself in the mirror. "Do something about it then," I muttered. "Since you couldn't help her before she died."

With one last, angry look at my defeated face, I grabbed my stuff and left. On my way down the street, my gaze fell on one of the posters Ginny had put up just a few days ago. It felt like years. One corner had come loose and flapped in the winter wind, sending Nicole's smiling face into animated movement. I averted my eyes and hurried past.

I made it to Pete's before them.

"Morning, Vi. You've heard?" He looked grim.

I nodded, feeling tears sting my eyes. "Yeah. Sucks."

"It does." He reached over and squeezed my hand. "I'm sorry. I want you to know I tried. A few times."

I sent him a questioning look.

"To find Nicole, or at least get a read on her. I had no luck."

Sounded familiar. "Thanks for trying. Can I get a caramel latte?"

"Sure, unless you want to try today's special." He pointed to his menu. "A peppermint latte with vanilla swirl."

"Sold." I pulled out my wallet and handed him my debit card.

Pete waved me off. "On the house. Let me know if you want to talk, okay?"

"I will." Once I picked up my coffee I grabbed a table in the back. Gabe and Zoe arrived five minutes later. Zoe said something to Gabe, then came over to join me as he headed up to the counter.

"Hey." She slid into the booth. "Gabe is grabbing our coffees. You need anything?"

I shook my head, holding up my cup. "All set, thanks. Hey, by the way. What was that whole thing with you and Ginny yesterday? About how you haven't changed? I didn't know you knew Ginny."

Zoe sighed. "It's not important. Really. Turns out Ginny went to my school for a while when we were kids. She's kind of . . . odd."

I rolled my eyes. "What, did she steal your lunchbox or something?"

"No," Zoe said defensively. "She just didn't fit in. The kids weren't very nice to her sometimes."

"Including you?"

"No," Zoe said, but it didn't sound convincing.

"What was the issue with her?"

"She was kind of out of her league. Her family didn't really belong. Her father is a half witch and didn't know it until later in life."

"Uh, Zoe? So was mine."

"Right, but her mother isn't a witch at all. So she's like, one-fourth witch. They kind of straddled the worlds for a while, but basically shifted over here to the mortal world. Ginny tried to go to one of our schools but she failed out. I'm not judging," she said again, with a touch of defensiveness.

"No, not at all," I said, deadpan.

"But I didn't think she dabbled much in the witch world anymore. So I was surprised when she got in a punch yesterday, metaphysically speaking."

"Why did you come with me if you were going to be mean to her? She's having a hard time."

"I wasn't being mean. She got mad at me. Gabe's coming," she said, inclining her head toward the counter.

I filed this conversation away for another time. "So what did you tell him?"

"Just that you and Ginny were pretty upset yesterday and need to know what's happening. He said he was sorry to drop the news on you like that but he was out at the scene and couldn't get into it."

"He doesn't need to be sorry. He was doing his job." I watched people hurry by outside, heads bent against the cold. I wondered how long Nicole had been outside. If she'd been cold. "You shouldn't have made him come talk to me."

"Don't worry about it."

"Worry about what?" Gabe slid into the seat next to Zoe and placed a cup in front of her, leaning over to kiss her cheek, then turned to me, his gaze sobering. "Hi, Violet. What are you worried about?"

"I know you probably can't talk to me, so you didn't have to come here," I said.

He shook his head. "She's right. Don't worry. How are you holding up?"

"Fine," I lied. "So what happened to her, Gabe?"

"We found her in the park, like I said. The autopsy is today, but I've got a pretty good guess on cause of death." He looked grim. "It appeared to be blunt force trauma to the head."

"Someone . . . hit her over the head with something?" He nodded.

"With what? Any idea who?"

"Could've been a man or a woman. No idea on the weapon yet."

"When . . . did she die? Was she dead this whole time?"

"ME said she'd likely been killed the night before we found her. About ten hours before."

So wherever she'd been, she'd been there a while. I wondered what she'd gone through before she'd died. It made me want to cry. "What about Chris Strand?"

Gabe's eyes turned hooded. "He's a person of interest." He took a sip of coffee.

I waited for more, but he didn't say anything else.

"Have you talked to him?"

Gabe shook his head slowly. "We can't find him," he said after a moment.

I sat back in my chair, trying to process that. "Can't find him? What do you mean? Like he took off?" I remembered Ginny saying Nicole's mother had tried to call him when she first disappeared and couldn't reach him.

"We don't know if he killed her. Apartment's tidy, no signs of a struggle. Car is gone. No one at his job has heard from him in a few days."

I sat back, trying to digest this. "So does that mean . . ."

"It means we're looking for him to answer questions about her disappearance and murder. That's all I've got right now."

"So are you looking at anyone else?"

"Why, you got someone else for me?"

I nodded. "Isaac Brady. The guy I called you about yesterday? He hated Strand and may have wanted to be more than friends with Nicole."

"Ah, shoot. Yes. I'm sorry. When you called I was . . . a bit distracted. I do have his name and I'll follow up."

"Good. Thank you. But you're still going after Strand."

"Of course. Him taking off . . . well, it makes him look really guilty. The chief wants to put all our manpower into tracking him down."

Something in his voice caught my attention. "What are you not telling me?" I asked.

Gabe drank some coffee, toyed with his cup. "This thing with Strand. It's not sitting right. I know it's obvious—man stalks woman, man kidnaps and kills woman, man goes into the wind. But I feel like that's only one possibility."

It was also a good possibility, but I agreed with Gabe. Leave no stone unturned. "If your gut is telling you something different, then it's not crazy and you should listen to it."

He kept his eyes on his coffee cup. "We could've done better," he said. "My colleagues. I can't help but feel like we could've stopped this." He sighed and met my eyes. "So Strand's a key suspect, but I'm keeping my options open. I'll put Brady on the list."

# CHAPTER TWENTY-NINE

*Sunday/Monday*

I told Josie I was sick Sunday and asked her if she could man the shop. I just couldn't face anyone, and I didn't want anyone to come in from town who wanted to talk about Nicole. Plus, I had the Magickal Council meeting on Monday and I wanted to prep for it.

But I had no energy. I spent most of the day in bed, trying not to think about anything. The one time I got up and thought about going to Pete's, I made it as far as the hallway when I saw a newspaper sitting on my mat. I didn't subscribe to the paper and figured someone had left it at the wrong door. But when I saw Nicole's smiling face above the fold, I couldn't help but pick it up and read the headline:

*Person of Interest Sought in Local Woman's Death*

I studied the photo. It was one I hadn't seen before.

She was dressed formally, as if she were going to some event. Her hair was curled and she wore makeup. She smiled straight into the camera. Like in the outdoorsy picture they'd used for the missing poster, she looked happy.

I skimmed the article to see if there was anything there that Gabe hadn't told me.

> *A local woman was found murdered Saturday in Wildflower Park. Authorities believe Nicole St. James of Beecher Street in North Harbor was killed in another location and brought to the park after her death. St. James had last been seen by family and friends on Monday.*
>
> *Police have identified Christopher Strand, also of North Harbor, as a person of interest in her death. The victim had reportedly recently ended a relationship with Strand. Authorities are asking anyone with knowledge of his whereabouts to contact them.*

The rest of the article didn't have anything new to say. Authorities were investigating every lead, and if anyone had any information about Nicole they should contact the North Harbor police.

I let the paper fall back to the mat and went back inside, where I remained for the rest of the day.

Monday dawned gray and dreary. I went through the motions of work and pleasantries, but my mind was elsewhere. And I couldn't help but feel like I was being led to the gallows as I walked into council chambers behind

Blake that night. He'd brought me a fix from the Potions Cafe—confidence and courage.

I really needed it tonight.

Despite Blake's promise that he would stop the questioning if he didn't like it, or if he felt it compromised me in any way, I still didn't feel good about this. I hadn't felt good about it before, but after hearing the news about Nicole I couldn't even think of anything else, let alone be coherent about something that had happened what felt like years ago at this point. Although someone else's life hung in the balance, which also stressed me out.

What I couldn't figure out was why anyone would think I had something to do with this in the first place. What possible motive would I have to do something so horrible to Mazzy? Yes, she'd messed with me and my shop, but we'd gotten that sorted out on the mortal plane and she did her best to rectify it. So what good would it do to want her punished so harshly in this realm?

"Ms. Moonstone."

My head snapped up as Oscar spoke my name in a voice so flat it made my skin crawl. "Yes?"

"I will be overseeing the proceedings, since your mother had to recuse herself from her chairperson duties. Given your relationship." He smiled, with a touch of glee, I thought.

I looked at Blake. "So what does that mean?"

"Not much." Blake smiled at Oscar, showing a bit of teeth. "Just that he can keep asking you to dumb it down, if he doesn't understand what you're saying." He steered me to my seat as Oscar's eyes shot daggers into Blake's back.

I sat down, still clutching what was left of my potion.

Chief Bell and First Deputy Merriweather were already present. Chief Lavender hadn't arrived yet.

"You okay?" Blake asked in a low voice.

I nodded. "They can't, like, decide to arrest me or anything, right?"

Blake smiled, a little. "They don't arrest people in the same way you're used to," he said. "But no. This isn't an interrogation, Vi. You're giving a statement. It will be fine," he insisted, when I looked doubtfully at him. "Just follow my cues. And stick to the facts like we discussed. Got it?"

"Got it."

He nodded and went to his own seat, where he pulled out some papers and started flipping through them.

I sat in my seat and watched as the rest of the council members arrived in various fashions. My mother, who hadn't been here a moment ago, was in her seat, talking to Hattie Blandon. My cousin Posey came in and took her seat, not speaking to anyone either. I didn't much feel like talking to her after what Blake had told me, so I avoided her eyes.

When everyone had arrived—including Chief Lavender and some mousy-looking woman I'd never seen before—Fiona rose. "I'm calling this meeting to order and turning the proceedings over to Mr. Sageblood." She sat down abruptly and went back to studying whatever paper Hattie had been successful at slipping in front of her.

"Thank you, Fiona." Oscar Sageblood also stood. Tonight he was wearing a long black cloak, like he was trying to get in character for something. Like a judge. Or the Grim Reaper. "I'd like to welcome our special guests from our Magickal Police Force, as well as Chief Lavender. Chief Bell?"

Bell stood with a nervous smile. "Esteemed council members, thank you for being here. And Ms. Moonstone, thank you for your willingness to participate and answer our questions for the formal investigation into the Mariza Diamond genieing.

"I'll be joined by my colleagues for certain areas of the questioning as needed. We've also got our Magickal stenographer with us to ensure we've captured the transcript of the interview." He indicated the mousy woman, who suddenly had a table with some kind of machine in front of her. Apparently even the court stenographers had powers around here.

"Well then, let's get started, shall we?" Chief Bell smiled again, then cleared his throat. He glanced back at the stenographer and nodded. She tapped her eyeglasses and a screen appeared in front of Bell. I couldn't see anything on it.

He turned to me. "Ms. Moonstone. Please run through the events of January seventeenth of this mortal year relating to what you know about the attack on Mariza Diamond."

I took a breath. "I went back to my shop, The Full Moon, in North Harbor, in the afternoon, after an event in the local park." Wildflower Park. Which reminded me of Nicole, and I cringed. "The door was locked. When I went back inside, there was a terrible smell."

"Describe the smell, please?" Chief Bell asked.

I had no idea if I could describe the smell. I couldn't even describe it that day. "It was bad."

"Bad," he repeated. "Bad how?"

I cast about for the words that would best describe what I'd felt that day. "Like rotten eggs. Or something dead." As soon as the words came out, a vision of Nicole's face flooded my mind again. My stomach lurched. I hoped I could get through this without getting sick, because that would certainly make me look guilty.

Chief Bell nodded and glanced at his floating screen, but before he could ask the next question, he was interrupted.

"Something dead," Oscar jumped in. "Can you possibly be more specific?"

I could see Blake out of the corner of my eye giving me that look that said, *Stay calm and just answer.*

I gritted my teeth and tried not to show it. "Something rotting. That's the best I can do."

Chief Bell glanced at Oscar and then back at me. "What did you find?"

"I went toward the back of the store and saw . . . a shoe." I remembered Mazzy's shoe because I'd actually liked her shoes, even though I hadn't told her. "I looked behind my counter and saw Mazzy."

"Mazzy," Chief Bell repeated. "You mean Mariza Diamond?" He twirled his finger and the screen turned my way. Mazzy's face filled the screen.

I nodded. "Yes."

"Can you describe her condition?"

I swallowed. I felt Blake's eyes on me, as well as the rest of the council. "She looked like she was melting into a puddle of slime. And it was kind of like a hologram. Like she wasn't real or something."

Posey snickered. I shifted my gaze to her and she looked away.

"So you had no idea what the condition was that you were looking at?" Bell asked.

I shook my head.

"Can you please answer with a yes or no?"

"No, I didn't," I said.

Oscar snickered audibly.

I glared at him.

"So what did you do next?" Bell asked.

"I called the police," I said.

"Which police?"

I flushed. "The North Harbor Police."

"And why did you call them?"

"Because I thought something . . . human had happened to her. I didn't know she was a witch."

"What did they say?"

"They arrived pretty quickly but by then Mazzy had kind of . . . evaporated. They thought I'd pranked them and urged me to be careful about my calls to them."

"And then what?"

I avoided looking at Blake, but could feel him watching me intently. I turned back to Bell. "I cleaned up the mess as best I could."

"So you didn't call anyone else?"

"No. I wouldn't have known who to call."

"Your mother, perhaps?" Oscar inquired, rising halfway from his chair.

I looked at Blake, hoping he'd say I didn't have to answer that, but he said nothing.

"No," I said. "I'd really just met her and it wasn't top of mind for me to just call her like that." I avoided Fiona's gaze.

"And there was no one else?" Oscar pressed.

I leveled my gaze at him. "I said no."

"Did you open the store after that?" Bell asked.

I shook my head. "It still smelled pretty bad. I saged and used a lot of incense." I trailed off when I saw Blake narrow his eyes at me. I was disobeying the rule about not offering details.

"So no one else was in the store when all this happened?" Bell asked. "Just you and the North Harbor police were in there that day?"

I kept my eyes firmly on Bell and willed my voice not to waver. "Yes."

"Thank you, Ms. Moonstone." Bell turned to his colleagues. "Anything further?"

Before either of them could say anything, Oscar stood. "I have one more question."

Bell nodded. "Please, go ahead."

"You said when you got back to your store the door was locked." He walked slowly around to stand in front of me.

I nodded. "Yes."

"Well, why wouldn't it have been locked?"

He was throwing me off and I wasn't sure where this was going. "I—I'm not sure what you mean."

"If you were out, it seems you would have locked up. That is, unless you expected someone else would be there," Oscar said patiently, like he was speaking to someone delayed.

"No, I just . . . no."

"But Josie Cook works for you," he said. "Wouldn't you have expected she would be at the shop that day?"

I squirmed a bit in my seat. "Not necessarily," I said. "Josie kind of keeps her own schedule."

"Really." Oscar crossed his arms. "Because I think—"

"Chief Bell, unless you have a specific question about this, I'm not sure it's relevant to inquire about Ms. Moonstone's employee roster," Blake said. "This isn't a cross examination."

Oscar smiled, and this time there was something lurking behind it. "Actually, it is very relevant," he said. "Because I received an anonymous tip that Ms. Cook was privy to this whole incident, and that she also facilitated the cleanup. Which would make sense, if Ms. Moonstone was as . . . clueless as she'd like us to believe." He turned to face the rest of the council. "I suggest we invite Ms. Cook to give a report as well about her relationship with Mazzy Diamond. And how the two of you conspired to get rid of Ms. Diamond."

# CHAPTER THIRTY

The entire council was silent for a beat. It felt like slow motion as I processed what he'd just said. They were trying to get to me through Josie, and I wasn't having it. For either of us. Blake rose, mouth open, ready to ream Oscar and try to get the cops to take control back. But I wasn't waiting around for him to save the day.

I stood up too, sending Oscar my best chilling look of death. I could see Blake behind him, trying to get me to shut up even before I said a word. I turned to him and gave him a mental shove in my mind, pleased to see him drop abruptly back into his seat as if I had, in fact, shoved him for real. Then I turned to Oscar.

"I have no idea what you're trying to do, Mr. Sage-blood, but the insinuation that Josie Cook and I are in any way involved in anything as terrible as this is absurd at best. Chief Bell, it's true that I don't know all the laws here yet, but I'd like to explore what charges can be brought against Mr. Sageblood for false accusations," I said, eyes still on Oscar. I took perverse pleasure in the look of absolute rage on his face.

Bell stuttered a little bit as he attempted to answer my question, but Oscar advanced toward me, his finger poking out of his long black sleeve like a skeleton's. "You disrespectful . . . I will see to it that we uncover the truth, no matter who your family is—"

The council erupted as Chief Lavender, who was closest to Oscar, reached out to keep him from coming any closer at the same time Blake and Fiona also jumped to their feet. But I'd had enough of this guy. I closed my eyes and lashed out with my hand in my best body combat block, the full force of my anger and rage behind it. Even though I was nowhere near able to reach Oscar, he tumbled backward like I'd just hit him with a club, nearly flipping over the chair behind him and landing underneath the long table.

I was getting good at this stuff, if I did say so myself.

"That's enough, all of you!" This time it was Merriweather, who'd been silent this whole time. He and Lavender hauled Oscar to his feet. Oscar shook them off, looked at me and muttered something I couldn't quite catch, then vanished out of the room.

"Ms. Moonstone is done," Blake informed the cops. "This was supposed to be a routine statement. You weren't supposed to allow badgering or other questioning. This isn't a trial."

"I'm very sorry," Chief Bell said. "I wasn't aware Mr. Sageblood was going to . . . go down that path. He is very familiar with how these proceedings work." He turned to me. "Ms. Moonstone, there are charges you can bring against Mr. Sageblood. Anyone who accuses someone of a crime like genieing without satisfactory evidence could be held to his or her own set of punishments. And for the rest of you," he said, raising his voice and looking around, "this is a closed-door session. What occurred in here is not to be discussed outside of this room, otherwise it's a violation of our privacy laws. Is that understood?"

When he was certain everyone had agreed with him in some form or another, he turned back to me. "Well, Ms. Moonstone? Would you like some time to think?"

I nodded. "I would. Thank you."

"Fine, then. You have my card." With that, he and his transcriptionist, followed by the other police, vanished from the room.

Fiona rushed over to me. "Violet, we're leaving." She motioned to Blake, who nodded, and the next thing I knew the three of us were in Grandma Abby's living room.

"Jeez," I said to Fiona. "I hope you check to see if Zoe's boyfriend is here before you do that. You know he's a cop and a mortal who knows nothing about this, right?"

"Not my problem," Fiona said through gritted teeth, then turned on Blake. "What in the name of the Goddess was that?"

"That was Oscar acting out," Blake said calmly. "Violet, you need to be careful. Oscar was not happy with you."

"I don't really care what Oscar was happy with or not," I said. "He's trying to bring Josie into this! Why is he doing that?"

Fiona turned to me, disbelief written all over her face. "Is that really all you're concerned about, Violet?"

"Of course I'm concerned about Josie. She didn't do anything."

"And yourself? Do you have no concept about what this could mean for you if someone decides you had a hand in this?"

"I didn't. And neither did Josie. So they should leave her out of it."

"She was there," Fiona said. "Somehow they found out."

"So what? You were too. Are they going to find that out?"

"Violet," Blake said through gritted teeth.

"What?" I rounded on him. "It's true. So Fiona, why didn't you tell anyone?"

"I should think that would be obvious," she said. "I was protecting you. All of us. Like I just told you. It was a mother's instinct," she added.

*Mother's instinct.* I nodded, a little surprised by the sentiment. I'd expected her response to be related to self-protection, but—if I was so inclined to believe her—it was related to me instead. Me, as her daughter.

She'd wanted to protect me.

I shook the sentimentality off. It sounded great, but at the end of the day somehow Oscar had found a way to throw Josie into it. And I would bet that my mother wouldn't be as quick to try to block that, unless it also involved me.

"Sure. And you were also trying to protect *you*," I said. "And Zoe. We were all there. I get it. It's fine. But if he has some way of knowing that, we could all get in trouble. Right?"

Blake and Fiona looked at each other.

"Right?" I repeated, more loudly this time.

Blake sighed. "There could be consequences for not reporting it right away, yes. And I have a feeling they're going to put on the pressure to go in and look around, even if it's just for show."

I stalked around the room, trying to make sense of this. "We also did Mazzy a disservice," I said. "We wasted time that could've been spent trying to find who did this. Maybe there was something at the crime scene that would've helped, but now it's lost forever because no one checked it out."

Fiona's laugh had sharp edges to it. "This is not one of your mortal television shows, Violet," she said. "We don't have DNA labs and forensic scientists. What happened to that girl wasn't your fault and I won't let them try to pin it on you, or any of us. That's exactly what our detractors want!"

"Well, if anyone believes what Oscar said, he just might get that. All he had to do was plant the seed, and he did a great job of that," I said. "Don't you think?" I turned to Blake.

He had been leaning against the wall this whole time, arms crossed over his chest. Now he looked at me, and I couldn't quite read his face. "You shouldn't have let your emotions get the better of you. It didn't help and it made it look like you had a temper."

"A temper? Are you kidding me? That dude was acting like I was on trial or something! You said so yourself. And everyone let him do it. You said this was just a formality. Really, it was an attack. And now Josie is going to get dragged into it."

"He doesn't know anything, Violet. What he knows is that Josie works for you, so he latched onto that. Your comment about the lock opened the door."

"Oh. Well, I'm sorry I said that my door was locked," I said, hearing the sarcasm oozing out of my mouth. "Maybe I should offer to tell the story over so everyone feels better about it."

"You're impossible," Fiona said, and with a flick of her wrist, she was gone. I didn't think the shower of glitter that rained down on me was accidental.

I was left with Blake, who wore an expression that I couldn't read at all. "So what now? Do I need to warn Josie? Is she going to be in any trouble? Do they really think we conspired to do this?" I couldn't make any sense of what had happened tonight, or how serious it was.

"He's reaching. And Josie isn't stupid, and she has a lot of friends in high places too," Blake said. "But if I were you I'd watch my back. You made Oscar angry— you made a fool of him—and you never know what he might try."

With that, he vanished too, leaving me alone.

# CHAPTER THIRTY-ONE

*Tuesday*

I barely slept at all that night. I kept having dreams about being in council chambers with black shadows surrounding me while Oscar Sageblood kept trying to talk to me. I used my powers against him but each time they seemed to get weaker and weaker until I couldn't keep him away from me.

When I finally woke up drenched in sweat, I gave up trying to sleep.

I needed to stop thinking about witches and genies. Not that the rest of my life was roses, but at least I could see how Ginny was. I hadn't heard from her since the day we found out Nicole was dead and I wondered if she'd talked to the cops at all since then.

I decided to go get breakfast at the diner and see how

she was doing. At least it would give me an excuse to get out of bed and out of the house.

But I didn't see her when I stepped inside, despite the usual weekday morning crowd. I wondered if she'd taken some time off because of Nicole. I chose a seat at the counter and grabbed a menu.

A minute later, Ginny rushed in, pulling off her coat and pulling on her apron at the same time. "Sorry," she called to someone out back, then headed behind the counter and stashed her stuff somewhere. She grabbed a pot of coffee and turned around, then realized I was sitting there. "Hey," she said. "What are you doing here?"

"I came to see you. And I'll definitely take some coffee."

"Of course." She grabbed a cup and poured.

"How are you?" I asked.

She shrugged. "Still here."

"You heard anything else?"

She shook her head. "You?"

"No. I talked to Gabe Saturday. He was looking into a few things. Besides Chris."

"Besides Chris? Why?"

I shrugged. "In case there was more to the story. You want them to be thorough, right?"

She sighed. "Yeah. Since they couldn't help her before, they may as well be thorough now."

"Have you talked to her family?"

She pulled out a pad and pen. "Yeah. They're devastated. And I think they're finally ready to believe Chris might've done it. What can I get you?"

I ordered a Greek omelet and home fries.

"You got it." Ginny disappeared into the kitchen. When

she came out again, she started making her rounds at the tables and booths.

I pulled out my phone to check email. A note from one of my suppliers telling me my shipment of fossils was going to be a couple of days late. I also had a missed call from a regular client. I listened to her voicemail—she needed an emergency crystal consult today if I could do it.

I checked the time. Eight thirty. A quick glance at my calendar showed me I didn't have any appointments until eleven. I shot off a quick text to my client asking her if she could come in at ten thirty. Then I texted Josie to see if she was coming in today. I needed her even-keeled energy. She kept me grounded. And now I felt like I needed to keep her safe.

Josie needed to know about Oscar and his threats, and his potential to open up the can of worms that involved my mother, my sister, and Josie's presence the day Mazzy was genied. Not that any of us had done anything wrong that day, but I understood what it could look like. The optics, as my dad used to say. At the time I didn't really understand what that meant, but now I saw the world a whole lot differently. If it looked like we had even remotely tried to hide something it would be bad for all of us. And now we had been put in the unfortunate position of facilitating this story that wasn't entirely true, because if it came out Fiona was there, it would look *really* bad.

Finally, I checked the local news site to see if there had been any updates on Nicole's case that Gabe hadn't called to tell me about.

There was nothing. I blew out a breath and put my phone down on the counter. I could hear my stomach

growling and drank more coffee to quiet it. The side door
to the counter opened and a woman walked in. She wore
a green power suit that blasted girl-boss energy out into
the entire diner. Her fiery hair was curly and untamed.
She carried a beat-up black briefcase.

Sylvia Townsend, Nicole's boss. In the flesh.

I tried not to stare as she walked around the counter
and headed for the booth in the back corner, diagonal to
where I sat. She slid into the booth, eye on the door, and
placed her briefcase on the table. She pulled out her
phone and called someone. "They aren't here yet," I
heard her say. "Make sure we're sending a bill. Even if
it's just for show." She put the phone down and opened
the menu.

I pretended to look at my phone, keeping one eye on
Sylvia. I wondered who she was meeting. As hungry as I
was, I hoped my food would take longer so I could justi-
fiably sit here and listen. Then the side door to the diner
opened and three men came in. Two of them wore suits
and ties, and the other a pair of khakis and a button-down
shirt. It took me a second to process that one of the suits
was Isaac Brady. He looked a lot different than he had at
yoga.

He recognized me at the same moment I recognized
him, but as I started to wave hello, he averted his eyes
and said something to one of the men he was with, someone I definitely didn't recognize. But I knew the other
man. It was Jackson Bogart, Nicole's former client.

They walked by me and went straight to the booth
where Sylvia sat. She stood to greet them.

"Sylvia," I heard the unfamiliar man say. "You're
looking well."

"Hello, Tim. You're looking like you're about to re-
gale me with meaningless compliments and a lot of
lawyer speak," she returned. "Mr. Bogart." The look she
gave him suggested she'd hoped she never had to see him
again. And Mr. . . ."

"Brady," Isaac said.

Fascinated, I watched this little power play until they
all sat. And realized Tim must be Tim Steele, Nicole's old
boss. Meeting with Nicole's former client and her new
boss. And a guy who possibly had been in love with her.
As I tried to process this without openly staring, Ginny
set my food down in front of me. "Here you go," she said.

"Thanks. Hey, don't turn around, but that crowd in that
booth behind you? The young guy on the right is Isaac
Brady."

Ginny frowned. "The one you told me about? Nicole's
coworker?"

"Yes. When you're walking around, see if you recognize him."

"I already told you I don't know him. And why are we
whispering?"

I didn't really know. I also didn't know why Isaac pretended not to know me, unless it was because he was at a
work meeting and he didn't want to seem unprofessional
or unfocused.

"I don't know. Just go see."

Another waitress started to make her way over to that
table, but Ginny intercepted her. She motioned to a table
on the other side of the restaurant. The other waitress
didn't look thrilled, but headed over there. Ginny glanced
at me, then walked over to Isaac's table.

"Good morning," I heard her chirp. "I'm Ginny and

I'll be your waitress today. What can I get you started with?"

Despite Ginny doing her charming waitress routine, they all still seemed pretty tense. The man Isaac called Tim barely acknowledged her, although Bogart was pretty charming. When she left the table, Tim leaned over and began speaking in earnest to Sylvia. But his voice was low and the white noise around us kept me from hearing anything. Sylvia looked more unhappy the longer he talked.

I picked at my omelet. It was delicious but I was completely unfocused. I desperately wanted to hear what was happening over there.

And I wasn't sure if it was my powers or just pure luck, but Sylvia's voice suddenly rose a few octaves, reverberating through the room.

"I don't care what you have to say. The evidence is the evidence, and I'm recommending we move forward. You'll be hearing from me formally."

Tim Steele didn't like that. He leaned forward to respond, but unfortunately he kept his voice low enough that I still couldn't hear. Frustrated, I leaned ever farther over on my stool, wishing everyone else in the diner would shut up.

And somehow lost my balance. I probably could've done something witchy to keep myself from falling if I'd realized in enough time that I was. But I surprised even myself and landed with a cry on the floor next to my barstool, taking my plate with me. Home fries rained down around me and my omelet went skidding halfway across the floor, landing near Jackson Bogart's foot.

He was out of the booth in a flash, rushing over to help

me up as the rest of the diner finally went silent as every-one gaped at the idiot who'd fallen out of her chair. I was too stunned at my own stupidity to move for a second. Then I felt hands reaching for me as Jackson hauled me up by my armpits.

"Are you alright?" he asked, as Ginny and one of the other waitresses rushed over. I could see Isaac out of the corner of my eye, staring openmouthed at me.

I tried to laugh it off as I straightened my skirt. "Yes, fine, just really clumsy. Thank you," I added.

Bogart picked up my jacket from where it had fallen, brushing at some splattered ketchup with a napkin, then hung it back on the hook under the counter.

"My God, Vi, what happened?" Ginny exclaimed. "Are you hurt?"

"Just my pride," I muttered, sliding back onto the stool as the other waitress bent to pick up my plate, which miraculously had broken clean in half. I bent to help her, but she shook her head.

"No, please, sit. I've got it. Would you like a . . . dif-ferent seat?" she asked.

"I'm fine. I promise I won't fall again," I said, trying to laugh it off as I sat back down.

"I'll get you some more food," Ginny said, heading back to the kitchen.

"No, Ginny, honestly, I'm fine," I said, draining my coffee. "I'm going to go, okay?" I was too embarrassed to stay and try to listen now. Plus they'd probably be hyper aware of me.

Jackson Bogart still stood there watching me. "Are you sure you're okay, miss?"

I tried to smile despite my embarrassment. "I'm fine. Really. Thank you," I said.

He nodded. "Anytime." He went back to his table and sat.

I grabbed my jacket off the hook. And with a cry, dropped it on the floor.

It had burned my hand.

# CHAPTER THIRTY-TWO

When I got to my shop a few minutes later, dragging my bruised ego behind me, Josie was already there. I was so happy to see her. Not just because we needed to talk about Oscar and Mazzy, but because I needed to feel like someone sane had my back.

"Jose. Thank God." I dropped my bag on the counter and hugged her.

"Wow. Hi, hon." She hugged me back, then pulled away to look at me. "You okay?"

"God no. It's been a week." I leaned against the corner of my desk. "I really need your expertise. Remember the stone that burned my hand?"

She nodded.

"Well, I just got my hand burned by something else that someone touched. Another mortal." At least I thought he was a mortal. Honestly, I had no idea anymore about anything.

Josie frowned. "Okay. That's weird."

"I know! Can you please help me figure out what it means?"

She thought for a second, then went out back. When she returned, she had her phone. "Just a sec," she said. "I know someone who might know. Ember. She's into all kinds of phenomena like that."

"Ember from the Magickal Council?" I was surprised, but maybe I shouldn't have been.

"Yeah." Josie glanced up from her texting. "We went to school together."

Small world, even in witch terms. "She doesn't seem that friendly," I said.

"Eh, you just need to get to know her," Josie said.

I watched as her fingers flew over her phone keypad. "They're both mortals, right?"

"Yes. One of them is—was—Nicole. The girl who was killed."

Her fingers stilled and she raised her eyes to me for a moment before she began typing again. "She said it could be a couple things, but most likely mortals who had some kind of contact with a dark force could hold onto that energy. It's not a supernatural thing, it's just an absorption of some kind of evil. And then they both came into contact with you, and you felt it—because you're a witch and you can feel things." She glanced up at me again, and now her gaze was curious. "I didn't know you felt things like that, though."

I didn't either. I frowned. "Mortal people encountering dark forces?"

"Yeah. It's more common than you think," Josie said.

"Mortal people can come into contact with all kinds of things they have no clue about."

"I felt a shadow around Nicole when she was here for her reading," I said. "It's actually why I felt like she was in trouble. But I didn't feel that with the other person."

"Were you reading the other person?"

I shook my head no.

She shrugged. "That's probably why."

"So he's in danger too?" I was getting more freaked out by the minute.

"I don't know," Josie said. She came and leaned on the counter next to me, sliding an arm around my shoulder. "This thing with Nicole. It's got you all messed up, huh?"

I sighed. "A lot of things do right now. Speaking of which, I need to talk to you about something else."

"Oh, boy. Sounds like we need some uninterrupted time for this." Josie waved a hand and the sign on the door flipped to closed at the same moment as the lock clicked. Then she turned and looked at me. "Well? Let's go."

I followed Josie out back, feeling kind of like I was heading to the gallows. I wondered if she had any idea what had gone on at the council meeting. Maybe she'd been expecting this conversation.

I realized I still didn't know much about Josie's witch life. She'd always been my friend here on the mortal plane, and that's how I still thought of her. But she was friends with Ember, and she knew things that I had no clue about, and she probably had powers I still couldn't even imagine.

It all made my head spin.

I pulled my desk chair over to the small table so we could sit together. "Hey, I did want to ask you. Did you order an obsidian scrying mirror?"

She looked blank. "I don't think so. Why?"

"There was one here the other day."

"Really? Where? I'd like to see it."

"It's, uh, gone," I said. "It broke. Anyways, no big deal. I just wondered where it came from."

"Syd, probably."

"Yeah. Probably."

"So what's up?" she asked.

"It's about the council meeting," I said. "The one where I had to give my statement. About Mazzy."

Josie nodded. "How did it go?"

I got up and got some water from the cooler to stall for a minute. "Not great. The cops don't really seem to know what they're doing. They let Oscar take over."

"Oscar?" Josie leaned forward to accept the paper cup I handed her. "Why?"

"Because he was acting as chair since Fiona had a conflict. You know, me." I turned back to get more water for myself.

"Ugh." She made a face. "I forgot he was second chair in cases like this."

"Yeah. Well," I cleared my throat, "he was a bit argumentative. Seems to really want to pin this whole thing on me for some reason."

"Violet, that's not going to happen. You didn't do anything wrong."

"I know, but . . ." I sighed and drained my cup. "Jose. There's no easy way to say this and I've been so worried about it since I left that stupid meeting."

"Sounds serious," Josie said with a smile. But her smile faded when she realized I wasn't smiling at all. "What, Vi? What happened?"

I forced myself to look at her. "Oscar said he got an anonymous tip that you were here. And he suggested that he was going to get the cops to question you too. That we conspired on this whole thing to get rid of Mazzy."

That was the second anonymous tip related to that day—the first being that the genieing had happened. I needed to dig into that more too.

"Vi, I told you, Oscar's reaching. He wants to cause trouble. And if he can cause it with your family, all the better. You know he doesn't like them. And you, by extension. I'm sorry you have to deal with that. But you don't need to let this guy get in your head."

"I'm not letting him get in my head. But I'm worried about you. Look, I don't know much about the witch's law enforcement code but I'm guessing that lying about who is at a crime scene is just as bad as it is down here in this world." I waved my arm around to emphasize our current environment. "So they can't know!"

"Vi, we didn't do anything. Nothing is going to change that. Just relax."

I couldn't believe she was so chill about this. Especially since I'd been freaking out about it for almost two days. "I haven't talked to my mother since then. I'm not sure if she's mad at me or not."

"Why would she be mad at you?"

I shrugged, a bit defiantly. "Because I used my powers on Oscar to put him in his place."

Josie started to laugh. "You didn't."

"I did. And Blake thought it made him mad and I should watch out. So now I'm worried about you because he seems to have his sights set on both of us."

Josie continued to look unfazed. "So what do you want to do about it?"

"I was hoping you'd have some ideas. I'm kind of new around here," I said.

"Let him blow off his steam. Chief Bell isn't going to give in to him just because of his family. He can come off as a little wussy but he does have integrity."

"That's your bright idea? Jeez, Josie." I crumpled my cup and tossed it in the trash. "Listen. We need to figure out who did this to Mazzy."

That caused some tension. I watched with interest as Josie's jaw tightened. "And how exactly do you propose to do that?"

"I've seen her, Josie," I said. "I've seen her in my crystals. She needs help and everyone else is taking their sweet time."

"Violet—"

"No, just listen," I said, ignoring the protest I saw building on her face. "Mazzy is on borrowed time. I mean, I didn't like her that much or anything, but I don't feel like she deserves this fate. And they're messing around worrying about you and me when they need to be focused on who is actually responsible for this!"

"That's right," Josie said, her voice dropping a few octaves. I recognized it as her stern voice. In the entire time I'd know her—nearly twenty years—she'd only used the stern voice on me one other time, when I'd had a fight with my dad and told him I wished he'd left me instead of my mother. "It's for *them* to focus on. The police. Not you."

"Yeah. Well, that'd be great, but they're not. So we need to figure it out. I thought you'd be all about helping. Don't you want to help?"

She pointed a finger at me. "Violet, don't let me catch you messing around with this thing. I mean it. I'll tell

Blake, I'll tell Fiona, heck, I'll tell the police. Stay away. Do you hear me?"

I wasn't sure what to say for a second. Josie was usually the first one to offer to help someone in need or right a wrong. Why was she resisting Mazzy's predicament? "Fine," I said. "But what if no one figures it out in time?"

Josie shook her head and pushed her chair back. "It's not your concern, Violet. You have a lot of other things to focus on now. Keep your head down, answer their questions, and let them do their jobs. Now I'm going to open the store."

I stared at her as she got up and headed out front. If I didn't know any better, I'd say Josie was scared. Was it what happened to Mazzy, or the whole Oscar thing? Was he more dangerous than I was giving him credit for?

# CHAPTER THIRTY-THREE

"Thanks for coming for dinner," Zoe said that night, surveying the pot bubbling on the stove somewhat frantically. "I hope it isn't terrible."

Judging from the sounds emanating from the pot I didn't have high hopes, but I kept my mouth shut. "So I'm a test case or something?"

She grinned. "Kind of. I really want to cook a nice meal for Gabe and wanted to practice. Did I tell you I signed up for a cooking class at the community college?"

"Oh, darling. How 1950s housewife of you." Fiona's lazy voice came from behind my ear. I hadn't even heard her come in, although that meant nothing.

We both spun around to find her lounging there, wearing what was, for Fiona, a casual outfit of jeans and a long, drapey sweater with silver sparkles.

Zoe shot her a dirty look. "What does that even mean?"

"It's not a compliment," I said. "At least not for us modern women."

"Right," Fiona said. "It's actually quite antiquated, Zoe, and I would expect better from you." She came over to peer into the various pans on the stove, sniffing the air. "What is that, anyway?"

"Risotto," Zoe said. We all surveyed the bubbling pot doubtfully. Zoe attempted to stir the contents, which just looked kind of lumpy and, well, stuck together if I was being honest.

"Want to taste?" She offered me the spoon.

I hesitated, but she looked forlorn enough about it that I figuratively held my nose and took a bite. It wasn't disgusting. Just . . . tasteless.

"I don't know, Zoe," I said. "Where did you get this recipe, anyway?"

"From my class. The teacher demonstrated a risotto last week. It looked easy enough." She sighed.

"Maybe it needs some salt," I suggested.

"Good idea." She snapped her fingers and a saltshaker hovered over the pot long enough to sprinkle its contents, then it vanished.

I had to laugh. "So when you cook for Gabe, are you going to present the salt and pepper like that?"

She glared at me. "Cut it out. I've been trying to remember not to do things like that."

"When are you going to tell him?" I asked.

"Tell him what?"

"Oh, come on. That you're a witch. That we're all witches. It kind of affects me too, so I need to get prepared. And I figure you owe it to the guy at some point, if you're going to keep seeing him. No?"

I could see Fiona's jaw tighten at this whole conversation.

"I can't tell him yet," Zoe said, avoiding my eyes. "I don't know how he'd feel about it."

Fiona rolled her eyes. "Of course you know how he'd feel about it. He'd think you were crazy, at first. Then he'd go through the stages: excitement, admiration, worry, and finally, it would become too big a problem for him and he'd be done with you. There you go."

We both stared at her, Zoe's face dropping with dismay. "Mother, that's so rude."

"I'm not trying to be rude, darling. I'm just telling you the truth," Fiona said. "And you," she turned to me, "as a businesswoman in this town, would be hassled just like that crazy woman who died was hassling you about being a psychic. Do you remember?"

"Of course I remember," I snapped. "I was almost arrested for her murder. How could I forget?"

"What do you want, Mother?" Zoe asked through gritted teeth. "I thought you were going out."

"I am. I need to talk to Violet." She turned to me. "It's about the Mazzy Diamond investigation. I've hired an independent PI firm," she said. "I don't quite trust our officers to be able to solve this. They're all too busy jockeying for position."

"What does that mean? Do you mean they're corrupt?" I asked.

"Corrupt?" Fiona narrowed her eyes. "What makes you ask that?"

"I don't know. Just a question. I mean, how do you know none of them are working with . . . people you don't trust?"

"I don't," Fiona said simply. "I'm giving them the benefit of the doubt, of course, but I also want to make sure we are covered. That's why I want to hire the lep-rechauns."

I blinked. "The what?" That was the second time I'd heard about leprechauns, and it didn't seem to be a joke.

"The leprechauns," Fiona said. "They have a wonder-ful private investigation firm. They are quite hard work-ers. And very committed to justice."

"Leprechauns," I repeated slowly.

"Yes, dear," Fiona said impatiently. "Do you need me to show you a picture?"

"No, I'm good, it's . . . it sounds weird."

"Well, that's because you've lived in this world for your entire life. In our world, it's not weird at all. Right, Zoe?"

Zoe, clearly still annoyed about Fiona's attitude to-ward mortal men, grunted in response.

"So what are the leprechaun PIs going to do?" I asked.

"Investigate," Fiona replied.

"Yes, but investigate what? Me?"

"Whatever they determine needs investigating," she said. "We need to trace this back to the person who not only did this, but the person who hired the doer. Which might require them to meet with you, yes. But they have no ulterior motive. You should offer them any help they request. Now," she said briskly. "I have to go. I have a meeting." Fiona snapped her fingers again and with a sharp crack in the air, disappeared from view.

I looked at Zoe, speechless.

Zoe shook her head. "She's so ridiculous."

"Leprechauns?" I repeated. "And hey, your risotto is burning." I pointed to the stove, where smoke had started to rise from the pan.

"Oh no!" Zoe rushed over and turned the heat off. "I don't suppose I can salvage this," she said, sounding defeated.

"How about this." I concentrated, then pointed my finger at the stove. The burned pan vanished. In its place, a pan of beautiful lasagna, still steaming, sat on the stove.

Zoe glanced at me, eyebrows raised. "That's pretty good, sis."

"Thanks. Hey, Zoe?"

"Yeah?" She was still admiring the lasagna.

"How are things really going with Gabe?"

She smiled. "Good. He's really sweet. I like him a lot."

"I'm glad. So despite what our mother thinks, are you going to tell him? About . . . us?"

"Well I'm going to have to eventually, right?" She brought two pieces of lasagna to the table.

"You are," I said.

"Then I will. When the time is right. But speaking of that." She glanced at me. I recognized the look. It said she knew I wasn't going to be happy about whatever she was about to tell me.

"Gabe's been really bothered by this woman's murder. I felt bad about it so I did a little innocent tuning in to the situation." She looked up at me. The only thing stopping me from blowing a gasket was the look on her face. "The boyfriend is in trouble too. I don't think he did it."

I stared at her, my fork falling to my plate. "What do you mean? How do you know this?"

Zoe leaned back, playing with her long, purple hair. "I can feel things."

"Feel things." I closed my eyes and rubbed my temples. "And you felt that her abusive boyfriend is innocent, and that's supposed to be the whole story?"

"No, that's not how it is. I mean, I can literally feel when things are a certain way. It's hard to explain."

"So can you see the truth? Like when someone's lying?" I knew I shouldn't even be thinking this way, but I was feeling kind of desperate. If Zoe could tell if this guy killed Nicole or not by a feeling—and she was right—then maybe she could see the real story too.

"No. But that would be a cool power to have. Listen. The guy didn't do it. I know he didn't."

"Well then who did?"

She shrugged. "I don't know. It doesn't work that way. That's what Gabe is working on. And you, I guess. Besides, I couldn't do anything about it anyway even if I did know. You know what Mom always says."

"Yeah, yeah. Don't meddle in the affairs of mortals if it could change the course of history." I sighed and picked up my fork again. I'd lost my appetite suddenly. "So what about Mazzy?" I asked.

"What about her?"

"You didn't know her, did you? Like you know Ginny?"

Zoe shook her head. "Never laid eyes on her."

"Do you have any feelings about what happened to her?"

"I don't. I never really spent much time thinking about it, though."

"There's an awful lot of people investigating, but no one seems to be getting anywhere," I said.

"Well, these cops aren't rocket scientists," she said. "Or even really high-level witches. A lot of them are here because of family ties."

Apparently that was the case in a lot of power structures in this world. "So I was thinking . . ."

Now she looked up. "What?"

"I need a way to figure out what Mazzy was working on for the newspaper," I said. "I feel like that could be key to all of this. And everyone is strongly encouraging me to stay out of it."

"Oooh, intrigue." Zoe grinned. "Let's have a drink." She snapped her fingers. Two beers appeared in front of us, floating just above the table.

"I don't like beer," I said.

"What do you want? Whiskey? Vodka?" She snapped again and a full tray of drinks appeared, hovering above the table.

I laughed. "That's pretty good. No need to go to a bar anymore anyway." That reminded me of Todd, so as soon as I said it I wished I could take it back. "I'll take the vodka."

"With tonic? And a lime?" Zoe winked. Another snap. The rest of the drinks disappeared and my fully made vodka and tonic floated over to me.

I plucked it out of the air. As I did so, I looked out the window and saw Sydney staring at us. She was heading into the side yard where her tiny house was parked. I swallowed hard and waved.

She shook her head as if to clear it, then waved back and hurried into her house.

"That was close," I muttered.

Zoe burst out laughing. "So you want me to tell Gabe, but you don't want to tell your friends?"

"Oh, be quiet," I said irritably. "We're talking about Mazzy and her reporting."

"Right. Mazzy. So who's telling you to leave it alone? And remind me again why you care so much? Didn't you have some kind of issue with this chick in the first place?"

"Zoe! What is *wrong* with you? Someone did a terrible thing to her. In *my* shop. And now people who hate our family are trying to suggest that I, or my close friend, had something to do with it. Of course I care. I just want to find out what happened to her and why it happened near me. Wouldn't you?" I held her gaze until she grinned at me and put her beer down.

"Just checking. I get it."

"Good. I don't need to argue with you too. I just had a whole thing with Josie about it today. And Blake has been telling me to stay away too. And our mother." Immediately my hand flew to my mouth and I looked around, expecting Fiona to swoop in and start lecturing me. She didn't.

But now Zoe looked interested. "Sounds like everyone else is giving up on her. So what are we gonna do about it?"

"Do you know anything about the Wicked Web?"

"Sure do." She narrowed her eyes. "How do *you* know about it?"

"I've heard things," I said noncommittally. "Anyway, is there some kind of hacker we could maybe hire to find out?"

Zoe grinned, those catlike green eyes flashing impishly. "As a matter of fact, I know a guy."

My eyes widened. It had been a shot in the dark, but maybe my sister could actually help me. "You're serious?"

"Of course I'm serious. You need a special witch to get access to the Wicked Web."

"A special witch?"

She nodded. "You really don't want to mess around with it if you don't know what you're doing. They can bewitch the space so none of the dark magic can attack them or you. If you're in that space it can be dangerous. I grew up hearing bad stories about people who messed around on the Wicked Web without the right kind of protections and . . ." she grimaced. "It's not pretty."

"Are you going to tell Fiona?"

"Of course not. She'll kill us. That was the one thing she forbade me to dabble in."

I glanced around, expecting her to appear in an angry shower of glitter, banishing us to some room for all eternity for even thinking about doing something like this. "You think she'll find out?"

"It'll be fine. My guy is discreet. Plus she wouldn't want you trying it on your own so it's actually better this way." She reached over and punched my arm. "Look at you, big sister. Getting into the witch world hardcore. I'm impressed."

I sipped my drink. "Be quiet and get me some more lasagna."

# CHAPTER THIRTY-FOUR

Their usual meeting spot was empty when Fiona landed in her shower of glitter after leaving her two daughters to cook up whatever scheme they were involved in. She'd brought extra glitter along as she suspected it was the only thing that ever brightened up this dingy place. The vampire behind the bar glanced up, saw her, and nodded.

"Where is he?" Fiona asked.

"Not here yet." His long side teeth glinted in the dingy light as he leered at her. "What can I get you?"

Fiona surveyed the sad selection of liquor behind him and decided they really needed to start meeting on her turf. "Nothing," she said. "I'll be outside. Tell him to come out."

She floated out the door and onto the sidewalk, taking

up a spot at the corner where she could watch the comings and goings of all the low-lifes who hung out in places like this. He insisted on meeting here to keep up the pretense, but at this point it was ridiculous.

He was late, too. Five more minutes and she'd have to send him a message that he wouldn't like very much.

Four minutes in and he appeared on the sidewalk in front of her. His expression remained serious as he walked toward her. His long dark hair was swept back in a ponytail at the nape of his neck. He wore all black.

"You're late," she said by way of greeting.

"Let's go inside."

"No. I hate it in there. From now on we'll meet somewhere else. I'll choose."

"Fiona—"

"Don't Fiona me. It's time. What were you thinking yesterday? Attacking Violet like that?"

"You know I had to," Oscar said. "They would expect it. And we need to keep up pretenses. And make sure we're stalling enough. You don't want anyone to get antsy with the police crawling all over this, do you?"

"It's causing other trouble," Fiona said. "They are going to look into Josie Cook now. That will send Violet over the edge. She has an annoying allegiance to her."

"Come now, Fiona. Aren't you just afraid they'll find out about you too?"

Fiona stepped up closer so their noses were almost touching. "You best keep your mouth shut about that."

Oscar sighed and looked around. "Of course I am. When have I ever betrayed your trust? And do you really want to stand out here on the sidewalk and talk about this?"

"I do. If that bartender leers at me one more time I'm going to freeze him like a statue."

This made Oscar laugh. "He has good taste. What else is there to say?"

Fiona wasn't in a laughing mood. "Someone is out for my daughter. And I know it's your family, Oscar."

He nodded, sobering. "I'm working on it. You know I have to do this carefully. Since they still trust me."

"Is it that boy?" She spat the word. "Todd?"

Oscar looked puzzled for a moment, then recognition dawned. "Him? He's a little worm. Nothing more than a spy. He couldn't orchestrate something like this."

"So who put him up to spying on her?"

"I have a feeling we'll find that out when we understand the whole story. Isn't Blake getting you any answers?" The sarcasm was light, but it was there. Even though Blake was a Sageblood by name, that was where the similarities ended. Unlike Oscar, he couldn't even pretend to be like them. He'd been the white sheep his whole life and Fiona knew it suited him just fine.

It also made him the subject of a lot of ridicule, which fortunately he was strong enough to rise above.

"He is. Don't you worry about Blake. I want to know who ordered Todd to spy on Violet, and who took down Abigail. Before anything else happens to this family that I'm going to have to put to rights. You know me, Oscar. I won't hold back next time."

Oscar laid a hand on her arm. Sometimes he could surprise her like that—when she expected an argument she got compassion. "I promise you. Nothing else is going to happen to your family. I told you a long time ago, I have your back."

"You better," Fiona said softly. She turned to go, but Oscar called her name.

"She's got a kick to her, Violet does." He rubbed his chest where Violet had psychically shoved him. "I have a feeling she can take good care of herself."

Fiona shook her head slowly. "She shouldn't have to. She has me to take care of her now," she said, then disappeared with a loud crack.

# CHAPTER THIRTY-FIVE

*Wednesday*

I jumped out of bed even before my alarm went off the next morning. I felt a little better today because I had plans. Zoe was going to help me get access to a Wicked Web specialist so I could get information on Mazzy. And as far as Nicole St. James went, I had a plan.

I was going to talk to Sylvia Townsend. And I was going to catch her early, before her day got busy.

I couldn't stop thinking about what Josie said—that both Nicole and Jackson Bogart's fiery touch could mean that they had both come into contact with some kind of evil. The people they both seemed to have in common were Isaac, Sylvia, and Tim Steele. Since I'd already turned Gabe onto Nicole's old firm, I figured I'd start with her new one.

There was plenty of information on Sylvia when I Googled her. She was one of those Annalise Keating-type lawyers, high-powered, no-nonsense, in-it-to-win-it types. I was actually surprised that she had represented the environmental crowd in this fight, instead of someone like Jackson Bogart, who had a lot of money and prestige and seemed to be more up Sylvia Townsend's alley. I searched for information on her ex-husband, the Hammerstein portion of her firm, but didn't come up with much. A reference to a Joshua Hammerstein, but I couldn't find anything recent on him.

I spent some time going through Sylvia's website—it appeared she had a few junior attorneys working with her, but no apparent partners—and reading a few recent articles she'd written. I saw her home office was in the fancy part of town. North Harbor had multiple personalities. There was the downtown area, where I lived, worked, and spent most of my time. Then there was the eastern side of the town, the business district with the larger office buildings, hotels, and the like. There was the more "urban" side, heading west past downtown, where the houses were smaller and closer together and there were more industrial-type businesses. Then there was the westernmost side of the town, which was also on the water, but separated itself from the rest of the city both by income level and attitude. That was where Sylvia had set up shop.

Traffic was light so it only took me about ten minutes to get there, and another five driving around her neighborhood before I located her home office, which was right on the water. The house was large but not ostentatious, with a lot of windows. A black BMW X5 was parked in the driveway.

And it must've been my lucky day, because she was outside with ice melt and a small shovel, chipping away at a patch of ice on her front stairs. I recognized the crazy hair even though she had a hat covering much of it. She turned to look at me as I pulled up to the curb across the street, pausing her work as I parked and got out.

"Ms. Townsend?" I asked, making my way across her driveway to the stairs.

"That's me," she said, resting the shovel against her railing. "I know you. You're the gal who fell off her chair at the deli yesterday."

I didn't know whether to be embarrassed or to laugh it off. Instead I shrugged. "Yeah, I've been going to yoga to improve my balance but it still needs some work."

Sylvia Townsend smiled. "I like a girl who can accept her own flaws. So, you need a lawyer?"

I shook my head. "No, but I hoped to talk to you." I took a deep breath. "It's about Nicole St. James." She didn't seem like the beat-around-the-bush type.

She didn't even flinch as she took that in. "Who are you again?" she asked. "I don't think I caught your name."

I guessed she wasn't mourning her new employee too much. Or else she'd mastered the art of hiding her emotions. "Violet Mooney. I'm a local business owner. I own a shop downtown."

"So you're not with the police?"

"No, I'm not with the police. I'm just helping. Unofficially. Nicole was a customer of mine. I saw her right before she disappeared. I felt sorry for Nicole when I met her and I feel even worse because I . . . couldn't help her." I felt my throat start to tighten with those words and forced myself to swallow.

Sylvia watched me for a long moment. I braced myself, expecting her to send me packing, but finally she nodded. "Alright. Come on in. You want some tea?"

I let my breath out in a whoosh of relief. I'd been ready to give her a little magickal nudge to welcome me inside if need be, but it looked like I wouldn't have to. "Tea would be great," I said, following her into the house.

The house turned out to be somewhat deceiving from the outside. It was much bigger inside than I'd imagined and the view of the Long Island Sound from the back windows was breathtaking. I figured in summertime with boats bobbing against the marina backdrop outside it would be like a postcard. She didn't take me into her office, like I'd anticipated, but led me into the main house. I was on high alert for any kind of bad vibe, but so far I hadn't gotten one.

"Have a seat while I put the water on." Sylvia pointed toward a sun porch. I headed out there. She joined me a minute later. "I have an electric teapot. Shouldn't take long," she said. "I hope this is okay. My office is there—" she pointed to a door off the kitchen—"but this is more comfortable."

"It's great. You have a beautiful place."

She inclined her head as if to say *I know*, then leaned back, observing me with those sharp eyes. "So, Violet, you wanted to talk about Nicole." Her voice trailed off slightly at her name, but it was the only sign that this affected her at all.

"Yes."

"You said she was your customer?"

I nodded.

"What kind of business did you say you ran?"

"I didn't, but I own The Full Moon. It's a crystal shop."

"Ah. I know it." Sylvia nodded. "Carla Fernandez thought you were public enemy number one. Thought you were doing voodoo in there." She smiled. "She was always a foolish woman."

I had no idea how to respond to that.

Sylvia chuckled. "I know, that was inappropriate. But very true. So tell me, Violet Mooney. What is it about Nicole that has you at my door? It's a terribly sad turn of events, but I'm not sure what I can do for you."

"She came to work for you. Recently."

The water bubbling in the electric teapot reached a crescendo. I heard a click, indicating it had shut off.

"Be right back," she said, and got up to get the tea.

I used the time to look around, trying to get more of a sense of her personality but her house itself didn't give me a lot of clues. I'd already snuck a glimpse of her aura and it was straight up red. Crusader color. Not surprising, considering her line of work.

"Actually," Sylvia said when she returned, answering my question from a few minutes ago, "she came to work *with* me." She placed a cup in front of me and sat. "Nicole and I go way back. We went to law school together. We'd always dreamed of opening our own firm."

That, I wasn't expecting. For one thing, Sylvia seemed a lot older than Nicole. "So what happened? She was working at that other place for a long time."

Sylvia nodded slowly. "She was. She went there after she left the firm we started together. I went to law school late," she said by way of explanation. "Met Nicole, we hit it off. Nicole always looked up to me as a mentor of sorts. I'd been working as a paralegal for a while so I had some experience and she was eager to learn as much as she could. She was good." Sylvia's gaze turned slightly wistful as she looked out over the water. "Fast learner, ambitious. When she asked me to go into partnership with her after we graduated, I said yes without a second thought. It was going to work." She looked back at me. "It was supposed to work." For the first time, the facade dropped and she looked sad.

I bit my tongue so I wouldn't start blurting out questions. I'd learned from my consults at the shop that trying to fill in the blanks could have the opposite effect on the speaker and effectively put an end to the conversation.

"Then we had . . . a falling out. We hadn't spoken in seven years when Nicole reached out earlier this year." Sylvia leaned forward and put her teacup down on the table. "At first I thought she just wanted to mend fences. Apologize, you know? But she wanted a job."

"What did you two have a falling out about?"

"Our morals," she said with a little smile. "We had a disagreement on a case. It took on a life of its own."

"Enough that you didn't talk for seven years. Then she wanted to work with you again?"

"She sure did."

"Why? Seems strange if you guys had such a fundamental difference."

Sylvia nodded. "We certainly had some things to work out. We had a couple of very deep conversations about our past history and why she felt the sudden need to work with me again. She had a good enough reason."

I assumed she wasn't going to tell me what that reason was.

She didn't. "I thought we were finally going to do great things together. It's such a shame. A senseless tragedy."

"Why did she say she wanted to leave her old job?" I asked.

Sylvia shrugged. "Time for a change."

"She represented Jackson Bogart. They opposed the bridge project. I heard it was the main case she worked on for the past year. Did she suddenly have a fundamental difference with them?"

Sylvia didn't respond.

"Why did you meet with that team the other day?" I pressed. "Did that have something to do with why she left?"

Sylvia's whole body language changed at that line of questioning. I could see her physically take a moment to gain her composure before she responded with the breezy tone she'd had up to that moment. "Now that, my dear, is confidential." She smiled and sipped her tea. "But I will say that if I had to work with that much testosterone, I'd want to leave too."

"Sylvia." I sat on the edge of my seat. "Nicole was really afraid when she came to my shop. She was having relationship issues."

"Not surprising," Sylvia said dryly. "The girl always had terrible taste in men."

"So I've heard," I said. "But her ex seems to be missing too." I wasn't sure if I was supposed to say that, but figured it couldn't be that big a secret.

But that caught Sylvia's attention. "Really," she said.

I nodded.

She ran her finger around the rim of her teacup, seemingly lost in thought. Then she snapped back to attention, as if she'd just remembered I was sitting there. "Well, I don't doubt it. When someone commits a horrible crime like that, they don't usually stick around to get caught. Trust me. I've seen it all," she said when I opened my mouth.

"So you feel certain it was him? Chris Strand?"

"Had to be."

"So you knew him," I said.

Now she looked wary. "No."

"But you're still certain? Do you know of any other issues she may have had? Work-related, perhaps?"

Sylvia shook her head slowly. "I don't. Listen, Violet. Like I said, this was a senseless tragedy. I've no doubt it was related to that man she was dating. The girl never did know her own worth. And look where it got her. Dead in a park. It's terrible. And I hope they get her justice." She glanced at her watch. "Now, I'm afraid my first appointment of the day is due. It was very nice to meet you, Violet."

# CHAPTER THIRTY-SIX

I left Sylvia's, replaying the conversation over in my mind, taking my time walking back to my car. I didn't see any clients pull up. I sat in the car for a few minutes, pretending to look at my phone. No one showed.

I guess Sylvia just didn't want to speak to me any longer.

Or something I'd said had unnerved her. I thought about her reaction to Chris Strand being missing, and my question about Jackson Bogart and the legal team at Nicole's old firm. She hadn't liked it.

Why had she met with them?

I pulled away from the curb. Then at the last minute, I went around the block and stopped at the end of the street facing Sylvia's. And watched her come out of her office, talking on her cell phone, and head to her BMW. She pulled out of the driveway and took off toward downtown.

Convenient. I was going that way too. Maybe her client had cancelled. Or maybe she was going to talk to someone who might give me a clue about her. I hung back to let a car get in between us, then followed her. Even her driving was aggressive. Confident. I followed her into town, almost losing her at the light near the Bean. She continued on, up past the train station, finally pulling into a parking lot of a small building. I paused just outside the lot, waiting until she got out of her car.

As I watched, a man walked slowly up to her from another parked car. They conferred for a moment, hugged, then walked together into the office.

It was Charlie Klein.

I waited until I was sure they were inside, pondering that turn of events, then drove in to read the sign on the door. Law Offices of Morley and Janssen, LLP.

Why was Sylvia meeting Charlie Klein and coming to see a lawyer after I'd spoken with her?

I jotted the name down and drove home, parked the car in my lot, and called Gabe. "I just went to see Sylvia Townsend," I said when he answered.

Silence. Then, "You what?"

"I went to see Sylvia," I repeated.

"Violet, I've been talking to you because I know you care about this case, but that doesn't mean you're working on it."

"Just listen. She was all about Chris Strand being the killer. But I don't think she knew him at all. And she seemed bothered that he's missing."

"You told her he was missing?"

I squirmed a little. "Not exactly. But I alluded to it.

What does it matter? You basically had a newspaper article put out that said that."

"Vi, you cannot be telling people—"

"Do you know the Law Offices of Morley and Janssen?" I interrupted.

"Sure. They're right near us. What does that have to do with anything?"

"She went there after I left."

Gabe sighed. "Again. So what? She's a lawyer. I'm sure she has lawyer friends."

"I'm sure," I said. "But what's her relationship with Charlie Klein?"

That made Gabe pause. "Charlie Klein? I'm not following."

"She met Charlie there. They hugged and then went inside together."

"Well, maybe she's helping him with another case? Something with Syd's shop?"

"Syd would've told me. And why wouldn't she have been there?"

"I don't know. Why do you think it's connected?"

"It's just weird," I said. "She lied and told me a client was coming. After I left she took off and met Charlie. The timing seems strange."

"I'll poke around a bit," Gabe said. "In the meantime, your other guy is a no-go."

"What other guy?"

"Isaac Brady. I checked him out."

"You did? He has an alibi?"

"Yeah. I went to see him at his office. His dad is in the hospital. Terminal. His family has been spending most nights there with him. He was there all week last week. The whole hospital staff on that floor vouched for him."

Well, that was cheery. "And still nothing on Strand?"

"Nothing." He hesitated. "But there was one interesting tidbit I picked up when I was at Brady's office."

My ears perked up. "What?"

"Apparently Nicole absconded with some client files when she left."

"Really? What files?"

"I don't know. Her boss mentioned it. That they'd filed a report with us. Asked if we'd located them when we searched her house."

I frowned. "Sounds like he's really broken up about her death if that's what he's worried about."

"Yeah," Gabe said dryly.

"Should you be looking at him too?"

"Already done. The guy barely does anything but work. When he's not working he's dad of the year. The day she was last seen he was at the office all day. Then he coached his daughter's softball team at night and took the whole team out for pizza and ice cream. They're also hosting his sister-in-law at his house and she vouched that he was there all night. The night Nicole died he was teaching a class at the community college and went straight home after."

"So then what were the files? They must've been important if he's so eager to get them back."

"He wouldn't say. Attorney-client privilege and all that crap. But I also think this guy is very by-the-book. The thought of his files floating around out there potentially able to cause a lawsuit on his firm could just give him anxiety. Anyway, he asked me to get a warrant to search Sylvia's office." Gabe chuckled at the apparent ridiculousness of that. "I told him it doesn't work that way. But he seems to think Nicole took them to her new job."

I hung up and tossed my phone into my bag. This left us right back where we started. With Chris Strand, who still hadn't turned up. Could something really have happened to this guy, or had he just taken off to try to avoid paying for what he'd done to Nicole? It could just be as simple as that, without me injecting some paranoid conspiracy theory into the mix.

But now I couldn't stop thinking about this mysterious Sylvia, who had a long history with Nicole. I wondered if this falling out they'd had was more serious than Sylvia had let on. Maybe she hadn't really forgiven Nicole. Maybe the whole job thing was a ploy to get Nicole close to her so she could get some sort of revenge. Maybe she just wanted those files—and once she had them she got rid of Nicole.

Ugh. That sounded like the plot of a bad TV show. I got out of the car, slamming the door harder than necessary, and went to work.

# CHAPTER THIRTY-SEVEN

I managed to get through the day but I wasn't really present. Syd had the day off, and Josie was in for a few hours but we were too busy to talk much. I was happy to lock my doors at six. I stopped to grab sushi and had just gotten home when I got a text from Syd.

*I have to talk to you. Can I come over?*

I wanted to politely decline. I loved Syd, but she could be very dramatic. I figured she was going to press me about Blake and Todd and I didn't have the energy for it. But she was my best friend, so I simply texted back, *Sure*.

*Good.* A second later, she knocked on my door.

"The joys of having your best friend across the hall," I said to Monty, going over to let her in. She stepped inside, Presley in tow.

"Hey, guys," I said, going over to give Presley a kiss.

She giggled and put her arms around my neck, squeezing me. "Hi, Auntie Vi," she said. Then she caught sight of Monty over my shoulder and let out a squeal. "Kitty!" And she was off and running. Monty, poor soul, tried to dive under my bed but he wasn't quick enough. Xander was nowhere in sight. I had a feeling he'd left the building. Literally.

"What's going on?" I asked Syd. "You don't mind if I eat, right?"

"Of course not. I just ate too. I have a problem." She went to my cabinet where I kept my (very small) stash of liquor, pulled out the bourbon and a glass, and poured herself one. "You want?"

I shook my head. The last thing I needed right now was booze. My head was foggy enough with everything going on. "Before we get to your problem. I have a question. Two, actually. First, is Charlie working with you on any legal stuff for your shop?"

She gave me a strange look. "No. Why?"

"Just curious. My other question is, did you put in any special orders lately? Like, for a scrying mirror?"

Her face was completely blank. "A what?"

"An obsidian scrying mirror."

"I have no idea what that is. And I don't order anything without checking with you or Josie, Vi. You know that. I don't know what I'm doing yet."

Which meant someone else had left it there. The thought chilled me. I did my best to shake it off and put it aside for later. "Okay. Thanks. So what's the problem?"

"It's Pete."

"Pete? What about Pete? Is he okay?"

"He's fine. Too fine, in fact." She dropped onto one of my barstools with a moan. "He asked me out!"

*Finally.* "He did? That's amazing!" I pulled out the stool next to her and sat. "Isn't it? You totally like Pete. Don't even try to tell me you don't. You guys flirt like crazy every time you're in the coffee shop."

"Of course I like him!" Syd dropped her head down to the counter. "That's the problem."

"I'm not following."

"What if we go out and he doesn't like me? Then not only will I be heartbroken and humiliated, but I won't be able to have coffee anymore. Or muffins. And Pete makes the best muffins." Sydney gazed at me, desperation written all over her face.

I stifled a sigh. Her drama queen was emerging but now didn't seem like the best time to point that out. There was also the other big issue here, which was not about Pete deciding he didn't like Syd, but Syd finding out he was a witch and letting that freak her out. Then again, that was also the problem with me and Syd. "Syd, why would he not like you? You two have been getting to know each other for ages. Pete's not dumb, and he's certainly not one to waste his own time. He's clearly interested in you and wants to take you out. I don't see the problem here."

"What if he doesn't like kids?" She motioned to where Presley was trying to dress an unhappy Monty in one of my sweaters.

"Once again, if he didn't like kids, he probably wouldn't have asked you out in the first place."

Syd pondered that. "You think?"

"I know. Look, Pete's a straight shooter." Aside from

the fact that he hadn't told her yet he was a witch. I guessed he'd want to save that for a second date at least. "If he didn't think you guys were somewhat compatible, he wouldn't have bothered."

Syd took a swig of her drink. "You're sure."

"Positive. You said yes, right?"

"I did."

"So when are you going out?"

"Well, that depends."

"On what? Your schedules?"

"Kind of." She was staring at me in a weird way.

"Syd. What's up? Why are you acting strange right now?"

She sighed. "Don't kill me. We were talking about Saturday night. And . . . the idea came up that we go out on a double date. You and Todd and the two of us."

I stared at her. "For your first date? You want to double date? With me?"

She nodded. "Please?"

"How did this idea come up?"

"I kind of suggested it. Don't be mad, Vi. Remember I'm your best friend and you'd do anything for me." She flashed me her brightest smile."

"You suggested it? Why on earth would you do that, Syd?"

"I don't know," she moaned, dropping her head on the table. "Because I wasn't sure if I could be entertaining enough to go out with him alone. I really like him, Vi."

With everything else going on, I certainly didn't need this right now. Sometimes I thought it might be easier not to have friends. "Do you have a sitter for Presley?"

"Josie is watching her. So is that a yes?"

I considered strangling her, but decided I'd eventually miss her too much. With a resigned sigh, I nodded. "Fine. Yes. Sure. But you owe me."

Syd jumped up and threw her arms around me. "Thank you, Vi!"

"Yeah, yeah." I extracted myself as my buzzer rang. Frowning, I glanced at my clock. Almost eight thirty. I wasn't expecting anyone. I went over to the intercom. "Hello?"

"Violet. It's Blake."

Blake? What the heck was he doing at my apartment? At least he hadn't just materialized in front of us both. That would've made Syd keep drinking for sure. I wondered if it was something to do with Mazzy. Or Josie and the investigation. Or maybe he was coming to tell me something bad about Oscar. I could feel my heartbeat start to race as I mentally sifted through all the worst possible cases and reasons for his visit.

"Hey, Blake." I tried to keep my voice normal as I glanced behind me at Syd. "One second."

She cocked her head at me and raised an inquiring eyebrow. "I didn't know you were expecting company," she said suggestively. "You can always bring him instead of Todd Saturday," she added in a stage whisper.

"Oh, be quiet! I wasn't expecting him." I hit the buzzer and unlocked the door. "He's a friend of my mother's, and she's trying to make sure I have all the protection I need for the store." I kept it as vague and as close to the truth as I could so I didn't feel like a complete heel lying to Syd.

"Mmhmm." She grinned and swirled her bourbon around in the glass. "And fancy, Vogue-type lawyers make house calls at . . ." she checked her Apple Watch, "eight thirty at night?".

Thankfully I didn't have time to answer because Blake rapped on the door and poked his head in. "Hello," he said, nodding at Sydney. "We meet again."

"We sure do," she said with a wink.

He gave her a funny look then shifted his attention to Presley, who ran over to him with poor Monty clutched in a chokehold against her chest.

"Hi," she said soberly. "Pet the kitty."

Blake grinned and knelt down, stroking Monty's fur with his big hands. "That's a pretty kitty," he said, glancing up at me. "Do you think the kitty needs to go night-night?"

Presley frowned and pulled Monty closer. Monty gave me a death stare out of slitted eyes. "No."

"I think he does," Syd said, sliding off her stool. "Because you have to go night-night, my dear."

Presley reluctantly let go of Monty, who made a bee-line for the bedroom and scrambled to safety under my bed.

Syd hoisted her daughter onto her hip. "Thanks for the advice. And the bourbon." She glanced at Blake, then grinned at me with her best Cheshire Cat look. "Have a good night."

# CHAPTER THIRTY-EIGHT

I waited until I heard Syd's door slam and lock across the hall, then locked my own and turned to Blake. "What's up? What are you doing here?"

"Not even a thank you for not just appearing? I thought about it, but didn't want to catch you . . . indisposed or something." Blake grinned at me.

I tried to ignore how hot he looked right now and rolled my eyes. "I did wonder about that. It's a good thing you didn't, because you would've given Syd a heart attack."

"I thought she was your best friend."

"She is."

"Then when are you going to tell her? About you? I mean, shouldn't she know she's working for a witch?"

"As long as her paycheck clears, I don't think it's part

of the deal. Besides, it's none of your business." I didn't need Blake to remind me I was being a bad friend. I pushed the niggling guilt I felt about that situation out of my mind. I didn't want to think about the Pete part either. If they started dating, he'd probably want to tell her. Which would mean I needed to tell her too, and probably first. Otherwise she'd never forgive me. She probably already wouldn't.

I did not need that headache right now. I refocused on Blake. "I'm sure you didn't come here to lecture me on my relationship with my best friend. What do you want?"

"I actually need you at the store."

"What store?"

"Your store."

"Now? Why?"

"Fiona hired her own investigators. To supplement the police work."

"I heard. She told me."

He raised his eyebrows at that, but didn't say anything. "They want to look at the scene."

I laughed. "The scene was disrupted a month ago. And every day since."

He gave me a look that suggested I was slow. "They are leprechauns. They have special powers of smell, for one thing. This isn't like your forensics shows on TV, Violet. They can . . . see things."

I thought of Mazzy's face in my clear quartz. "Like, what kind of things?"

He sighed, somewhat impatiently. "I'll explain later. Look, I got another request from Chief Bell. I can't keep ignoring him. It's important Mac and his team get in there first. Can they go in and take a look?"

"We seriously need to do this now?" I'd been looking

forward to crawling into bed and getting—hopefully—a full night's sleep before whatever fun tomorrow would bring.

"Yes, now. They want to be sure they have a full picture before the police bring their team in. And I have to talk to you about that too. Why don't you sit." Blake nodded at my recently vacated stool.

I crossed my arms over my chest, mostly to try to keep my heart from beating straight out of it. I didn't like the look on his face. "I'm fine. What's going on?"

Blake sighed and closed his eyes. The next thing I knew, I was on the stool.

"Knock that off!" Outraged, I tried to jump up but he held up a hand. And I realized I couldn't move. Like he'd glued my butt to the chair.

"Oh, I swear to the Goddess." I glared at him. "I have no idea who you think you are, but—"

"Violet. Be quiet and listen to me. There's a special unit investigating you in this Mazzy debacle."

I stared at him. "What . . . what do you mean? What kind of special unit?"

"The Stalker Squad. They look into the worst crimes witches and other beings commit against each other."

The Stalker Squad? Sounded like a club of creepy men to me. "So what does that mean? What about Chief Bell?"

Blake shook his head. "They decided to use this team instead. I was starting to wonder why it was taking him so long to request a specific time. This is why. It's a separate unit that's not under his jurisdiction."

"So like a PI firm?"

"No, because they are governed by the commissioner. So they have a lot of authority." He hesitated. "I don't know who requested their involvement, but I'm guessing it's coming from pretty high up."

He looked serious. More serious than I'd seen him look since I'd met him, except for maybe the other night when I'd shoved Oscar Sageblood over a chair. I felt a twinge of fear in my stomach. "This is Oscar, isn't it?"

"Like I said. I don't know."

I searched his eyes to see if he was telling me the truth, but of course, I had no way of knowing. I knew nothing, really, about Blake Alexander. He could've been the one who started the investigation, for all I knew. How well did my mother really know this guy? I felt chilled at the thought of just how much I didn't know about my new world, and all the potentially dangerous people waiting to take me down just because of who I was.

It didn't feel very good.

"Then I guess I just have to figure this out for them so I can make sure it doesn't get pinned on me." I went to get up and realized Blake still had me held on the chair. The heck with this. I had powers too. I concentrated really hard and shot out of my seat, landing halfway across the kitchen.

Much better. I turned around with a slow smile, enjoying the look of surprise on his face.

He covered it up quick. "Very nice," he said, but his words were tight. "You're learning. But Violet—for the last time, you need to stay away from this thing."

"Really. How am I supposed to do that? I'm in it. I've been in it this whole time. And now you want me to go downstairs and confer with leprechauns about it, then meet up with some black ops squad. But I'm not supposed to look into it myself? For my own protection?"

He was in my face from across the room before I could

even blink. "I'm telling you, Violet. You have no idea what you're doing, and this is not something you need to mess around with. You wouldn't have the first clue how to start, for one thing. I mean it."

*Oh no, he did not just challenge me like that.* Blake Alexander obviously didn't realize who he was talking to. Or that my sister had some sort of in with a Wicked Web expert. I arranged my face to be carefully blank and held his gaze long enough that I could tell my lack of reaction was bothering him. "Fiona doesn't know about this?"

Blake shook his head slowly. "Not yet. But she will soon, and, well . . ." He smiled a little. "You know her. She'll fight it, but I don't think even she will win this one."

"Then how did you find out?"

"I have my contacts," he said evenly.

"Ah. Contacts." I nodded earnestly. "Great. So when is this Stalker Squad coming, then?"

He studied me as if he couldn't figure me out. "As early as tomorrow."

"Well, they can't just barge in whenever they want. I have a business to run."

"I don't think they'll care. But let's take care of one thing at a time. Mac and his team are waiting. Come on." He grabbed my hand and I felt that weightless, slightly drunk feeling I got when I teleported. The next thing I knew, we were standing in my shop in the dark.

"We could've just walked over," I muttered, going over to flick the light switch. And jumped a foot when I saw three small men clustered near my counter. "Oh! Uh, hello." I couldn't help but stare at them, even as I mentally kicked myself to stop. I'd never seen a leprechaun before—obviously—aside from the St. Patrick's Day depictions of little men with pointy shoes and top hats sitting in a pot of gold at the end of a rainbow. I had no idea if that was reality, although these men were half my size so that, at least, seemed to jive with folklore. They were not, however, wearing suits and pointy shoes. They wore all black—black jeans, black hoodies, black sneakers. And for people with access to a lot of gold—if that were true—they didn't look very happy. In fact, they looked downright surly, almost like a street gang but, well, smaller. And certainly not like they were the mascots for a rainbow-filled day.

They all stared at me like I'd spoken a different language. Had I? I had no idea if they spoke English. I glanced at Blake for help.

"Mac, this is Violet Mooney," he said. "Fiona's daughter. Vi, Mac Finnegan. His firm is the top of its kind."

The smallest man stepped forward, offering his tiny hand. I reached over and shook it. It was dry to the touch, and didn't feel quite human. Which made sense because, well, he wasn't.

"Nice to meet you, Mr. Finnegan," I said.

He didn't suggest he felt the same. "It's Mac," he said in sort of a growl. His voice was deeper than I'd imagined. "Shiloh and Goldie." He indicated his counterparts. "We need to get a sense of what happened here. I'm guessing from the smell the incident occurred right here?" He gestured to my counter area.

"Smell? It doesn't smell anymore." I looked at Blake, who remained silent. "Jo—I had it cleaned. By one of the witch cleaning services."

Mac stepped over so he was toe-to-toe with me. I had to look down to meet his eyes, but somehow I still felt very tiny under that stare. "So you're a smell expert?"

"Um. No. I just can't smell—"

"Exactly. We are experts in smells. Especially smells like this. So why don't you leave it to us."

I flushed. "Listen, Mister . . . Mac, there's no need to be—"

"Hey, Vi, can I talk to you?" Blake interrupted. He didn't wait for my answer before he grabbed my arm and pulled me out back.

I wrenched myself free and glared at him. "What?"

"Don't."

"Don't what?"

"Don't make them mad. You want Finnegan on your side."

"How am I making them mad? I just said I couldn't smell anything!"

"I know, but they can be . . . a little sensitive. Just let them do their thing. They're the best in the business, which is why Fiona hired them."

I opened my mouth to argue but found I didn't have the energy. I'd imagined myself on my way to bed, but instead I was standing in my shop arguing with a leprechaun about the smell remaining from a witch who'd been slimed weeks ago. The words from an old eighties' song ran through my mind: *Welcome to your life, there's no turning back . . .*

I let out a long sigh. "Fine. Let's go finish with the leprechauns so I can go to bed." I turned and flounced back out into the main shop.

They were all crowded around my counter. One of them—Shiloh, I think—was on the floor, his nose pressed against the floorboards. I thought of how I hadn't really washed the floor since the Mazzy debacle and wrinkled my nose. Let him roll around on my floor. What the heck did I care? As long as they got off my back.

Mac knelt down next to him and said something in a language I didn't understand. Goldie raised his head and nodded.

Mac looked at me. "Who else was here?"

Nervously, I looked at Blake. "What do you mean?"

Mac stepped up to me. He reached just past my waist but I still felt like squirming under his gaze. "Don't play games with me, Miss. I'm trying to help you."

"Just tell him, Vi," Blake said. "The same rules don't apply here."

"My sister Zoe came in right after I found Mazzy. She summoned my mother. Josie Cook was with my mother at the time, so they both showed up."

Mac muttered something to the other guy, who still lay face down on my floor. As I watched, his hand disappeared right into the floor.

My eyes nearly popped out. I looked at Blake. He shrugged.

Goldie muttered something else in that language I couldn't understand. It was kind of driving me crazy.

"Do you know what they're saying?" I asked Blake in a low voice.

He shot me a dirty look just as Mac turned around and leveled me with a stare that made me cringe. "We can hear you."

"Well, great. I can hear you too, but I can't understand you. And this is my shop, and this whole thing has an impact on me, so I'd really appreciate it if I could!" I hadn't meant to yell, but this whole evening was frustrating the crap out of me. Also the fact that I was arguing with a lep-rechaun and his team made the whole thing that much more ludicrous.

"Ms. Moonstone. If you want our help, you'll stay quiet and stay out of our way. Am I clear?"

Blake raised his eyebrows from behind Mac in an in-furiating *I told you so* look.

"Sure. Fine. Clear," I muttered, then turned to Blake. "Since I can't ask any questions or know what's going on, I'm going home. Make sure you lock up when you leave."

I was already back in my apartment when I realized my parting line was pretty stupid, since they were all just going to beam themselves in and out of there. I paced around my apartment, getting angrier—and more nervous—by the minute. I had to rely on a team of leprechauns to save me? I was new to this life, but it still seemed a little ridic-ulous.

This just clinched it. I had to figure out what happened to Mazzy myself. In between figuring out what happened to Nicole, of course.

I slumped miserably onto my bed. How did I end up in any of these situations?

# CHAPTER THIRTY-NINE

*Thursday*

One of the things I hadn't tried a lot was summoning. Like how Zoe had called for my mother the day we found Mazzy at the shop. The next morning I tried it with Zoe. I didn't feel like going over there, possibly bumping into Syd. And I certainly didn't feel like seeing Fiona.

I needed to figure out this Mazzy thing. Now. And I also needed to figure out why Charlie was meeting with Nicole's new boss days after Nicole was murdered. I wished I could find out more about why Sylvia and Nicole had stopped speaking. If it had been that bad, what had compelled Sylvia not only to forgive her but to hire her as soon as she came knocking? It didn't sit right with me. But the minute I started to put my energy and attention into that puzzle, something else happened in my new world to snap it away.

First things first. I had to ward off whatever was happening with all these different investigations into Mazzy's situation. Between the regular police force, the leprechaun squad, and this special squad Blake had dropped on me yesterday, I felt like the odds were starting to pile up against me. And if whoever hated me most got their way, I wouldn't be able to do a thing for Nicole. Or save Mazzy. Because since I hadn't actually done this to her, if they pinned it on me and left it at that, she'd never be free from her imprisonment.

I closed my eyes and concentrated on contacting my sister, and asking her to get here immediately. When I opened them, there she was.

I grinned. "Hey. I *can* do that."

She high-fived me. "Nice job, sis. I could've said no if I wanted to but I figured I'd give you a win," she said with a wink. "So what's up?"

"We need to talk to your guy. Like now," I said. I filled her in on the leprechaun squad and everything I'd learned last night, as well as Blake's continued insistence that I leave it alone. "I'm so tired of everyone saying that."

"Well, you're in luck. I talked to him yesterday and gave him the high-level details. He said I could bring you anytime to talk more about it. So we can go today if you want."

"Really? That's amazing. Thanks, Zoe." Although I was worried about missing more time at my shop. I wished I could figure out how to stop time for certain things. "How does it work? Do we pay him? Does he like, hack into things? How does he do it?"

"Let's just go talk to him," Zoe suggested. "Now's good, yeah?"

Before I could respond, she had grabbed my hand and with a crack, I felt that sucked-into-the-vortex feeling and we were hurtling through black. I still hadn't stopped closing my eyes when this happened, especially if someone else was "driving." When I felt myself land I tentatively opened them, looking around.

We were in a large, sunlit room overlooking some kind of lake. Beautiful diffusers were set up around the room, emitting colorful, scented plumes that reminded me of the bottles in the Potions Cafe. The decor was tasteful but cozy—the black couch looked like something I could've curled up on and slept for days.

The only thing that suggested we were where we were supposed to be was the computers hovering around the room. At least six of them, all levitating above their surfaces. I turned to Zoe, a question in my eyes.

"What?" she asked. "Were you expecting a room in someone's basement? That's how your hackers do it. Hey, Solomon! We're here."

When Solomon walked in a minute later, he also was not what I expected. To Zoe's point, I probably held a vision of my stereotypical hacker—some greasy kid with a Cheeto-stained shirt who hid in the dark and played on the computer all day. With his sleek suit and cool demeanor, Solomon would've fit in well at Nicole's old law firm or some other big fancy corporation, with one exception: his dark blond waist-length hair, which hung in a long braid. I couldn't tell how old he was, although as Blake told me age didn't matter so much in their world, but he was probably close to Pete's age.

Whatever that was.

After a curious glance at me, he approached my sister and kissed both her cheeks, squeezing her hands. "Zoe. Lovely as usual. And this must be your sister."

Zoe nodded. "Violet, Solomon."

He came over and gave me the same greeting. "Delightful to meet you. I have heard a lot about you, but I'm sure you hear that often."

I smiled. I couldn't help but like him immediately. He gave off a comfortable, safe vibe and I could see a lot of clear yellows and greens in his aura, which were good signs. Focused, smart, business-minded, but also generous and trustworthy.

I had to admit I was relieved. I still didn't know what to make of Zoe sometimes, so I'd been wary of the company she kept.

"So I hear you need my help. I'm ready for you." He swept a hand around the room, motioning to the computers. "In fact, when Zoe called me it sounded urgent, so I got a head start. Would you like to sit? Lemonade, tea, coffee?"

"Coffee, please," I said. I hadn't had any before Zoe had swept me out of my apartment.

"Same," Zoe said.

He snapped his fingers and three coffees appeared on a table in front of the couch. "Please, sit." When we did, he crooked a finger nearly covered by a thick silver skull ring at one of the computers. "Let me tell you what I've found."

I felt my heart skip with excitement. Could this guy have solved the whole Mazzy thing already? If it was this easy, why hadn't anyone done it before? I'd had no idea what to expect here, but it certainly wasn't this well-oiled machine of an operation.

"I had my team start by looking into Mariza Diamond's life and work."

"Your team?" I repeated, glancing at Zoe. We were supposed to keep this on the down-low.

"Solomon runs what you guys would call an information technology business," Zoe said with a straight face.

Solomon nodded. "Some of what we do is perfectly legal. And then I have my other team." He smiled. "So as I was saying. Her life, not that exciting. Then again, she was young. Very typical activities. Partying, dabbling in some illegals, the usual." He waved that off. "But her work was very interesting. She was a junior reporter, but ambitious."

I remembered the story she'd done about fraudulent psychic types in my world. "Yeah," I said. "I was acquainted with that side of her. Was she working on something that would've been bad for someone?"

"She was poking a lot of bears, I believe is the phrase you would use," Solomon said. "Some of them I wasn't as interested in. But one in particular involved you."

I felt the color drain from my face. "Me? Another story about me?" Here I was, worried about her being stuck in a bottle forever and she was still trying to throw me under the bus.

Solomon held up a hand, then crooked his finger at the computer again so it turned to face me. "Before you jump to conclusions, see for yourself."

I scanned what was on the screen in front of me—a report that Solomon's team had created. I skimmed the intro about who Mazzy was, where she worked, her questionable contacts, until I got to the part that interested me.

*Ms. Diamond uncovered evidence while researching a corruption story involving high-profile witches that someone was monitoring Violet Mooney for the past five years. The observation was allegedly ordered by an anti-fraud task force as part of a broader investigation. Ms. Mooney was one of many people being surveilled. To date, we have not located the source of the investigation. According to Ms. Diamond's notes, there were concerns about where Ms. Mooney's powers were being used in the mortal world and for what purposes.*

*As part of the investigation, a specialized remote-viewing wiretap was authorized. Authorization was in the form of a court order based on evidential concerns. The court order was granted. Ms. Mooney was apparently included on a long list and Ms. Diamond obtained the list. Ms. Mooney was referred to as a "renegade" because of what she could do in the mortal world.*

*Upon further investigation and according to her transcripted notes, Ms. Diamond believed that it wasn't a justified remote viewing of Ms. Mooney, as she had nothing in common with the other people under surveillance. She intended to find out why. According to her notes, she obtained copies of the "Violet tapes" and saw that they were watching her, who she spent time with, and had even begun viewing her boyfriend, Todd Langston. [Notes suggest there is more information on this person in Ms. Diamond's files, which we have not yet found.]*

*Ms. Diamond intended to publish the story—
potentially a series—in the* Magickal Times. *Her
editor had approved the reporting, which wasn't
complete at the time of her genieing.*

My head spun as I looked up from the computer,
which returned to Solomon's side once I stopped reading.
"So what . . . what does this mean?" I asked. My throat
felt like I'd swallowed some needles. The words were
hard to push out.

"We're still working on retrieving all of Ms. Diamond's notes. As I said, this was very preliminary after
Zoe rang me. I should have more to report shortly."
Solomon reached out and made a come-hither motion
with both hands. All the computers flew to his side. He
scanned them all quickly, then nodded. They returned to
their original hovering positions. "Checking on my
team," he said with a smile. "They're all hard at work.
Shall I reach out to Zoe when I have more news to report?"

"That would be great," Zoe jumped in, looking at me
anxiously.

I nodded. "Yes. Great. Thank you."

"Anytime, my dear. Zoe is one of my favorite witches."

Before we left, I turned back to him. "Are you able to
find out who did this to Mazzy?"

He gazed at me with a serious look, tapping his
menacing-looking ring against the table. "If they've left
any traces, I'll find it. But it will take me time. That, I
cannot leave to my team."

He bid us goodbye with another kiss on each cheek.
By the time we landed back at my apartment I felt like
crawling back into my bed.

"You okay?" Zoe asked.

"No. Not really, Zoe. I mean, I just found out people have been watching me. *For five years*." And something else niggled at the back of my mind. It took me a minute to put my finger on it, then I remembered. "And what was the other information about Todd that they referenced?"

Zoe shook her head slowly. For once, she had no flip remark to offer. I think she was just as shaken as I was.

"You can't tell Fiona," I said. "Promise, Zoe."

She thought about this. "Normally I would agree. She wouldn't like that we were poking around in the web, Solomon or not. But given . . . what we heard, she could probably help—"

"No. I don't want anyone to know about this yet. Besides, she'd probably fly off the handle. No pun intended." I paced the room, trying to figure out my next move. I felt even more of an obligation to help Mazzy now—since she had actually been trying to help me.

"Blake, then? Violet, you need to tell someone who . . . knows how to handle stuff like this."

I knew she was right. The problem was, I didn't know whom to trust at that moment.

# CHAPTER FORTY

After Zoe left, I realized I needed to get a move on and get to my shop. I glanced at my phone to see what time it was. Eight o'clock. I frowned. Wasn't that when we'd left to go see Solomon?

Then I broke out in a grin, remembering my wish to hold time. Apparently I'd done it.

My phone buzzed, signaling a text. Syd.

**So we on for Saturday? :)**

Shoot. Saturday. Our double date. Which meant I had to talk to Todd.

*Why was Mazzy investigating Todd?*

I texted her back and told her I'd check with Todd today, and that I'd be in the shop by ten. Then I went to get ready.

The Todd thing bothered me almost more than the rest of what I'd read. I wished Solomon would hurry up and figure out that piece. While it was disturbing that people were investigating me, it was even more disturbing that Mazzy was looking into my boyfriend. I'd learned by now that Mazzy didn't do anything unless there was a darn good reason—and usually something in it for her, like a career move—to do it.

I went into the kitchen to make more coffee—Solomon's had been good but I hadn't had a chance to finish it, given that I'd been distracted by the report I'd been reading. Immediately, two furry bodies twined around my legs, looking for breakfast. I obliged, at the last minute conjuring up some sardines to put on top of both their bowls. I didn't have any handy and wanted to make sure they had a special treat this morning.

I also thought I needed to talk to Pete. He seemed like the best choice. I'd always trusted him, and he hadn't let me down yet. So I decided to tackle two tasks at the same time.

I texted Todd.

**Meet me for coffee?**

His response was nearly immediate, which was also surprising.

**Yes of course. Pete's?**

Todd usually wasn't super attentive, sadly. Which didn't say much for me since I'd stayed with him all this time and put up with it. But when he was wrapped up in his work, hours could go by before he responded to a message from me. It didn't bother me much these days when I was feeling so ambivalent toward him, but I could remember times in the not-so-distant past when his seeming lack of interest had really hurt me.

I gritted my teeth and focused on the job at hand. Which had initially been to get through the weekend for Syd and Pete, but now I really wanted to know why Mazzy was investigating Todd. If I dumped him too quickly, I might not find out.

**Yes. I'll be there in fifteen.**

I fired off the text, then tossed my phone into my bag. I flipped my head over and sprayed hairspray into my roots to get some volume going. I was feeling kind of flat today and didn't want my hair to reflect that.

I dressed in a pair of jeans and a T-shirt, then dressed it up with a long, flowing, sleeveless wrap and a tangle of crystal necklaces. I put on long silver earrings that brushed my shoulders and my trademark purple combat boots, then grabbed my coat and bag.

I was on a mission.

Todd was already waiting at a table at Pete's when I walked in. He also had two cups in front of him, so I figured Pete had suggested something he knew I would like. Todd wasn't really a coffee guy, so he had never paid a ton of attention to what I drank. Pete, however, knew exactly how to match me with the perfect coffee. It was a trick of the trade, sure, but if my barista could do it, why the heck couldn't my boyfriend?

Why on earth had I stayed with this guy so long?

Annoyed with myself, I stalked over and dropped into the chair opposite him. He'd started to rise and lean forward for a kiss, but I didn't leave him the option.

He sat back, awkwardly. "Hey, Vi."

"Hey."

"Got you a caramel macchiato." He slid the cup over to me.

"Thank you." I removed the stopper and took a sip. As always, Pete's coffee was to die for. I glanced over to the counter. Pete was watching us. I raised the cup in a salute, then turned back to Todd. "It's good."

"Pete made it, not me."

"I figured. I'm sure he chose it, too." I didn't mean to sound so snarky but I couldn't help it.

He gave me a funny look. "I'm glad you texted. I miss you."

"Want to go out with Pete and Syd Saturday night?" I asked.

He looked taken aback for a minute, then he recovered. "Pete and Syd? Like on a date?"

I nodded.

"Since when are they dating?"

"Since Saturday night, if all goes well."

"And you want us to double date?"

"Yeah. It would make Syd more comfortable."

Todd glanced over at the counter as if trying to get a better picture of Pete so he could imagine him with Syd. Then he looked back at me. "Okay."

"What about the bar?"

"I said okay. I'll have someone cover for me. It's been a while since we've been out on a Saturday night." He smiled a little. "Where we going?"

"No idea. I figured I'd let Pete pick so he can impress Syd. I'll go tell him." I got up and went to the counter where Pete was making drinks.

"Hey, Vi. Looks like a happy conversation," he said.

I grimaced. "Yeah, it's fine. Listen, we're on for Saturday night."

Pete put down his almond milk and grinned. "Perfect. We'll see you at eight."

"Where we going?"

"Let me think about it. I'll run it by Syd and then text you, okay?"

I flashed him a thumbs up then turned to go back to my table and almost slammed into someone. "Oh, sorry," I began, then realized it was Blake. "Blake. What are you doing here?" I hoped he was going to tell me what had happened with the leprechaun squad after I'd left them in my shop last night, but figured that would be a stretch. Nobody seemed to want to tell me anything, even when it directly involved me.

"Hey, man! Long time no see!" Pete leaned over the counter and did some kind of fancy handshake thing with Blake that made me roll my eyes. Men.

"Good to see you, buddy. And you too, Violet." Blake smiled that lazy smile at me. "Have time for a coffee?"

"No. I'm . . . with someone. I'll talk to you later."

"I can wait," he said as I walked away, his voice loud enough that I know Todd heard him because he was watching the encounter so intently.

"That guy again?" Todd asked when I returned to the table. "What's he doing here?"

"Getting coffee, I would assume. Plus he's friends with Pete." I nodded to where they were huddled over the counter, talking in low voices. I wondered what they were talking about.

"Is he why you've been so busy?" Todd crossed his arms over his chest and fixed me with a stare that managed to be both innocent and hurt at the same time. I'd forgotten how good he was at this kind of thing.

"He's helping me with some insurance policies for the shop and we're trying to get it finalized," I said through gritted teeth. "And I don't know why it matters. I don't recall you being forthcoming about a lot of things. Carla Fernandez, for one. Mazzy Diamond, for another." I watched him closely.

A flicker in his eyes, but nothing else. He was good.

"I don't know what that's supposed to mean, but I told you a long time ago, I don't know her."

I nodded slowly. "I know you did. And I don't believe you."

"What does *that* mean?"

"She knows you," I said. "Actually, I heard she was investigating you. For some story she was doing." I hadn't meant to disclose that, but it slipped out. That was my problem—when I had something important to say, I usually just said it.

Todd stared at me like he'd never seen me before. "What . . . what are you talking about?" he asked, but his voice wasn't as confident as it had been a moment ago. "A story about what?"

I raised my hands, palms up. "Not sure. Was hoping you knew."

He frowned. "Well, I don't. So I think you must be mistaken. Why don't you just ask her?"

If only it were that easy. "Mmm," I said noncommittally. "I'll think about that. I have to talk to Pete before I go to work. I'll see you Saturday?"

He watched me for a long minute, then reached over and squeezed my hand. "Vi. I know I've let you down. I'm really trying to make up for it. But you have to give me a chance, okay?"

I said nothing.

He sighed and let go. "Fine. I'll see you Saturday."

# CHAPTER FORTY-ONE

I watched Todd walk out the door and turn in the direction of the bar, then made my way to the counter where Pete and Blake were both watching and trying to pretend they weren't.

"What?" I said when I reached them.

"Nothing," they both said in unison.

"You need more coffee?" Pete asked.

I nodded. "Please."

"Coming right up." He went to make it.

While I waited, I could see Blake watching me from the corner of my eye.

I turned to face him. "What?"

He leaned closer, crooking his finger at me like he wanted to tell me a secret. Despite myself, I leaned in too, bracing myself for some new revelation about the witch world.

"When are you gonna dump that guy?" he asked instead in a stage whisper.

I stepped away, glaring at him. "Oh, be quiet. It's none of your business." I turned back to Pete as he approached with my coffee. "Do you have a few minutes?" I asked him.

He nodded. "Of course. What's up?"

I glanced at Blake. He didn't look like he was going anywhere anytime soon. "Sylvia Townsend. You know her?"

Pete shrugged. "I know of her. She comes in here sometimes. Why?"

"Nicole St. James went to work for her not too long ago."

"Is Nicole St. James the woman who was killed?" Blake asked.

"Yes," I said through gritted teeth. "She wasn't . . ." I lowered my voice, ". . . a witch or anything."

"So what? That doesn't mean I don't care," Blake said easily. He sipped his coffee.

I turned back to Pete. "I went to see her."

"The lawyer? Why?"

"Because I saw her having a conversation with all the people Nicole used to work with. And then she lied to get rid of me and went to see another lawyer." I pulled out my phone where I'd noted the name of the firm. "Law Offices of Morley and Janssen, LLP. She met Charlie Klein there."

Pete frowned, thinking, then shook his head slowly. "Don't know the firm. I mean, I've heard of it but I don't think I know anyone there. In any case, I'm sure all her friends are lawyers, no?"

Same thing Gabe had said. "But what about Charlie?"

"I don't know. Maybe she's helping him with something? His will, maybe?"

I didn't think that was it, but really, what evidence did I have otherwise? I sighed and slumped against the counter. Maybe I was crazy. Maybe I was trying too hard to solve something that really was obvious—the missing boyfriend did it. Her other possible boyfriend had an alibi and really, why would her new boss kill her? Maybe all of the crazy stuff that had happened to me in the past couple of months was getting to me and I was having some kind of mental breakdown.

Pete and Blake were both watching me with some level of concern.

"Stop looking at me like that. Forget I mentioned it." I turned to walk away but Pete called my name.

"Let's go out back and sit for a bit," he suggested. "You said you wanted to talk."

I hesitated. I did want to talk to Pete, but not necessarily in front of Blake since I was blatantly ignoring his directive to stay away from the Mazzy thing.

To his credit, Blake read the room. "I'm leaving," he said with a nod to Pete. "Vi—we do need to catch up soon. I'll be in touch." He lifted a finger to his watch.

For a second I was afraid he would pull a real vanishing act in the middle of the cafe and out us all, but he simply checked the time, nodded at us again, and strolled out the door.

Pete stifled a smile, then motioned for me to follow him out back, calling over to his other barista that he'd be back in a bit.

"What's going on?" he asked when we'd sat down in his break room. "The Mazzy situation?"

I nodded, dropping my head into my hands. "Everyone's investigating me, Pete. Now there's some special squad involved."

"Special squad? Not the Stalker Squad?"

I didn't like the look on Pete's face. "Yeah. Why? You know them?"

"I know of them. They're only called out for the big-time cases."

I had no idea what that meant in witch terms but it might be best if I didn't. "Mazzy keeps . . . showing up in my crystals."

"In your crystals?"

"I was trying to use them to see if I could help Nicole," I said miserably. "Instead I just keep seeing Mazzy. And someone . . . there was a scrying mirror in my shop. I used it and it went kind of bad." I told him the story. "Blake came in. He destroyed it. But the thing is . . ." I hesitated. "Neither Syd or Josie bought it."

"You think someone put it there?"

I rubbed my arms, trying to take the chill out of them. It had nothing to do with the temperature in the cafe. "There was another time when I felt like someone had been in my shop. I didn't get that feeling when I found the mirror but I can't help but think . . ."

"What does Fiona say about all this?" Pete asked.

I said nothing.

He sighed. "You didn't tell her?"

"No. Listen, Pete—I need you to be totally honest with me. Can I trust Fiona?"

His eyes almost popped out of his head. "She's your mother, Vi."

"So what?" I shoved my chair back and stood up, pacing the small room. "There are plenty of mothers out there whose kids can't trust them. And it's not like I know her well."

"Why would you think that?"

I told him about how Fiona was hiding the fact that she and Zoe had been in my shop the day I found Mazzy. "She said she's doing it to protect me, but . . ." I shook my head miserably and sat back down. "I don't know what to think. And she just put these leprechauns on the case and expects me to trust them too. The whole thing is just weird."

"Listen, Vi. Fiona is a complicated witch. There's no doubt about that. But I know how much she loves you. I know," he repeated, cutting off my objections. "You have to believe me on this one. If she's doing something, it's to help you. We may not understand it, but Fiona has been leading things for a long time. She understands the rules and she knows how to get around them when she needs to. She also understands the politics. You have to trust her."

When I didn't answer, he reached over and grasped my arm. "You have to trust her," he repeated. "I wouldn't steer you wrong, okay?"

I sighed. "Fine. I hear you."

"Good." He let go. "And Blake too."

I arched my eyebrows at him. "Now you're pushing your luck."

"Fiona asked him to help and he takes his responsibilities seriously. And he loved your grandmother, Vi."

There it was. I'd been wanting to ask, but the time hadn't ever been right. And I wasn't sure what he would tell me anyway. "He did?"

Pete nodded. "She was like his own. He doesn't . . . have much of a family. By choice."

I wanted to ask more about that, but it seemed intrusive. "So he knew about me? Like before now?"

"Of course. You were always kind of a legend," he teased.

"Blake told me to stay away from the Mazzy thing and I can't, Pete." I took a breath and met his eyes. "I have someone looking into her life. Someone Zoe introduced me to."

Pete's eyes darkened. "Who?"

"I don't think I can say. But I need to know why this was done to her and what it has to do with me." I rose again and walked around the small room. "Look. All these people are *investigating*," I used air quotes, "but nothing is getting done. It all seems like a smoke screen to try to put the blame on me and stall things. We only have thirty days left to free her! Why doesn't anyone seem to care? She was a pain in the rear but that doesn't mean she deserves what happened to her, especially if someone was using her as a pawn to get to me."

Unlike everyone else who threw a fit when I said that, Pete listened to my entire rant and took a moment to think before he responded. I loved him for being so thoughtful about everything. He was just what Sydney needed.

"Vi, I get where you're coming from," he said finally. "And I know you feel guilty, and that the Nicole thing is adding to it. But I want you to be careful. You're right to be wary of people right now. I don't know who Zoe's person is, but I hope she made sure they were trustworthy."

I nodded. "I think he is. There's one more thing, Pete. This guy found out that Mazzy was investigating Todd." I didn't want to mention the surveillance on me. That would send Pete through the roof, and he would probably run right to Blake and Fiona. I wasn't ready for that.

"Todd? You're sure? Why?"

"They're still looking into it. They found some notes on him in her files, but nothing yet that indicated why." I asked the other question that had been plaguing me since I'd heard this. "I know Mazzy dabbled in the real world too, but unless I'm interpreting what this guy told me incorrectly, it sounded like this investigation was part of . . . our realm. So why would that be?"

"I don't know," Pete said slowly. "But now I want to find out."

I shook my head. "I don't want you to do anything. Best to stay out of this. There's already a lot of people involved. I just wanted to run it by you."

I could tell he wasn't entirely convinced that was the best course of action, but there wasn't much I could do. "I'm glad you did," he said.

As I got up to leave, he called me back. "Be careful, Violet. Until all this gets sorted out, be very discerning about who you trust."

# CHAPTER FORTY-TWO

I left Pete's with a lot to think about and a date with Charlie Klein on my to-do list. I couldn't do it now since I had a client coming in soon, but at my first opportunity I'd sneak out to talk to him. Syd had the shop open when I got there, and she was cheerfully ringing up a pretty big sale—one of my giant pieces of amethyst, as well as a malachite pendant and a moonstone bracelet, two new items I'd gotten in this week.

"Impressive," I said when the customer had left. "I don't think I've seen her before."

"Nope. First timer." Syd grinned. "I'm good at making people think they need extra stuff. Comes from years of selling complete outfits."

"Speaking of that," I said, tossing my bag behind the

counter. "I wanted to talk to you. I know I've been distracted lately, and you've been such a lifesaver."

"I know this Nicole thing is hard on you," Syd said. "I wish I could do more to help."

She didn't know the half of it. "You've been helping. And I don't know what plans you have for your shop right now, but I wanted to offer you the position of my shop manager."

Her eyes widened. "Really?"

"Yeah. You'd be doing me a huge favor—" My words were cut off as she flung herself at me, wrapping me in a giant hug.

"Yes! I would love to. I have to figure out my next moves with the shop, but it's going to cost me some money and I'm just not ready yet. So, this is perfect. Thank you, Vi."

"Thank *you*," I said. "You're a natural. Hey, are you excited for your date Saturday?"

She grinned. "I can't wait. I really like him, Vi."

Aww. She sounded like a teenager with her first crush and it was adorable. I also felt a little pang of jealousy. "I'm glad," I said. "He likes you too. But you know, Syd, you didn't have to wait for me to go out with Pete. He's not that scary, you know."

"I know. I just . . ." Syd ran a hand through her hair, which she hadn't tamed today. Corkscrew curls stuck out around her head like a halo. "I feel comfortable when you're around. And I want to be comfortable when I go out with Pete. You know? I know it sounds dumb."

"It's not dumb at all," I assured her.

"I know it's a little weird with you and Todd right now so I extra appreciate it."

"Yeah," I said. "But it's fine. I'll figure it out."

Syd studied me for a second. "You will. Meantime, if you don't want to bring him on Saturday, bring someone else." She winked at me.

"Someone else? Like who?"

"Like him." Syd pointed behind me.

I whirled and felt my face turn red. "Blake, what are you doing here? And you cut that out," I hissed, turning back to Syd.

She held her hands up in mock defense. "I'm just saying."

Blake regarded me with amusement. "Got a minute?"

"Not really. I have an appointment coming in," I glanced at my watch, "five minutes. Actually, she's early," I said, as my client walked in as if on cue. "Hey, Julia. How are you? You can go have a seat. I'll be right there." I waited until Julia settled onto the chair in the back of the store before I turned back to Blake. "What do you want?"

"I can wait. I'll be out back." And he strolled past me into my back room like he owned the place.

I looked at Syd. She looked at me. Then she shrugged. "At least he's cute. Hey, I'm finishing unpacking that new box. Where do you want the pyrites? I love the cubes." She held up one that she'd left on the counter. "I may need one of these."

That almost made me laugh. Syd had gone from wanting nothing to do with my woo-woo stuff to becoming a crystal junkie. "Pyrites are great power stones," I said. "They're all about wealth and abundance."

"God knows I need more of that," Syd muttered.

"You can put some in that smaller window, and then maybe some on the main case there," I pointed, "and the rest over there in that smaller case?"

Syd gave me a thumbs up and got back to unpacking her box. I focused on Julia as best I could but couldn't stop thinking about what Blake wanted now. I wondered if Pete had told him about our conversation.

Once I'd sent Julia home with her crystals and waited on a woman who needed something to help her son with his studying—I gave her a beautiful sodalite and a carnelian—the shop was empty and I headed out back. Blake was at my desk and Syd leaned against the doorframe, and they were laughing. Xander lounged on the desk, nuzzling against Blake's hand.

I strode to my desk and planted myself in front of him, arms crossed over my chest. "What's so funny?"

Syd gave me a strange look. "Nothing. Blake was just telling me a funny story about a case. I didn't know he did, like, court cases. I thought he just did the boring paper stuff."

"I only do the boring paper stuff for special clients," Blake said with a wink.

I didn't smile.

Syd took the hint. "I have to get back to work. See you, Blake." With a last, curious look at me, she headed back into the shop.

"What do you think you're doing?" I demanded, whirling on Blake. "Why are you stalking me?"

He laughed. "Stalking you?"

"You showed up at Pete's, now you're here."

"I showed up at Pete's to get a coffee and see an old

friend. I wasn't aware I was intruding on you and your boyfriend." His tone fluctuated slightly on the last word, sending my hackles up even further.

"So I guess I'm imagining it being weird that you showed up there."

Blake shoved the chair back and stood. "What's the deal with that guy anyway?"

"What guy?"

"Your boyfriend."

"What do you mean, what's the deal?"

"How well do you know him?"

That knocked me off track. "I would say pretty well, since we've been dating for a while." I narrowed my eyes. "Why do you care?"

He stepped up, so close to me that I could smell his cologne and the faint scent of coffee. He smelled good.

Too good.

"Who said I cared?" he said softly.

I had no idea what to say to that, so I said nothing. We stood way too close to each other through this uncomfortable silence, until I tore my eyes away and stepped back.

"Blake, why are you here? I'm sure you didn't come here to talk about Todd. Especially since you don't care." I used air quotes on the last words.

He sighed. "It's about last night. When Mac and his team were here."

"And?"

"And they found something. There was still some . . . residue under the floorboards."

I remembered that guy's tiny hand disappearing through the floor. "Okay. What does that mean?"

"They tested it. It came back as a substance that's only been used in very few of these incidents."

"Very few? I thought there weren't many of these *incidents* in the first place," I said.

Blake gave me a look that suggested I wasn't following. "Not in recent years, no," he said.

I waited for him to say more, but he didn't. "Okay, then, so is that a good thing? If it's a substance they recognized, then won't it be easier to track the . . . bad guy? Or girl?" I had no idea what to call the kind of villain who turned people into a slimy genie.

"Not really. I know that's what all the cop shows you watch might tell you to think, but that's not the way it works in our world."

"Okay. So what do the test results mean?" I pressed, after a full minute of silence.

"The test results suggest that these guys are pros. It wasn't a subpar copycat attempt, or even a junior genie. That's really all I can tell you, but I wanted you to know."

"Wow. Truly enlightening. Since you still have nothing of any substance to tell me, I need to get back to work." I turned to go, but felt a hand on my shoulder. I hadn't even seen him move from my chair but on second thought I guess he didn't need to actually move.

I turned to face him, stepping away from his grip. "What, Blake?"

"Since I have the feeling that you're going to do what you want anyway despite all my warnings, I'm going to give you some insight into genies and what this all means. Maybe that way it will sink into that thick head of yours that you need to let the pros handle this."

This guy was really starting to get on my nerves, no

matter how hot he was. "I really don't appreciate your insults," I began, but he cut me off.

"There's someone I need you to meet. Tonight after work. I'll pick you up." And with that, he was gone, leaving the now familiar scent of palo santo in his wake, leaving me no opportunity to protest or even ask who this mysterious being was.

# CHAPTER FORTY-THREE

"**I**'m bringing her to Sulamith. Tonight."

Blake and Fiona sat outside on Fiona's back porch. Fiona had called him there after she got off the phone with Mac. Now, she stared up into the field beyond the house. She could still imagine Abigail and her friends there, under the light of the moon. She wondered if they'd spent a lot of time discussing Violet and possible scenarios, and if any of those scenarios involved Abigail's eventual death, or if that was never even imagined.

"Why?" she asked.

"She needs more information. I don't trust her not to poke her nose where it doesn't belong. Where she could get into trouble." Blake glanced at Fiona out of the corner of his eye. "So what did Mac say? All he told me so far is that it was a pro job."

"That's one way to put it. He traced the source back to the Fernsbys."

Blake's head snapped around to look at her. "You're kidding."

"I wish I was," Fiona said. She'd been disturbed to hear the news too. For one of the original families in last century's genie wars to be back in action was not a good sign. It meant that not only had they been building up their power all this time, but that they had help.

And it was that help that was worrying her right now.

"So what's going to happen? Is Mac able to pinpoint any specific people?"

"He's working on it. It's a slow process," Fiona said. "He also found traces of surveillance equipment in Violet's shop. He wants to look in her apartment. I may just let him go in without telling her. I don't want her to know."

"Surveillance? What kind of surveillance?" Blake's voice was sharp.

"Whoever set it up had a number of protective, blocking spells on it so it couldn't be traced. He's still working on it. Meanwhile, he's uncovered additional information." She looked at him. "On Abigail."

She heard his sharp intake of breath, and knew that this news would enrage him.

"Okay," he said after a moment. "What was it?"

"Mac found evidence that she was being targeted for quite some time. I don't know by whom," she said as he opened his mouth to ask the next question. "But whoever it was must have also been building up to this slowly. Targeting her powers, trying to chip away at her very being."

"Why didn't she—"

"Stop them?" Fiona broke in. "I figured you'd ask

that. I had the same question. Because clearly she knew what was happening. A stupid woman Abigail was not." She sighed. "They threatened Violet. If she fought back at all, they were going to . . . well." Better to spare him the details of what Mac had told her. Leprechauns weren't known for their tact. Not that she'd wanted him to hold back. It was time to hear all of it.

Fiona could see the emotions playing out on Blake's face as he processed all of that information. She'd gone through it too. It had given her a grudging new respect for Abigail, although she did think the woman had let her emotions rule her. She could've come to her. Together they could've stopped this *and* saved Violet. But Abigail was prideful, and she would've acted alone and un-selfishly with Violet in mind.

Foolish woman. Not because she'd given her life for her granddaughter, but because she'd given her life for her granddaughter without thinking through all the options—and Violet was still in danger. But Blake had been much closer to Abigail and Fiona understood she needed to let him mourn this too.

Although he'd better do it quickly because there was work to be done.

Once he was ready to speak again and had ultimately decided not to smash anything or cause any magickal mayhem, he looked at her. "Mac doesn't have the full story yet?"

Fiona shook her head.

"Where did he—"

"I didn't ask and I'd rather not know. That's why I hired him," she said.

Blake went silent again. "So what now?" he asked finally. "We just wait?"

"Of course not," Fiona said. "We need to stick closer to Violet than before. I know she's running around trying to save everyone, but we can't let her out of our sight. Especially with that Todd character in the picture." She fixed that death stare on Blake, the one that he'd seen turn many people into sniveling morons. He wasn't about to turn into one of the sniveling morons—she understood that quite well—but she was counting on his feelings for Violet.

He met her eyes. Something dangerous glinted in his. "I don't plan on it."

# CHAPTER FORTY-FOUR

Blake must've been watching me. As soon as Syd left the shop and turned the corner, he appeared in the middle of my shop floor, in exactly the same manner in which he'd left this morning. "Ready to go?" he said without preamble.

The guy had plenty of nerve. He was acting like I needed to follow him around like an obedient schoolchild with no explanation about who I was even meeting. And I didn't like it. I also didn't like anyone watching me, especially given what Solomon had told me about me being under surveillance. I'd been creeping around my own store all day, unsure of who was seeing what. I'd managed to completely freak myself out at this point.

"I don't know yet. Where are we going, exactly?" I asked.

"To talk to someone who can give you all the gory details of things you need to know," he said. "Just what you wanted, no?"

I folded my arms across my chest. "I want to know where you're taking me and who I'm meeting."

Blake muttered something that I assumed was a curse. Before I could blink he was across the floor, right in my face. He grabbed my arm and pulled me in to him, leaning down so close our faces were only inches apart. I hated myself for it but I felt time stop as I wondered . . . was he going to kiss me?

It felt like years but then he spoke. "You," he said through gritted teeth, "are freaking impossible sometimes."

Unexpected disappointment washed over me like a wave and I shoved him away. "Me? Have you met yourself?"

"Just be quiet." He grabbed my hand, and then we were tumbling into that black void. I closed my eyes and held on.

When I opened them again, we were in a room that looked like something out of a Victorian romance novel. The walls were a deep maroon fabric that felt suspiciously like velvet when I brushed my hand against it. Little jewels were embedded into the fabric, giving it a royal look. A matching sofa and chairs were scattered around the room. I stood on a white rug that felt like a cloud under my feet. Little bottles of all shapes and sizes sat on a tray on a velvet ottoman.

A woman with army-short white hair perched on one of the chairs. She looked mostly human but something about the shape of her face suggested . . . maybe she wasn't. She wore a thin strand of beads around her forehead that clasped behind her head and hung over one shoulder of her simple black dress. She smiled at me, rising with one hand extended. "Hello, Violet. Nice to meet you. I'm Sulamith."

I glanced over my shoulder at Blake, who nudged me forward. I shook her hand. "Hello."

Blake stepped over and engulfed her in a hug. "Thanks for seeing us."

"Anything for you," Sulamith said to him before returning her attention to me. "Please, sit, Violet."

I did, choosing the sofa across from her. Blake sat next to me.

"Violet is looking for some history on genies," he said to Sulamith. "And given your . . . unique insights, I thought you would be her best resource." To me he said, "Sulamith is part genie. She's also a genie historian."

I didn't quite know what to say to that. Part genie? I thought genies were off-limits to the rest of the witch world. They sounded so . . . ominous.

Sulamith read my mind. "I'm sure that's worrisome given what you've heard," she said to me. Her demeanor was kind, genuine, almost like a favorite aunt. I tried to get a read on her aura but I couldn't, and I didn't want to be rude by forcing it. "I resisted my heritage for a long time because of what happened a century ago. But once I realized I could use it for good, to help people understand the plight of genies, I decided that would be my life's work. It's difficult sometimes, given people's prejudices, but I've largely been successful." She reached for the tray of liquids. "Would you like a drink?"

I wasn't sure what was in those bottles so I politely declined. Blake took one and drank, then leaned back, crossing his legs like he was getting ready for a show.

"Where would you like me to start?" Sulamith asked Blake.

He smiled. "How about the beginning?"

She nodded. "It's as good a place as any, I suppose." She turned to me. "I heard there was a recent genieing that people are now attributing to a hired genie assassin."

I frowned, trying to take that in. "A what?" Blake definitely hadn't said that when he'd told me the preliminary results of Mac's tests. Although the word "pro" could've easily suggested it.

"Meaning that it wasn't a random genie performing a malicious act at someone's bidding," Blake chimed in. "Mac found evidence tracing what happened to Mazzy back to one of the original dark genie families, which indicates it was a professional job. And they were known as assassins." He motioned for Sulamith to take over.

"A century ago, genies ruled our world," she began. "They held the balance of power, and other species were definitely the weaker minority. There were good genies, of course, but like any other species—both supernatural and mortal—the bad ones tended to be the ones who rose to the top. So most of the land lived in fear of genies.

"Of course, this eventually caused a war—genies versus all other beings. It lasted for a hundred years, and during that time genie assassins were the darkest, most dangerous enemies in our world. Genieing someone was only one of their terrible punishments, but it was the most effective one they used. The fact that it could be reversed added an extra layer of torture when they used it on someone, because it kept the person in a horrible, painful limbo, and it kept their loved ones in the same kind of limbo. Back then it was pretty nearly impossible for anyone to reverse a genieing. Because the assassins were so dangerous, no one wanted to test them, and so they got away with this for a very long time. A lot of lives were ruined."

I held my breath, trying to imagine a reign of terror lasting that long, where the stakes were so high. I knew similar tortures were true in other countries in my own world, both past and present, but I was blessed enough never to have lived through something like that. "So what happened?" I asked finally.

"Once the witches and other beings were able to band together, they used their collective powers to destroy the genies. It was the first time so many different beings were able to put aside their differences and come together for the common good. If they hadn't, our world probably wouldn't have lasted. Or else the genies would've destroyed every other species and found a way to take over the human world as well." She eyed me. "That's how dangerous they can be, Violet."

I tried to absorb that.

"When the war ended and the genies were defeated, they were put into subservient, powerless positions. But they were also desperate, so the assassins taught others how to commit a genieing in the event they could use the masses to rise up again, if given the chance. So a lot of less powerful but still dangerous genies were also causing havoc where they could, trying to find favor with those who had opposed the war.

"Genies also ended up being sold on the black market by people who wanted to perform evil acts. Anyone using genies for nefarious purposes was considered a traitor. Today, it's a crime to own a genie. There have been rumors that some people still employ dark genies, but it's very dangerous for them to do so. If they are caught there are grave consequences. Also, by entering into these relationships with a genie . . . if they get any inkling of power back, they will seize it and this time, they won't allow themselves to be defeated. It's also very dangerous to go into a deal with a dark genie because their powers are slippery and they can turn the tables on people very easily—and they desperately want to get back into power too. But there are ways that people can still call on them. They're still sold via an underground network, for instance.

"But the new generations of genies are just trying to survive and keep to themselves. It's very difficult for them as a species, given their history. There is also a terrible phenomenon where genie children are kidnapped and raised into the radical beliefs of the past. Genie parents have to give their children strict rules in order for them to avoid being kidnapped by a genie with bad intent. It's rarer nowadays, but still real."

"Like trafficking?" I asked. This story was getting crazier by the minute.

Blake nodded. "Exactly like that."

"That's awful. Did the person who hired the genie used against Mazzy get it on the underground network?"

Sulamith smiled a little sadly. "It's very likely. Good genies wouldn't be involved in any of that. Most people in our world understand that the kind of genies who can be bought usually have bad intentions. And that there is no loyalty. So someone who engages with them has to think like them. And be ready for whatever could come their way if they enter into a deal with them."

"This is why I've been telling you to stay away, Violet," Blake said. "This is a bigger problem than Mazzy. Let Mac and the PIs handle it. You have no idea what it's like to go up against a genie."

"I never said I wanted to go up against a genie," I snapped. "I said I wanted to help find out who did this to Mazzy so she can be freed. Is that possible?" I asked Sulamith.

"Anything is possible, my dear. It's also very dangerous."

"Would you know if a genie was in your space?" I asked.

"Why do you ask?" Sulamith said, with a glance at Blake.

"I'm curious. I feel like I should know in case anyone is trying to do something like that to me."

Sulamith was quiet for a long moment. Then she leaned over and handed me one of the glasses off her tray. I hesitated, then took it and drank. It tasted lovely, almost like lemonade.

"Anyone unsuspecting can't feel a genie coming for them," she said. "They are able to hide very well. But for those who may be able to sense more than others, they'll feel the shadow."

# CHAPTER FORTY-FIVE

*Friday*

I had to put a small sleep spell on myself after the visit to Sulamith's, which thankfully worked because otherwise I wouldn't have gotten an ounce of sleep. I woke Friday morning with a pit in my stomach and a swirling brain. I was worried about beings with bad intent creeping around my store, and now I'd started to worry that someone had hired a genie to get me.

Although Fiona's presence in my life would hopefully discourage that.

I rolled out of bed and checked my phone to see what time it was. Seven ten. If I got ready quickly I could catch Charlie Klein before he went to the diner to meet his friends, which was his usual routine on Fridays.

I fed the cats and got dressed, skipping my first cup of coffee in favor of getting information. It wasn't until I got out on the street that I did the mental head smack. I needed to get used to using my powers to make my life easier. It still wasn't second nature to me. I could've had my coffee and gotten ready with a snap of my fingers. I'd probably look a lot better than I did now, too.

I cut through the back alley and my parking lot, crossing the street to Charlie's lot just as he emerged from his doorway. He lived above his barbershop—had for the past fifty or so years. His lot looked so empty without Syd's store.

Charlie saw me coming and raised his hand in a wave. I hurried over and fell into step beside him. "How are you, Violet?" he asked.

"I'm doing okay, Charlie. You?"

"Any day on this side of the dirt is a good day," he said with a grin.

"I completely agree. Hey, do you have a few minutes to talk?"

He looked at me curiously. "I'm on my way for breakfast with the boys, but I can take a few minutes for a pretty lady, sure thing."

"Thanks, Charlie. Pete's okay?"

I knew it wasn't—Charlie liked Pete just fine, but he wasn't big into "fancy coffee," as he put it. But today I didn't wait for an answer, just linked arms and steered him there.

I bought him a black coffee and we settled at a table in the back. "What's so important that you brought me to this fancy-pants place?" he asked, looking around as if he were on another planet.

"Charlie, how do you know Sylvia Townsend?"

He looked at me curiously. "Now why do you want to know that?"

I shifted a little self-consciously in my chair. "Because I saw you with her at that law office earlier this week."

"Did you now?" He sipped his coffee. "Well, that's right. Sylvia and I had some business a few years back, and we were thinking of revisiting that business."

It sounded very stealthy. I tried not to show my impatience. "I'm asking because . . ." I trailed off, not entirely sure how to articulate this. "I got kind of pulled into this Nicole St. James mess and I told Ginny I would help her look into it. She was worried that the police . . . weren't taking it seriously enough. And since Nicole worked for Sylvia and they'd been on the outs until then, I was curious."

Charlie didn't speak for a while, just sipped his coffee and studied me. Finally he spoke. "If you're thinking Sylvia had something to do with that woman's death, you're dead wrong."

I blinked. That was pretty direct. "Okay. Why do you say so?"

"Why would you think she did?" he countered.

"Because it seems weird that they didn't talk for years, then all of a sudden Nicole leaves her job and goes back to work for her and they're friendly again, then she ends up dead and Sylvia was meeting with her old firm and an old client right after that." There. I'd said it out loud.

Charlie sat back in his chair. "So you think she just, what? Lured her back into the fold so she could take her to the park and beat her over the head? You've certainly cut right to the chase, haven't you?"

It sounded a little silly as he said it, but people have done worse. "Look. I just want to know what the deal is," I said. "I know they're looking at her boyfriend, but he's missing and I started to wonder, what if it's shortsighted to just assume it's him?"

Charlie didn't answer, but he seemed to be deep in thought.

"Charlie?" I prompted after a minute.

He refocused on me.

"You want to tell me what's going on?" I asked. "Because it's been almost a week now and they don't seem to have any leads. Except Strand, who they can't find."

"You remember Eddie Mathers?" he asked.

I racked my brain for the name, which sounded familiar. Then it hit me. "Your friend," I said. "The one who was forced out of his store."

Charlie nodded. I could see the sorrow in his eyes. I'd recently learned that Eddie Mathers—who'd been Charlie's best friend for most of his life, including through their time in Vietnam together—had been forced out of his store when the city council had raised rents. The store had been his life. He'd owned it forever and his wife had passed away so he didn't have much else. Once he'd shut down, he moved to Florida and committed suicide not long after. I knew Charlie still mourned his friend, and it was one of the reasons why he took a contrary view to a lot of the city council's actions. But I had no idea what he had to do with Nicole St. James.

"Eddie had a son. His name was Ed Junior. Would've been close to fifty now. Was a local businessperson, too."

I frowned. "Would've been? Did something happen to him?"

"He went missing. About fifteen years ago. Rumor was, he'd embezzled funds and cheated his business partner, then took off. I never bought it." Charlie's watery eyes held mine. "He loved his dad. His mother got sick right around then, too. He wouldn'ta left like that. And he sure as anything was no thief."

"So why did everyone think that?" I asked.

"Everyone didn't," Charlie said. "But it was the story that got told so much it became fact."

"Okay. So who told the story?"

"His business partner," Charlie said. "Jackson Bogart."

I let that sink in. The memory of searing my hand on my jacket after Bogart touched it rushed into my mind.

"What was their business?" I asked.

"Contractors," Charlie said. "The business Bogart still owns."

"Okay," I said again, trying to piece this together. "I still don't see—"

"I helped Eddie try to get justice for his son. Eddie believed that something had happened to Ed Junior. He didn't trust Bogart one whit, especially when he began trashing Ed all over town. We tried to get the police to investigate more but they didn't seem to want to put in a lot of effort. Bogart has a lot of money." He said the word like it was a curse.

"So what happened?" I asked.

"They couldn't prove anything, and Bogart used his money to shield himself. So I reached out to Sylvia. She knew my daughter."

Charlie's daughter had also died years ago. He and Eddie Mathers had a lot in common, I realized. But Charlie found a reason to keep living.

"Sylvia tried to put together a civil suit against Bogart years ago, claiming they'd covered up misconduct relating to Ed Junior. The court eventually threw it out for lack of evidence. Nothing ever came of it."

"So you and Eddie thought . . ." I lowered my voice

and looked around the cafe. No one paid any attention to us. "That Bogart . . . did something to Ed Junior?"

Charlie nodded grimly. "There was no other good answer. Ed and Bogart had their differences over the years. Unfortunately Ed had gotten himself into some trouble back then that, well, made the story of him stealing and running easier for some to swallow. Not his family. They knew him enough to know that was all nonsense."

"Charlie, what were you and Sylvia doing at that law office the other day?" I asked.

"Sylvia is working on a new case, based on new information. That's all I can tell you," Charlie said.

"A new case involving Ed Junior?" I asked.

He nodded.

"And Jackson Bogart," I said.

Charlie held my gaze but said nothing.

I took that as a yes.

# CHAPTER FORTY-SIX

I left Pete's a few minutes later, intent on calling Gabe to tell him about this conversation as soon as I got to work. I also wanted to ask Josie about the burn phenomenon. She'd said it meant they'd both come in contact with the same dark force, but what if one of them *was* the dark force? Was that possible? I burst into my shop, hoping she'd be there. Instead, I found my sister waiting for me.

"We have to go," she said. "Solomon wants to see you ASAP."

I frowned. "Is that good or bad? I really can't right now, Zoe—"

"He called. We have to," she said impatiently. Without waiting for an answer she grabbed my hand.

Next thing I knew, I was back in Solomon's sunny kitchen with the floating computers.

"Zoe, Violet," he said, rising from his seat in front of one of the machines to do the cheek-kissing thing with both of us. "Thank you for coming so quickly." His hair was loose today and he reminded me of one of those men on the cover of a romance novel.

"Of course," Zoe said, with a sideways glance at me. "Happy to."

"Did you find out more about Mazzy?" I asked.

"Please, sit," he said, indicating the living area. Zoe and I sat next to each other on the sofa. He sat across from us, motioning for a computer. One floated toward him. He reached for it and pulled it in front of him, scanned it, then looked at me. "Todd Langston."

My stomach dropped. "What about him?"

"I told you Ms. Diamond was investigating him."

I nodded. "Did you find out for what?"

"I found out his real identity. Are you familiar with the Sageblood family?"

I literally felt the blood drain from my face as Oscar's image floated in front of my eyes. My head started to spin and I worried that I might pass out. *Get it together*, I commanded myself. "Yes," I said when I felt like I could speak again. "I am."

Solomon nodded. "Well, Todd Langston is part of their family. Langston is a mortal name he assumed."

I looked at Zoe. She looked dumbfounded. Probably as much as I felt. I wasn't sure how to process this at all. "Are you . . . are you telling me Todd is a witch?"

Solomon nodded.

"From the family that hates my family?"

He nodded again.

"And he knows this?"

"Vi," Zoe snapped. "Shut up and let him talk."

"It's okay, Zoe. I figured this would be shocking news." Solomon focused on me. "Todd isn't a prominent member of the family. He's actually been in the mortal world with hardly any contact with his relatives for most of his life. He adapted too well to the lifestyle and stopped most communication."

"So maybe he didn't know," I said hopefully. I didn't want to believe Todd had been lying to me all this time. Then again, I'd been lying to him—or at least omitting the truth—since I'd found out, so I wasn't really any better.

At least, that's what I tried to tell myself.

But Solomon shook his head. "He knew. He chose the mortal life, yes, but his family . . . felt he owed them for some things they did for him in his younger years. They reengaged him and gave him a task. That task was you."

"Me? What does that mean?"

"He was asked to make contact with you. To spend as much time with you as possible." Solomon looked me straight in the eye. "To watch you. Mainly, to report back about if and when you learned who you were, who your family was, and if you intended to take action on that."

I slumped back in my chair. Todd had never really loved me. I was a job for him. A family obligation. From a family who meant me harm. What was I supposed to do with that? And why didn't anyone know about this— any of the people who were supposed to be looking out for me?

But something else was bothering me even more than that. "Why would they do that, though? How would they know that I was going to get back into this life? Grandma

Abby wasn't going to let it happen. If she hadn't died . . ."
I looked at Solomon, the realization dawning. "They knew something was going to happen to her."

Solomon reached up and smoothed his hair down. His skull ring glinted in the morning sunlight. "I haven't quite gotten to the bottom of that yet, but there is record of contact between your grandmother and someone from the Sageblood family. I haven't been able to identify who yet."

"Contact? Like what kind of contact?" My grandmother wouldn't have willingly been communicating with them if they were as bad as Fiona and Blake said. "It had to be Oscar. He hates me. He's been gunning for me since the minute I set foot in this world. He did something to her, didn't he?"

Solomon held up a hand. "Let's not jump to conclusions. I will get to the bottom of it, Violet. I promise you. But this tells me that Mazzy had likely found out something about this and that's why she was looking into Todd."

I swallowed hard. I knew intellectually that none of this was my fault, but it made me feel even more responsible for Mazzy's situation. Even though she was likely pursuing it as the scoop of the century rather than trying to actually help me. "Then it had to be one of them who did this to her, right? So she wouldn't blow everything out of the water?"

"Can we tell the cops? About Todd?" Zoe asked.

Solomon shook his head. "I haven't found that he did anything illegal. He wasn't the one responsible for putting the surveillance in Violet's store, so we can't get him on that. Although there is one interesting thing that I am trying to confirm. I believe he made the anonymous tip about Mazzy to the police. Which means he knew it happened. Don't blame yourself," he said to me. "Even Blake knew nothing about this."

"Blake?" I wasn't following.

Solomon nodded. "I know he doesn't associate with his family much, so I'm not surprised. There's a mutual disrespect there."

Now I was really confused. "I'm sorry. I don't know what you mean."

"You don't . . . Ah, that makes sense. I'm sorry. Blake's mother is a Sageblood so he is also technically part of the family."

Now I really felt like I might pass out. Blood rushed through my ears, pounding like waves in a turbulent ocean. I leaned forward, putting my head between my knees, willing my body to return to equilibrium.

Blake? A Sageblood? I'd trusted him. What if he was part of all of this?

As if he'd read my mind, Solomon reached over and laid a hand on my back. "Blake is not your enemy," he said. "He's the 'white sheep' of the family who doesn't associate with his relatives. He has no dark side, and for that reason he's highly trusted among the community. That's why he holds the position he does.

"I know this is a lot. We're going to unravel this, I promise. In the meantime, you must be careful, Violet. You can't let on to Todd that you know about any of this. If he alerts anyone else, it could send them into desperation mode. And you don't know what desperate witches are capable of."

# CHAPTER FORTY-SEVEN

"I told Todd," I said. Zoe and I were back in my apartment. Xander and Monty could tell I was upset and were both cuddled up with me. I wanted to crawl into bed with them and stay there for the foreseeable future, but she didn't give any indication of leaving. I think she was as shocked as I was about what we'd just heard.

"What do you mean you told him? Told him what?"

I sighed. "I saw him yesterday morning. I asked him why Mazzy was looking into him. I had no idea it was a witch thing," I said when Zoe turned a shocked look on me. "She was a regular reporter too."

"You still should've kept your mouth shut. You heard Solomon. Now he's going to tell his disgusting family. I need to tell Mother."

"No you don't. Do not," I said, grabbing her arm. "Promise me. You can't yet, Zoe. She'll go off half-cocked and do something."

Zoe snatched her arm away. "She's gonna kill me when she finds out," she muttered.

But I couldn't get my mind off of Todd and this incredible betrayal. "I'm supposed to go out on a date with him tomorrow night like nothing is wrong, too," I said. "When he's been spying on me. When he only dated me because he his family told him to watch me. And Blake? Seriously? All those warnings about that family and he's *one of them*?"

"I'm not worried about Blake," she said. "I completely believe that he's trustworthy. I'm sure he was warning you about them. He must know them better than anyone. And what they're capable of. It's more reason to believe him."

My head snapped up and I glared at her. "Did you know?"

She shook her head slowly. "I didn't, Vi. I swear."

"Does Fiona?"

"That, I don't know," she said. "You know Mother. She's got her own set of rules about life. I would guess there isn't much she doesn't know."

"So she's been keeping this from me." The anger gripped my entire body with a ferociousness that surprised me.

"If she has, it's because she didn't think it was important, Vi. She wouldn't have put him in charge of you if she didn't trust him."

"Does she know about Todd?" I asked through gritted teeth.

"I seriously doubt that," Zoe said. "She would have re-moved him a long time ago."

I had no idea what to doubt and what to believe any-more. "I need you to go," I said. "I need to be alone for a bit."

"Vi," she began, then stopped and stood. "Never mind. I get it. Really, I do. I'll check in on you later, okay?"

"Fine. Thanks for bringing me to Solomon. At least someone told me the truth. And don't tell Fiona."

Zoe stood to go. "As long as you don't let on to Todd that you know any more about this. Especially his family. Promise me, Vi. Solomon's right, you don't want to back him into a corner. If he only thinks you know Mazzy was a mortal reporter, he might think he's still in the clear." With those parting words of wisdom, she tugged on her long string of beads and was gone.

After she left, I sat on my bed for a long time thinking about what to do. Part of me wanted to go confront all of them—Blake, Fiona, Todd. But Solomon was right. That could just be disastrous. I had to bide my time.

I sent Syd a text to tell her I wasn't coming in today, that I had a few things I needed to take care of. She wrote back:

**You okay?**

I replied:

**Fine. Looking forward to tomorrow night.**

I added a smiley face so she wouldn't worry, then put my phone on do-not-disturb.

I went to my grandmother's book and concentrated on finding something about boundaries or blocking. Mean-ing that I didn't want Blake showing up out of the blue. Or Fiona, for that matter. I must've been getting more in tune with the book because a page flew open with a short spell on how to "close your cloak." I shut all the blinds in my apartment, lit some incense, and sat down on my bed, letting the words run through my mind once before I spoke them out loud:

*Rays of sun, rays of light*
*Elements of fire, water, earth, and air*
*I call upon you to create a cloak of protection*
*from all directions*
*Cast white light around me like a cloak and*
*keep out all who may mean me harm.*

Once that was done, I grabbed my giant selenite sphere. I wasn't sure it would work the same way my clear quartz had, but one of the first things I'd learned about stones was that it was all about your intention more than anything else. And since selenite was also a clearing stone, it felt like a good choice. I closed my eyes and set the intention that it would give me answers but keep me protected.

Then I opened my eyes and tuned in. I wasn't sure what I even wanted right now. There were so many emotions flooding my mind and my body that I couldn't focus. Nicole, Mazzy, Blake, Todd, my mother . . . where did I even start? Finally I just closed my eyes and let go, hoping that the right answers would find me.

When I opened them again to focus on the crystal, the sphere was full of images. It seemed to mirror the clutter in my mind—faces of everyone I'd been thinking about collided in the familiar rainbow of colors that I'd come to recognize as Mazzy's hair. And one other image that I knew I had also seen before.

That building. The one I'd seen last time, with the large, arched windows. Why was I seeing that place again? While I couldn't shake the feeling that I'd seen it before, I still couldn't quite place it.

And instead of Mazzy stealing the show, like what usually happened in these visions, today that wasn't the case. The rainbow colors were fading, and for a moment I started to panic that the shadow being was returning, especially now that I knew there were dark forces working against me.

But it wasn't the shadow. Instead it was Nicole, and more surprisingly, the face that I now recognized as Chris Strand. Growing more prominent the longer I focused on the crystal, almost like he was gaining in size and strength. I watched, captivated, until I felt a presence around me. Unlike the shadow incident, it didn't feel ominous, but it still started to freak me out—especially when it felt like a hand grabbed mine.

And then I was catapulted out of my apartment. I may have cried out, but I couldn't be sure. *It finally happened,* was all I could think. *I was concentrating on something wrong and mistakenly teleported myself somewhere.*

When I felt myself land, I was on the floor in a completely unfamiliar place. An apartment. A nice one, actually, I realized, when I looked around. New. And seemingly empty. I paused, listening, but didn't hear anyone or anything except some noise outside. The room smelled stale, like no one had been in it for a while and had left food behind, in the trash or something.

I got up, making sure I was still in one piece, and looked around. A couch, chair, and small desk in the corner of the living room were the only pieces of furniture.

Nothing on the walls but a giant TV. No curtains. The layout was open for the main kitchen and living areas, but there were two doors suggesting a bedroom and bathroom. I crept over and put my ear to one of the doors. Nothing. I pushed it open. A bathroom. Empty. I did the same with the other door. Bedroom. Also empty. Not much in there but a bed and a dresser. One nightstand with a lamp and a couple magazines. I went back to the middle of the living room and looked around again. Another door in the hall revealed itself to be a hall closet. There were a bunch of tools in it, along with workboots and a few jackets.

Where the heck was I?

I spotted some mail on the kitchen counter and went over to sift through it. And my eyes widened when I saw whose name the top envelope was addressed to.

Christopher Strand.

Holy Goddess. Was I in Chris Strand's apartment? Had he . . . brought me here? How could he do that? I flipped through the rest of the mail. All the envelopes had his name on them.

I went to the window and peered out. Across the street, the familiar view of the local North Harbor Marina and the sparkling water beyond. I was a couple of blocks away from my own apartment, in a missing murder suspect's home.

And I had no freakin' idea how I'd gotten here.

I debated trying to summon Zoe, but decided against it. I was here for a reason, so I'd better figure out what it was. I hoped the intuition or whatever that had brought me here showed me what to do next.

I headed for the little desk in the corner. It was empty save for an abandoned plug, presumably for a laptop the cops had taken in their search for him, and a couple of pens. I opened the drawers. Odds and ends, old papers, some blueprints and architectural drawings—nothing that looked out of the ordinary for a contractor. I did find a photo buried under a tangle of paper clips and some old business cards. Chris and Nicole smiled at me, arms around each other. She had long hair in the photo, and he looked definitely younger than the pictures I'd seen in the news. They looked happy. And it all went to crap, like most relationships.

Ugh. I didn't want to think about that. I shut the drawers and looked around. By the looks of this place, this guy was definitely a bachelor. I remembered hearing he'd just moved here. The building was definitely new. Maybe in transition from his relationship with Nicole he'd lost any interest in decorating? He didn't seem to read books, either. The only reading material I'd seen was a bunch of magazines. I went through those, just for kicks, but they were all about architecture or cars.

So why was I here?

I went back to the mail, mostly because I couldn't think of anything else to do at this point, and went through it again. This time I looked at the return addresses instead of the recipient's name. Electric bill, car payment, junk mail from credit card companies, a catalog from something called Northern Tool.

And on the very bottom, a large envelope from Townsend and Hammerstein.

My heart started to pound. I grabbed it and opened it with shaking fingers, acutely aware I was committing a felony by reading someone else's mail. But the feeling that I'd just found what I came for was pretty overwhelming.

I got the envelope open somehow and read the cover letter. It was a subpoena for Strand to give a deposition in a potential civil matter against Jackson Bogart, citing that Strand had important information related to the 2005 disappearance of Eddie Mathers, Jr.

# CHAPTER FORTY-EIGHT

My heart was pounding so hard in my chest I thought it was going to deafen me. I flipped to the next page, which showed a rendering of a building.

A building that looked just like the one I'd been seeing in my crystal vision attempts. The large, arched windows were exactly the ones in my visions. So what did this building have to do with anything? I looked more closely at the address. 800 Main Street, North Harbor, Connecticut. I'd heard it before. But where? I closed my eyes and concentrated. And saw Bogart's face the night he'd spoken at the city council meeting, the night Nicole had failed to show up. *"Jackson Bogart . . . owner of the building at 800 Main Street."*

I went back over to the drawer where I'd seen blueprints and yanked it open, pulling out the papers.

They were old, original drawings of 800 Main Street.

Why had Chris Strand held on to these drawings all this time? That building, by Bogart's own account, was fifteen years old. Had he helped build it? Did he know something . . . about what happened to Mathers, if something had actually happened to him? Had he been part of it?

The next page of the packet looked like a photocopy of someone's handwritten notes, with a paragraph highlighted.

*Strand worked on the original building with Bogart's crew. Foundation was poured two days earlier than scheduled. He recalled b/c he'd tried to take time off but was denied because Bogart allegedly needed the crew there when the cement was poured. But no one ended up being onsite. The last time he saw Mathers was the previous evening, and he and Bogart were having an argument.*

Then, all in caps:

*NEED HIM TO TESTIFY ON THIS TO GET ANY MOVEMENT SINCE BOGART'S ADMISSION TO ME IS PROTECTED!!*

I sat there for a long time, rereading the same words over and over again. Unless my imagination was running wild, Nicole and Sylvia were trying to get Strand to come forward with potential evidence that Bogart had done something to Mathers.

Had he killed him and hidden his body in this building? Is that why he was so adamant that it couldn't be torn down, even though the town had likely offered him a very large sum to do so?

And if Nicole and Strand both knew this . . .

My brain was working overtime, and the pieces were all starting to click for me. It made sense. Too much sense.

Somehow, while Nicole had been representing Bogart, she'd learned what he'd done. Attorney-client privilege prevented her from telling authorities. So she left the firm and took her evidence to Sylvia, ostensibly to get help in putting some kind of case together.

A case in which her ex-boyfriend was also instrumental.

So had Bogart found out and killed Nicole, and possibly done something to Strand too? Or had Strand really been the culprit all along because he didn't want to upset the equilibrium with Bogart? Or maybe he'd gotten paid off years ago and was afraid of what Bogart had on him?

I had to go to this building. I should at least be able to feel something there to let me know if I was right, or if I was crazy.

I pulled up in front of 800 Main Street an hour later and gazed at the building. I knew it from passing. It was on my usual route to the grocery store. I'd never actually gone inside it, but it definitely had a presence. It was just . . . there.

Possibly hiding secrets for more than a decade.

There were lights on inside, but the kind of lights office buildings left on for the cleaners. It was Friday evening, after hours for most businesses. I hadn't expected anyone to be around. I'd texted Gabe the address and told him there might be something here, just in case. And I'd brought Xander with me. I had no idea what my magickal cat was capable of, but it couldn't hurt to have added protection.

I surveyed the parking lot. There were two cars parked there. I also knew there was a small garage underneath, so there were potentially more people here. I looked at Xander. "Stay here," I said, although I didn't have high hopes for that. I cracked the windows, locked the car, and headed over to the building.

I wasn't exactly sure what I would get by coming here, but hoped for an intuitive hit, some kind of strong feeling that would tell me if I was barking up the right tree. My gut feeling wouldn't convince the police force if there really was something here, but I'd have to worry about that later.

I'd brought a small clear quartz with me, along with a selenite wand, thinking they might help. I'd also tucked my stainless-steel water bottle into my bag in case I needed some kind of mortal weapon. That thing seemed like it could hurt.

But that was a last resort. Risking looking like a weirdo to any passersby, I pulled the wand out of my bag and waved it in a figure eight motion as I walked, trying to clear the air around me of anything negative.

I circled the building. It seemed . . . ordinary. I'd imagined a place like the Overlook Hotel in *The Shining*, but so far, nothing like that.

At least on the outside.

I went up to the front door and tried it. It was unlocked. I pushed it open and stepped inside, reaching automatically for my phone and turning on the light. There was a small light on in the foyer, but everything was deserted. I stepped to the directory and shined the light on it. A bunch of businesses I didn't recognize and one that I did: Bogart Enterprises, Inc. Third floor, unit 307.

I wondered if I could get inside his place like I'd gotten into Strand's. But that was different. It was like Strand himself wanted me to go there versus it being my idea. But something told me the answer I was looking for wasn't going to be in a file cabinet in Bogart's office. If there were skeletons—literally—in this building, I assumed they wouldn't be that easy to find.

I paused, getting my bearings and determining my next move. Now that I was here, it seemed like maybe I had jumped the gun a little. I checked my phone to see if Gabe had responded. Nothing. Then I realized I had no service.

That was weird. I looked around. I was still in the foyer, and there was nothing to suggest this was a dead zone. I walked closer to the front door, holding my phone up. Still nothing. No bars. Still a big line of text reading *No Service*.

Awesome.

I used my selenite to try to clear my phone. When that didn't work, I stuck it in my pocket. I'd just take a quick walk around. See if anything felt off. Then I was outta here. I'd go talk to Gabe and he could figure out what to do.

I went down the hall, looking for the stairwell. I found it near the back of the building. Only the emergency lights were on back here. I pushed open the door tentatively and stepped in, propping the door open with a door stopper I found in the hallway so it didn't lock shut. I went up to the third floor and started there.

Bogart's office was locked and dark, as was every other office on the floor. I paused outside of it and risked closing my eyes for a minute, trying to get a sense. I'd always done aura work only on people, but it had to work the same way for places like this. Any physical location that had absorbed some kind of energy had to have its own soul. I truly believed that.

But I didn't feel anything.

I took a pass around the second floor. Nothing. I thought I heard a voice somewhere, but couldn't pinpoint it so I moved on.

When I went back to the first floor, the door exiting the stairwell was closed—not as I'd left it. I pushed against it.

It wasn't just closed. It was locked.

My heart sped up as I pushed the heavy bar to open it, throwing my entire body weight behind it. It didn't budge.

I muttered a curse and pulled out my phone again, praying for service.

Nothing.

*Okay, don't panic. There has to be a way out of here,* I told myself.

But how had the door gotten locked in the first place? Had I not placed the door stopper tightly enough and it had closed on its own? Or . . . was someone in here? Someone who didn't want me to leave?

I followed the stairs down one more flight, thinking there might be another exit into the garage or something. The door there had a giant red sign that read NO ENTRY —BUILDING MAINTENANCE ONLY.

I pushed at it and it opened. I stepped into some sort of basement.

My skin immediately started to crawl. I couldn't tell if

it was a reaction to a gut feeling, or to whatever smelled so bad down here. A punch of nausea hit me in the gut and I put my hand over my mouth, whirling around to run back upstairs. I didn't even want to stay and try to figure out what this feeling was. Mostly it wasn't good, and I was scared.

But as I pushed open the door, I came face to face with Jackson Bogart.

# CHAPTER FORTY-NINE

I stared at him, the fear clenching my throat. I knew I still held my wand and felt stupid. Mostly because even if I tried to hit him with it, it would break. Selenite was a soft stone and not ideal for a weapon.

"Violet Mooney, right?" he said, as if we'd just bumped into each other on the street and he was trying to recall my name.

I didn't answer. I took a step back, into that disgusting basement.

"What are you doing here? Did you get lost?" he continued, moving forward so I had no choice but to keep stepping backwards. "I'm afraid not much is open right now."

"It was you, wasn't it," I said, finally finding my

voice. I held my selenite in front of me, a poor excuse for a defense at the moment. "You killed Nicole."

Bogart's expression didn't change. Anyone watching this would think I was the crazy one, stumbling around the basement of a building where I didn't belong waving a crystal wand around, while Bogart looked his usual expensive, sane self. But all my senses—both witch and mortal—were screaming at me that it was him.

He stepped forward and cleared the door, letting it slam behind him. I was truly trapped now, with him standing between me and the exit. It was too dark to see if there was another exit anywhere else, and I was afraid of what I would find down here.

"I wish you wouldn't have figured that out," he said. His tone was so . . . mechanical that it was spooky. "I didn't want to. We were a good team. She actually earned my full trust—but when she got it, she couldn't handle it." He spread his hands. I could see a ring glinting on his right hand, the only flash of light aside from a very dim window somewhere to my left, just above my eye level. "She left me. And not only that, she tried to destroy everything I'd built. Literally and figuratively."

"You killed Ed Mathers. And Nicole found out."

Bogart laughed. It was an ugly sound. "She found out because I volunteered it. Otherwise, she never would have. My secret has been safe for this long, and that won't change. If the town couldn't do it, one foolish girl couldn't do it."

"Did you kill Chris Strand too? Or was he in on it with you? Since he hated Nicole anyway." I took another couple steps back, away from him. I was closer to the window now, trying to gauge the height of it. Out of the corner of my eye, it looked big enough that I could get through it.

If I had to break it, I would. I just had to get up there first.

But Strand's name bothered him. I could see it in the way his whole body tensed, even though I couldn't see his face well in the darkness.

"That moron? He signed his own death warrant years ago," Bogart said. "He knew everything, but he couldn't just leave it alone. Like you, I guess. You just couldn't leave it alone."

I shook my head. "It wasn't me. Everyone was going to find out anyway, because Chris and Nicole were working against you with Sylvia. They were filing a suit and they were going to bring it to the police. You're done, Jackson. It doesn't matter what you do to me. It's already out there."

He was quick. If it wasn't for that stupid ring, I wouldn't have seen him lunge at me. As it was, I only had a split second to react. I threw myself out of his way, landing on the floor and scrabbling backwards like a crab, praying I didn't touch anything disgusting on this bare cement floor. He lost his balance and went down, and then came after me. I reached for the selenite and brought it down hard, hearing a crack as it connected with his face, and his subsequent curse. It broke in my hand, but hopefully had bought me a moment or two while I assessed my options.

I realized that I didn't know if any of my powers would work against mortals, even if I'd gotten a good shove in on Oscar Sageblood. I also didn't know what would happen to me if I tried. Fiona had been adamant that witches shouldn't interfere with mortals in that way.

But did life and death situations count?

I pointed at him and concentrated hard, waiting for what had happened to Oscar earlier this week to happen again.

Nothing. And now he was on me again, his hand around my ankle, the other hand reaching for my hair. With a cry of frustration, I used my other foot to stomp on his hand until he let go while simultaneously sinking my teeth into his wrist. When he howled in pain I wrenched free, then scrambled toward the window.

And saw flashing lights outside. *Gabe.* He must've gotten my text.

But he'd never find me down here and Bogart wasn't about to let me go. And now he was mad. I felt his breath on my neck before his hand went around my throat, squeezing. I used my last reserve of energy to grab my bag, which still hung across my body, and use my water bottle to at least stun him again. Thankfully my aim was somewhat on point because he let go. Still coughing, I reached into my bag and pulled out the bottle. Holding it by the skinny end, I turned and delivered another blow to his face and head. When he dropped to the ground, I turned to the window.

It was open.

I blinked. It hadn't been a second ago. I knew it hadn't been. But there was no time to think about it now. I screamed as loud as I could as I grasped the sill for purchase and hoisted myself, using my feet like Spider-Man would to climb the wall. I heard shouting from somewhere close by. Then I felt hands on my shoulders, pulling me out to safety.

# CHAPTER FIFTY

"You sure you're okay?" Todd asked for the third time. We were outside the restaurant the next night, waiting for Pete and Syd. She'd insisted I was off the hook if I needed to recover from my ordeal, but I wasn't having it. I had no desire to sit home alone and think about how Jackson Bogart could have easily killed me just like he had Ed Mathers, Jr., whose body he'd hidden in the foundation of his building at 800 Main Street fifteen years ago; Nicole St. James; and as they'd learned early this morning, Chris Strand, whose body had been found in an abandoned construction site—Bogart's—on the other side of town. If it hadn't been for Xander—who I knew in my soul had opened that window—I might not be here. But my magickal cat had gotten out of the locked car and led the cops directly to that basement window.

Good thing Gabe had read his text eventually and brought a team out with him to Bogart's building.

"I'm fine." The bruises on my neck had been apparent enough that I'd needed to wear a scarf, but aside from that I was none the worse for wear.

Physically, anyway.

"Why did you go there alone, Violet? That wasn't a great decision."

"Right, you would have gone with me. Since you're always around when I need you," I said, my voice dripping sarcasm.

Finally, a flash of anger as his face reddened. But before he could respond, Syd and Pete walked up to us.

They looked cute together was my first thought. And she looked awesome. Her usually unruly curls were tamed but still buoyant, and she wore a beaded dress that looked like it had come from her store. Pete just looked happy.

They both wrapped me in a hug at the same time.

"You can't stay out of trouble, can you?" Pete said softly into my ear.

I laughed. "I'm fine. Really. And look, we got justice for Nicole." Ginny had barely been able to talk but she had called me the minute she'd heard and told me how she'd be grateful to me forever. I still thought it would've been better if I'd figured it out before Nicole died, but that was my own guilt to carry.

"Well, we're not going to talk about that tonight," Syd declared. "Only happy things." She squeezed my hand, then looked at Todd as if just realizing he was there. "Hey, Todd."

"Hey," Todd said. He nodded at Pete.

Pete's return nod was curt. "Let's go in," he said. "We have reservations."

He took Sydney's hand and led the way inside. Todd and I followed. We didn't speak again until we'd sat and given the waitress our drink order.

I looked around, feeling like everyone was looking at me. It had been all over the news today about Bogart and his crimes, and the whole town was abuzz about it. I hadn't seen Charlie Klein yet, but I hoped he was pleased that his friend's son would finally be put to rest.

I wasn't the only one who noticed people staring though. "You're a celebrity now," Todd said to me.

I couldn't tell from his tone if he was proud of that or if he was being snarky. I brushed off the comment, but Pete watched him with narrowed eyes.

The waitress came back to take our orders. I ordered a salad, figuring I could choke some of that down even though I still had no appetite, and pretended to be engaged in the conversation Syd and Pete were having about some of Pete's customers. He always had the best stories about his cafe.

But my mind wasn't totally engaged, until I heard Todd mention "the lawyer guy."

Immediately I snapped to attention and realized they were all looking at me. "Sorry, what?" I asked.

"I said, what's the deal with that lawyer guy who you've seen way more than me lately?" he said.

"Why are you asking me that?" I said.

"Because here he is again." Todd pointed. "Seriously, Violet, is there something I need to know?"

Had Todd lost his mind? I twisted around in my seat, then froze. Because the lawyer guy in question *was* here, coming toward our table. What on earth was Blake doing here?

"Actually," I said, "the real question would be, is there something *I* need to know? Since you two are related and all."

That knocked him back in his seat. And the second blow came immediately following as Blake reached the table. "You," he said, pointing at Todd. "Come with me."

I could see Todd prepare to get mouthy and silently willed him not to. He didn't listen. He rose in his chair, and the "Who do you think you are" was barely out of his mouth when Blake reached both arms straight up in the air, palms facing out, and said something I couldn't quite make out.

Everything around me stopped. Everything except me, Todd, and Pete. The witches among us.

"Sorry man," Blake said to Pete. "I just need a minute."

"No problem," Pete said dryly.

"Did you seriously just freeze time?" I said to Blake. "Can you teach me how to do that?"

"Not now, Violet." He had his hand around Todd's wrist, as if he were afraid he was going to take off. "You're both coming with me."

"Coming where?" I asked. "I'm kind of busy at the moment."

"We have a few things my long-lost cousin and I need to get to the bottom of," he said, eyes on Todd. "Let's let these people get back to their date, shall we? You're not needed here anyway, Vi. They've got this." With his free hand, he grabbed mine, and the next thing I knew the three of us were outside.

I assumed everything inside had gone back to normal.

"Blake, is this really necessary right now?" I demanded. "I don't even have a coat!"

"It is," he said through gritted teeth. "Would you be quiet and let me handle this? Mac has some news. And I think the three of us need to hear it together."

Todd looked like he might be sick on the sidewalk.

I didn't feel so hot myself. I wasn't sure I wanted to hear whatever this news was, not so soon after everything else. "Blake—"

"Violet. Please. I know you know my family history and I'm sorry I never told you. But unlike him"—here he gestured at Todd with disgust—"I wasn't doing it to fool you. I don't have anything in common with my family and don't want to be tainted by them. I know what you've heard and I didn't want you to think of me that way." He took a step closer to me, so close I could feel his breath on my face. "And I care about you. You have to believe me."

I felt it again—that rush of anticipation, the desire to feel his lips on mine. Even right here on the street, in front of Todd. More importantly, I felt an indisputable knowing all the way in my gut that he was telling me the truth. "I believe you," I said softly.

He smiled. "Good. Because I'm going to make sure you know everything."

But once again, he didn't kiss me. Instead, he stepped back and took my hand. I hesitated, then squeezed it tight, trusting him to take me where I needed to go.

# Connect with